BY LONNIE BUSCH

(More about Busch's books at the end of Cargo Hold 4)

CARGO HOLD 4

LONNIE BUSCH

Human Authored Reg #: 1028416, https://authorsguild.org/human

UBiQ PRESS

No AI was used for any part of this book

CARGO HOLD 4

Copyright © 2024 by Lonnie A. Busch

A UBiQ PRESS BOOK

North Carolina, USA

https://lonniebusch.com/

Cover Art by Lonnie Busch

ISBN: 978-1-964024-91-2 (hardcover)

ISBN: 978-1-964024-00-4 (paperback)

Library of Congress Control Number: 2024905698

First Paperback/Hardcover Editions, April 2024

Human Authored Reg #: 1028416, https://authorsguild.org/human

CARGO HOLD 4

CHAPTER ONE

THE POUNDING AND SCREECHING COMING FROM CARGO HOLD 4 was nearly unbearable. Then the moaning. Followed by deep guttural cries resonating through the ship, vibrating the metal bulkheads. The commotion shocked the crew, as if something was trapped within the walls of the space craft trying desperately to escape. The harsh disturbance summoned First mate Berlin from her work station to the craft's holding area.

Standing next to the massive titanium door, she listened, trying to figure out what was going on. Everything they'd discovered on Planet J-78 was stored in Cargo Hold 4, but none of it was organic, according to their scanners.

As if a switch had been flipped, the hold fell silent, the storage area of the vessel mute as a tomb. The way it should be. She eased closer, trying to quell her scudding heart, until a loud scream sent her leaping backward, her legs shaky, unsteady. The scream came again, like someone, or something, being skinned alive.

They had disembarked from the planet over a week earlier and hadn't heard a thing from the cargo area until thirty minutes ago. Now the racket was nearly nonstop, except for intervals of silence followed by shrieks and unintelligible shouts and wailing. Then the banging would start again.

Captain Desna walked up next to her, listening, obviously perplexed by the commotion, the hammering like metal on metal. After a few minutes, she looked over at Berlin. "What the hell?" Captain Desna said.

Berlin could only shake her head, hoping the big door would hold under the constant assault. The clunking and knocking grew louder, the intervals of quiet growing progressively shorter until the ruckus resembled the steady assault of an automatic weapon, huge rounds slamming the titanium door.

They both eased away, their attention trapped by the disturbing phenomenon.

Two more crew members joined them, moving up slowly, cautiously, whispering to one another until Captain Desna silenced them with a quick movement of her hand.

A moment later, a heavy hush fell over the vast storage area. Berlin let her eyes travel the full length of the immense enclosure, all forty cargo holds peacefully innocuous, seemingly unaffected by the freakish event in Cargo Hold 4.

"How long before we get to XB-92?" Captain Desna said, nearly in a whisper, as if any sudden sound could set off the disturbance again.

Skip told her about eighty-six days and change, his voice low, trying to match her whisper.

"Is there anywhere to put down before XB?"

"I'll check." He turned and left the cargo vault.

Berlin had remained silent, but couldn't any longer, not at all liking the idea of landing just anywhere. "You think that's a good idea, Des?" she said. By order of the captain, the crew had dropped the formalities of addressing her by rank after sixteen months into the long mission. That was over three years ago.

"Any suggestions?" Desna said, addressing her First mate.

"Why aren't there cameras in these holds?" Berlin couldn't understand why the mission planners hadn't installed them everywhere. She looked over at Desna wondering why she was getting the stink eye. "What?"

"Do you have a camera in your closet?" Desna said. "Or in your refrigerator?"

Berlin regarded her with confusion.

"This is a storage area, Berlin! Why would they install cameras inside storage areas?"

Berlin bristled under Desna's rebuke. She could see she was bothered by this development, and was uncharacteristically testy. Berlin didn't like the situation any more than the rest of the crew, but putting down seemed chancy on some random planet, especially if something went wrong, causing the interior cargo hold doors to automatically open. It had happened early into the mission during a faulty set-down. Something malfunctioned in the computer system, initiating the open function. The crew's provisions spilled out everywhere. Now, the risk felt greater than ever for a speculative landing. The potential for releasing this angry stowaway from Cargo Hold 4 was one she didn't want to contemplate.

"We could inspect the hold from the outside," Berlin finally said, not sure this type of maneuver was any safer than putting down. "The window on the small door."

Gretel had exterior hatches to the cargo bays, making supplies and gear easily accessible at any docking station without entering the vessel. Alongside the massive outer hatches were individual doors for each bay, each one fitted with a small window of tempered glass.

"Go wake Chelsey," Desna told Berlin, then turned to go back up to A-Deck.

Assistant Science Officer Hurd stepped forward, and spoke softly to Berlin. "Very risky. Chelsey won't like it."

Berlin turned away from the odd man, knowing Hurd was right, but it still seemed a better bet than putting down somewhere. Before she made it to the stairwell, Cargo Hold 4 came alive again, the screeching and crying nearly unbearable, then the pounding. Before reaching the top of the stairs, she half-expected to hear someone screaming, *"LET ME OUT OF HERE!"*

Hurd followed her up the steps, then disappeared down A-Deck corridor before she could completely form her response to his negativity; now it no longer mattered. Hurrying toward Chelsey's quarters, she couldn't help but wonder why no one had uttered the question that had to be on everyone's mind: How could anything survive in that cargo bay? There wasn't any air. Not breathable air.

When she reached the door, she raised her knuckles to the metal surface and rapped lightly a few times, hoping not to startle Chelsey from a deep sleep.

"I'm up. Come in!"

Berlin swiped her palm past the door open sensor. Chelsey stood in the middle of the room, wiggling into her jumpsuit.

"Hey, Berlin. What the heck is going on in Cargo Hold 4?"

"You heard?"

"Cap called down here a few minutes ago to give me the news."

"You okay with this?"

Chelsey fidgeted in front of the mirror, combing her fingers through her hair while trying to zip her suit at the same time. "Sure. Why wouldn't I be?"

Berlin felt silly reminding her of the perilous spacewalk she'd executed only four months earlier that almost ended with her lost to space forever. That one hadn't been Berlin's idea, but she felt horrible just the same.

"Fawn must still be in sick bay..." Chelsey said, then focused on the zipper, turning toward Berlin. "Otherwise, she'd probably be doing this. It's cool."

Chelsey was covering. Berlin realized the young woman was scared shitless but was more afraid of admitting it. A second later, the low growling from Cargo Hold 4 echoed through the floor, the eerie chatter coming from everywhere at once it seemed.

"Dang! That's Cargo Hold 4?" Chelsey said, glancing once more at the mirror before spinning her attention to Berlin. The alarm sounded throughout *Gretel,* an all-hands-on-deck alert. When it ended, a deafening caterwaul burst up from the hold, sending gooseflesh up both women's arms. Chelsey, for the first time since Berlin had entered her quarters, looked petrified.

Berlin wanted to assure her she'd be safe, that nobody expected her to actually enter the cargo bay, just observe and report from the window. Desna would have explained that to her. Even so, performing any kind of spacewalk was fraught with danger; there was much more that could go wrong than right, and Chelsey knew that better than anyone... she'd managed to live through one such event not long ago.

CHAPTER TWO

CHELSEY DISEMBARKED *GRETEL,* TETHERED TO THE SHIP BY AN umbilical cord feeding her oxygen and heat. Strapped to her back was a contour-fit streamline aux tank in case something went wrong with the lifeline, holding enough O_2 for fifteen to twenty minutes, depending on her stress levels. In place of the aux tank, she had planned to wear a SAFER—a self-contained jet pack—until Captain Desna suggested she may have to enter the purge vent, making the use of the SAFER impossible. It was far too large and cumbersome.

Navigating the outer hull of *Gretel,* Chelsey pulled herself along using the metal-tube railings that ran the full length of the spacecraft, as well as circling the ship's circumference in numerous sections down its length, making exterior repairs easier to accomplish. Once she was close, she would use the vertical metal railing to work her way down to the cargo hold hatches. The captain and crew monitored her progress from the bridge. Everyone was on full alert, Berlin manning the remote controls of the bright-yellow CPV-drone they called *The Yellow Submarine,* which maneuvered a safe distance out from Chelsey, following her every move, its bright spotlight illuminating her progress.

"Nearing Cargo Hold 4," Chelsey said, her voice muted and hollow inside her helmet.

"Check the window first," Desna said, leaning forward on the console, her eyes trained on the huge monitor across the bridge.

Chelsey planned to, not wanting anything to do with entering the purge vent. No way was she crawling into that skinny duct unless it was absolutely necessary. The tight space was claustrophobic, and gave her the creeps.

"Nearing the window." Chelsey knew what her voice must be sounding like on the bridge. Months earlier, she'd heard Wurther and Fawn when they'd perform repairs on the hull, their voices sounding a million kilometers away. It was chilling. And if Fawn weren't battling some bizarre illness Doctor Karl couldn't puzzle out, Chelsey knew that the young girl would be the one out here getting ready to play peek-a-boo with whatever perversity had taken up residence in Cargo Hold 4.

"You okay, Chelse?"

"You bet, Cap!"

"Don't get cocky! Just check the window and report back."

"My eyes are your eyes!"

The Yellow Submarine was tracking Chelsey's trek down the side of the ship, staying a safe three meters away; close enough to catch her if she *fell,* yet far enough to prevent hindering her movement. What a strange thought, as if *falling* in outer space were even possible.

Chelsey hadn't meant to take a deep breath when she pulled herself closer to the window; it was an involuntary response.

"Everything okay?" the disembodied voice inside her helmet said.

"Good! I'm good. Getting ready to meet our visitor."

Chelsey secured herself by clamping her boots into the quick-release cleats on the metal landing at the base of the small titanium door. Once secure, she released the handles and rubbed her gloved hand over the window, cleaning away debris and dirt from their scavenging missions on numerous planets. Once the glass was cleared, she brought her helmet closer until the face of the shield touched the glass. The cargo hold was pitch black, *The Yellow Submarine,* as well as her own helmet, reflecting in the glass. They had planned to leave the lights in the cargo bay off, so whatever it was wouldn't be alerted or spooked and go crazy, possibly damaging the ship. But it was useless; Chelsey couldn't see a thing.

"I'm going to switch on my helmet lights, see if they'll penetrate past this glass."

Nothing came back from the bridge. The CPV-drone edged to the side, using its cameras to record the event for further analysis.

When the helmet lights snapped on, Chelsey moved her head, trying to find the perfect angle to illuminate the gloom inside and be able to see at the same time. The light fell on certain objects, cutting the interior into useless slivers of abstract and unintelligible shapes. As she was getting ready to tell them to turn on the cargo bay lights, something shot past the beams from her helmet.

"There was something!" she said, her heart racing.

"Calm down, Chelse. Your blood pressure's rising."

Chelsey took a few deep breaths, trying to gather herself, then moved her helmet closer again to block out extraneous light from *The Yellow Submarine*. Something slammed against the glass. Chelsey pushed away from *Gretel*, dislodging the soles of her boots from the cleats, hurtling away from the ship. By now she was in a spin, moving farther and farther, her mind trying to process what she saw, unable to accept the phantasm as fact.

She was growing faint, the umbilical cord wrapping around her like a serpent. People were screaming into her helmet comm, telling her to hang on, panicked voices, telling her that Berlin was guiding *The Yellow Submarine* right to her. Before Chelsey could register what was happening, the umbilical broke loose from her suit, the aux tank on her back instantly sending fresh air, red lights flashing as she tumbled through space. A second later something grabbed her and dragged her back toward *Gretel*, transporting her safely back to the capture bay. When the airlock closed, she hurriedly wrenched the helmet off her head, dropping it on the deck. Within seconds, Doc Karl and Wurther were at her side, hauling her toward the doorway to the waiting gurney, rushing her to sickbay.

By the time the captain reached the medical facility, Doc Karl had placed Chelsey in a cleared-domed quarantine capsule.

"Is she okay?" Captain Desna said.

"She's in shock. She'll be all right. I gave her a sedative and put her in a Q-Cap because I still haven't figured out what's going on with Fawn."

Nestled comfortably inside the capsule, with no sense of her physical presence, Chelsey could hear every word they were saying, but strangely couldn't communicate back, as if she were monitoring everything from a separate consciousness, one outside the corporeal world. As if on cue, the metal walls and floor began to reverberate with a deafening snarl. She couldn't see the captain or Doc with her eyes, but could see their every action in her head, watching them react to the horrifying baying, shifting their attention from the bulkheads to the floor, then the ceiling, the entire ship wrapped in an unnatural din.

CHAPTER THREE

BERLIN AND DESNA WERE ON THE BRIDGE CONSIDERING THEIR options, waiting on Skip to return some encouraging news from his station across the room. Since the outer inspection had failed, with Chelsey slipping into a coma, there was no one else to try again, no one small enough to enter the purge vent to see what was going on. The commotion in Cargo Hold 4 had not dissipated one iota, and in fact, was growing worse, making it difficult for the crew to get satisfactory sleep, the unholy tumult unyielding.

One option Berlin floated was opening the main exterior hatch to Cargo Bay 4, allowing all their research samples to be sucked into outer space. They'd lose everything they'd gathered on XB-92.

Desna was considering it, though that gambit seemed a bit drastic considering they had no idea what they were dealing with. What if this *thing* managed to avoid being jettisoned into space, attaching itself to the exterior hull, damaging the ship irreparably? In Cargo Bay 4 it was at least contained, though allowing it any egress without knowing its capabilities seemed foolhardy.

Bringing up the manifest for XB-92, Desna and Berlin studied the contents of Cargo Hold 4, their eyes traveling down the list of minerals and fossils they'd found, proof of life many millennia ago. However, what they'd experienced was a planet virtually barren, most likely destroyed by some kind of cosmic event that had wiped out all life. Desna was just beginning to drill down into the extensive collection of bone fragments when piercing screeches seized everyone's attention. The tortured shrieks continued, growing exponentially louder, as if whatever had been trapped in Cargo Hold 4 was now free and roaming the enormous ship.

Hurd had just entered the bridge, coming on his shift, when he stopped cold and looked down at the floor, then over at Desna. Desna and the crew sat unspeaking, unmoving, suspended in the high-pitched wailing that boomed through the bridge, the painful clamor underpinned by raspy deep growls that shook the displays and terminals. Desna glanced at her water glass sitting nearby, the surface rippling from the fracas. Quartermaster Wurther entered the bridge, clearly vexed by the disturbance, and started to speak to Desna when she threw up her palm to quell whatever he was about to say, everyone fixed by the ungodly disruption.

Desna trapped Hurd's eyes, trying to read the spiritual liaison's unwavering expression, wondering what his take on this situation might be, yet couldn't bring herself to speak in the presence of this aberrant cacophony.

The noise was obdurate, driving down into her chest and abdomen, crowding out her thoughts. It continued unabated, its intensity never waning, until it stopped, leaving in its wake an odd residue of sound, a sort of oscillating clang in Desna's ears. The new hush was like a shrill vacuum no one could escape.

The crew was motionless until Desna spoke to Hurd. "What do you make of all this?"

His eyebrows arched briefly. "I'm not sure," he said, in an academic tone. "An incorporeal entity, maybe? Possibly not even organic..."

"Incorporeal!" Desna jerked forward in her seat. "What made you go there?"

"The fact that it can survive in the cargo hold. I mean, we haven't seen it yet. Our only experience of it is auditory... discarnate spirits, ghosts for instance, often communicate audibly..."

Desna looked over at Berlin. Berlin shrugged, then blurted out with a tremor of fear in her voice. "Chelsey saw something!"

Desna nodded, reframing Berlin's claim back to Hurd. "Something freaked her out..."

"True, but it could have been an apparition, visible to human perception. Or an energetic presence. That would not make it corporeal, though. Or organic."

Desna sat back in her chair, taking her eyes to Berlin, whose face was wrecked with worry and concern.

"We have to find out what the hell's in that hold!" Berlin stated, sucking in a deep breath as if to steel herself against unthinkable possibilities.

Desna agreed, but how? She glanced back at Hurd, who, as if convinced the conversation was over, had placed himself at his terminal, perusing a constant stream of data.

"What about you, Hurd?" Desna said. "Could you enter Cargo Hold 4 through the exterior hatch?"

The crew let out audible gasps, spinning with obvious disgust toward Desna, shocked by her outrageous suggestion.

"You can't be serious, Des!" Berlin shouted.

Desna knew the crew would react this way. Hurd had become part of the team, fitting in perfectly. Nonetheless, he was a hybridized human, most of his biology consisting of artificial components. She could never be certain where the human stopped and the android started. It was probable, if Hurd was correct in his supposition, that he would be unaffected by this entity. After all, he lacked human perception in terms of psychological investment. He wasn't prone to fear and superstition the way humans were. He didn't process events emotionally, which could protect him from shock and the acute fright Chelsey had experienced. Plus, his mostly faux biological structure would make it easy for him to withstand the harsh environment of Cargo Hold 4. He'd still need an aux tank (for all his ersatz components, he did still breathe oxygen) and a pressurized suit. Nevertheless, he was protected from the mental fallout which was difficult for other crew members to guard against. Chelsey was still in a shock-induced coma, according to Doc.

"Well?" Desna grew impatient waiting for Hurd to respond, feeling all eyes on her.

Before he could say anything, Skip rushed down from his station. "We've got bigger problems, Desna!" He appeared harried, his eyes flashing between her and Hurd. "We're coming up on BC-1!"

She shifted toward him. "That's not possible!" She was confused, knowing *Gretel* shouldn't reach BC-1 for at least another six to eight months.

"It may not be possible, but that's what the readings show."

"Put them up."

The big screen displayed their current position in relation to BC-1. They'd reach the first Breadcrumb in less than two weeks. Desna shook her head, a thousand imponderables shuffling through her brain. Would there be time to slow *Gretel* enough to rendezvous with BC-1? How would the docking work with this new issue in the storage area. Could an attempt to link with the supply pod disrupt the hold area, upset the status quo and free this entity from Cargo Hold 4? Was the crew even ready for their first fling with a supply pod? Everything about the process was theoretical at best. Skip, as the pilot of *Gretel*, had practiced exhaustively on the simulator to learn how to do it, but it was *simulated,* and already the speculative scheme was breaking down. Fawn had also practiced the maneuvers on the simulator. She was the youngest member of the crew, joining the team when she was eleven, and could conceivably be the only surviving member of the mission. She had learned how to dock with a pod so she could resupply on her own in the event no one was left toward the end of their expedition. But she was ill in quarantine, and unavailable for their first docking attempt.

A decade before *Gretel* was launched, the planners had fired supply pods into space at two- and a half-year intervals along the same trajectory as *Gretel*, the idea being that this trail of "breadcrumbs" would be accessible to a faster spacecraft which would eventually catch up to the supply pods just as the crew's provisions started running low, greatly extending the mission for decades. The overall plan was, once *Gretel* reached the final pod, BC-4, the ship and crew would load up with fuel and food and everything they needed to start their long journey back to Earth. New pods launched after *Gretel* entered outer space would aid their expedition all the way home, possibly as much as fifty years from the time they'd departed Earth. Some of the crew may not make it, but everyone knew the risk. Nevertheless, it was worth it to bring back artifacts from across the unseen regions of the universe.

Not even five years into their mission, they had already amassed an incredible collection of data, minerals, recorded video, photographs, soil samples, as well as sealed containers of air and gaseous compounds. Now, it seemed, they'd attracted a life form they had no idea how to cope with.

However, the long-range planning and hypotheticals were coming apart. Why were they already intercepting the BC-1 pod? Had they been traveling too fast? Had the pod been deterred by something, maybe an asteroid strike? Or some other unforeseen anomaly hindering its progress?

"What do you want to do?" Skip asked.

The process for intercepting the pod was complicated. Desna knew that *Gretel* would have to reduce its speed incrementally, eventually matching it to the supply pod to prevent shooting right past BC-1 with no chance of going back due to fuel consumption. This was a one-and-done situation; if they failed to match the speed of the pod in time, and dock successfully, they were screwed.

"Start the process," Desna told Skip. "We have no choice. Berlin, go check with Doc and see how Chelsey and Fawn are doing?" Desna stood from her chair. "We're going to need more hands if this docking maneuver is going to work."

Berlin said, "I can do it, Desna."

"Do what?"

"Perform a spacewalk to inspect Cargo Hold 4 before we dock with BC-1..."

"You're gonna put on a spacesuit and muck around out there for an hour or more?" Desna said, scoffing. "I don't think so."

"Look, that was one time. I got scared. I'm over it."

"I'm not," Desna said with a dismissive wave of her hand. "Wurther, are you up to speed on this docking attempt?"

He nodded, turning from his display.

"Hurd?" Desna said, waiting for the curious man to respond. "Can you enter Cargo Hold 4 safely or not?"

As if on cue, the hellish howls, the pounding and clunking, rushed up from the hold area below the deck of the bridge. The racket built with such ferocity that crew members gripped their desks and seats, as if the sheer severity of the riot could dislodge them from their stations, carry them off the ship.

Desna lowered herself slowly back into her chair, clutching the armrests, her heart rate matching the fervor of the entity's bleating. The ship grumbled and shook, or so it seemed, everyone silenced by the harsh protestations of the aberration, whatever it was. It went on for a good fifteen minutes, the crew frozen with worry and trepidation. Desna knew they had to resolve this before reaching BC-1. When she looked up to find Hurd, he was gone.

CHAPTER FOUR

When the dreadful keening and yowling finally stopped, Desna was frazzled, the aftermath of the furor echoing on her eardrums, a monotonous high-pitched drone. It had gone on nearly nonstop for the past three days since they'd learned about their interception with BC-1.

On little sleep, due to the ceaseless upheaval emanating from Cargo Hold 4, Desna, Wurther and Skip worked nonstop trying to get clarity on the details outlining the docking procedure, which was less than eight days away. They had yet to develop a strategy to deal with the outraged entity, but they needed to, the constant assault affecting their work. Hurd had not responded positively to her call for help, saying that he lacked the necessary skills to perform such a task.

"What skills!" Desna had shouted at the peculiar man, perturbed that when she needed him most he bailed. They hadn't spoken since. Berlin tried to soften Desna's stance toward him, but she was having none of it, sarcastically stating that he had to do more than listen to people's fears and dreams. Hurd served as the ship's psychologist and confessor, and guru of all things spiritual. Desna didn't give a shit. She needed him to step up, and he wouldn't.

Berlin came over to where Desna, Wurther and Skip were

working and asked if she had a minute. Desna excused herself and followed Berlin into the corridor outside the bridge.

"I needed last night, Berlin," Desna said, touching her First mate's hand and sighing.

"Yeah, so did Wurther!" Berlin seemed agitated with Desna.

"I'm glad he doesn't mind our little trysts." Desna leaned in to kiss Berlin on the lips. They held the embrace for a moment before Berlin drew away.

"He doesn't mind because he doesn't know," Berlin said, obviously a bit miffed about something. She let go of Desna's hand, then cleared her throat. "Why don't *you* mind? That's the bigger question!"

"Baby doll, life is too short for that." Desna wondered what was going on with Berlin. Even so, whatever it was, it would have to wait until—

Loud banging and screams shattered her thoughts, the sound roiling up from below, an explosion of shrieks and howls and grunts. Metal against metal, the clatter ringing through the ship, crying and baying, then more banging!

"For the love of *God!*" Desna covered her ears with her palms. "We have to make it stop!"

"Hurd will do it!" Berlin shouted over the clamor.

Desna met Berlin's eyes. "You sure?" she shouted back, leaning in closer.

Berlin nodded, a tear slipping down her cheek. Desna took her hands in hers, squeezing them. "I'll make sure he's safe, all right? Don't worry. I promise!"

Desna went back to the bridge where Wurther and Skip were planning out the docking with BC-1, trying their best to ignore the commotion, stopping occasionally to check the entrances, the ceiling and floor. She hurried over and told them to put everything on hold, that they were going to deal with Cargo Hold 4, that Hurd agreed to do it. The two men's expressions soured, squinting up at her, not trying very hard to conceal their disgust.

"It has to be done," she shouted over the grizzly cries and mind-numbing pounding. "I'm going fucking crazy here!"

They nodded reluctantly, then left the bridge to help Hurd

get ready in the airlock. Hurd arrived an hour after Desna had alerted the crew about the spacewalk. When Desna entered, the peculiar man was suited, sitting, breathing pure oxygen to flush the nitrogen from his bloodstream. Even in the secured environment, Desna could still hear the muffled cries and protestations of the thing in Cargo Hold 4. It seemed that it hardly stopped anymore, a constant reminder that they were no longer alone.

Wurther spoke to Hurd through his helmet comm. "Can you hear me okay, Mr. Hurd?"

He raised his hand and gave Wurther a thumbs up.

"No, you have to respond over the comm so I know it's working."

"Yes, no problems here." He looked at Wurther, smiling.

This was a mistake. Desna could already feel it. Hurd was too timid and naïve for this kind of operation. He'd be eaten alive trying to reason with this maniacal entity. Fear under these conditions might be the only thing to keep someone alive, a very necessary emotion to have when one's survival was on the line. Is this what he'd meant when he said he didn't have the "necessary skills?"

She was about to call it off when the pandemonium beyond the airlock reached a new crescendo. Even with the shrieks and screams inside the compartment muted, they were no less disturbing. Berlin entered the airlock and looked over at Desna, then at Wurther. Desna shook her head back and forth, out of Hurd's sightline, rolling her eyes. Wurther shrugged, a noncommittal gesture that didn't shout confidence. Berlin came closer to Hurd and bent over, bringing her face close to his tinted shield. He had his eyes closed. She knocked on the shield lightly. He brightened, and nodded, then grinned like the village idiot.

"That's it!" Desna screamed. "Get that suit off him. He's not going out there."

Berlin appeared relieved. Wurther wasted no time getting Hurd's helmet off, then started undoing his suit.

"I don't mind doing it, Captain Desna," Hurd said. "Really... I'll be just fine."

Desna rushed from the airlock, wondering how she'd gotten into this situation. None of the crew had military training, except for Skip, who'd been in the Navy for ten years after high school. And Wurther seemed to have some mercenary background, but didn't like talking about that time in his life. For the most part they were scientists. Desna had been a professor at a university, teaching space sciences, going through a messy divorce. Berlin had been one of her students, and the cause of her messy divorce. Fawn showed Alan Turing math skills by the time she was six. Her parents, two lifer astronauts, practically raised her for space travel. Fawn, at age nine, upon learning of the mission, urged her parents to sign her up early so she could be included on the team. She was the brains, but for now, was riding the bench in sick bay with some pesky, unknown virus. Chelsey had been a Space Camp phenom, rock climber, backpacker and all-around wanderer, and wasn't about to miss the adventure of a lifetime.

Taking the steps too fast, Desna stumbled hurrying down to the storage area, her mind juggling a passel of disquieting realities about the expedition. The uproar in the cargo vault was deafening, as if amplified through a rock concert sound system, the groaning and whimpering otherworldly, larger than life. Standing before the Cargo Bay 4 hatch with her hands pressed over her ears, she tried to imagine what life force was so distraught on the other side. She imagined it to be immense, maybe even too big for the airplane-hangar-sized hold. What did it want? To be set free? Was that its only desire? Or was it something far more odious? They had to get eyes on it, whatever it was, and figure out how to banish it from *Gretel.*

Desna was about to head back up to the bridge when someone spoke behind her. She spun around to see the young child.

"Fawn, what are you doing out of quarantine!" Desna shouted. The young girl's eyes were sunken, ringed with darkness, her skin pasty white. Like a wraith. "You shouldn't be down here," she yelled toward the young girl.

"I'll go in," Fawn said.

"I can't hear you! Let's go up to A-deck!"

The pounding started, the banging so loud it seemed as if the hatch could blow at any moment. The hammering came quicker, stronger, as if something were beating the titanium door with a metal post the size of a telephone pole. The pinging echo burrowed down into Desna's eardrums, the sensation intolerable.

"I said, I'll go in! I can do it!" the girl screamed, seemingly using all her strength in the process.

Desna ran over to Fawn, grabbing her arm to help her up the stairs. Her flesh was like ice.

"You're freezing to death. Come on!"

She hauled the girl up the steps. Dr. Karl met them at the top, quickly wrapping a blanket around the child's shoulders. He looked at Desna, his eyes pleading, his expression lost. He shrugged, as if giving up on trying to overwhelm the noise, mouthing something to Desna she couldn't understand. She frowned, pointing at her ear.

They rushed into the closest compartment and shut the hatch. The ruckus was more muted, but still a powerful presence.

"That decibel range is going to render us all deaf!" the doctor shouted toward Desna, even though she was standing only a meter away. He pulled the girl close to him, trying to warm her.

"Why is Fawn out of quarantine?" Desna shouted back, unsure if Doc could hear her.

He rocked his head back and forth, sad, as if he had no idea. Then he pointed toward sick bay and started guiding the girl from the compartment. Desna nodded, watching Fawn shuffle away, knowing what she had to do.

CHAPTER FIVE

"That's insane!" Berlin screamed. "No way! You're not doing it!"

It didn't matter what Berlin said, she'd already made up her mind. "I want you operating *The Yellow Submarine* in case I get into trouble," Desna shouted. "You're the only one I trust."

"You can't do it! You won't even fit!"

"I'm the same size as Fawn, and you know it!"

Desna won the brief staring contest. Berlin, hugging her arms across herself, started to sulk, then cry, her lower lip puckering as it always did when she didn't get her way. She stomped her foot. "No!" But the command was weak, had no gusto, her face twisted with defeat. Desna could tell she was fading, giving in to the inevitable. The young woman folded down onto the divan, quivering, tears flowing down both cheeks.

Desna would have loved to console her, but there wasn't time. The noise had made it nearly impossible for anyone to concentrate or work, the BC-1 merger rapidly approaching. Intervals of silence were becoming ever rarer, nearly nonexistent.

Wurther, Skip and Hurd were supposed to meet her in the airlock twenty minutes earlier and she was already late. "I've got to go! Please don't let me down!" She patted Berlin on the leg and hurried from her compartment.

Desna was rushing down the corridor, hoping the *thing* in

Cargo Hold 4 didn't rip the ship apart, when everything fell quiet, a residual hum the only sound lingering in her ears. By far this had been the worst assault yet. Desna closed her eyes and took a deep breath, drinking in the hush, letting her body regroup before the next attack. Any second she expected it to start again. Unsure how long the peace would last, she decided it best to get to the airlock and begin her acclimation, hoping Berlin didn't forget to get the CPV-drone ready.

She was nearly out of breath when she reached the airlock, the ship still silent as space. Odd, she thought. What was going on? Had the *thing* finally freed itself after its mighty struggle with *Gretel?* And at what cost to the ship? Or had it died? Regardless, she welcomed the new tranquility, her heart realigning to its naturally-paced rhythm.

When she entered the airlock, she was surprised to find no one there. Wurther and Skip were as reliable as the sun, while Hurd, well, she didn't know what to make of a hybridized human. He was strange. She wriggled into her spacesuit and adjusted her helmet over her head, then secured it. She switched on the oxygen and started breathing slowly, regularly, closing her eyes to enjoy the new calm.

"Captain?" someone whispered in the airlock.

Desna spun toward the sound and spied Hurd standing in the doorway. "Where is everybody?" she said, her voice distorted by the helmet. Hurd looked as if he didn't want to come any closer. His eyes were pained, his expression dark. She'd never seen him so apprehensive. "What's going on?"

His lips buckled as if what he had to say was going to upset her. "I think I made a huge mistake," he finally managed to squeeze out. "I think you should come with me."

"I'm in the middle of acclimating. Can't it wait till we're done with this?"

He shuffled his feet, unable to meet her gaze. "I don't think the spacewalk will be necessary."

"What?"

"Please, just come with me, okay?"

Desna lifted the helmet off her head and set it on the bench next to her, then twisted out of the suit, letting it crumple to the floor in a heap. All she had on was her leotard, but she wasn't about to go back to her compartment and get dressed.

Hurd turned away, as if he expected her to follow. When he reached the stairwell, she knew he was leading her down to the cargo holds. At the bottom of the steps, standing in front of Cargo Hold 4, were Wurther and Skip. Berlin was over to the side in the shadows when she saw Desna and ambled over.

"What's going on?" Desna's eyes ratcheted between the crew members. Before anyone could answer, she spotted what this little pow wow was about.

"What the hell happened?"

The titanium hatch was damaged, covered with huge helmet-shaped dents pushing out, the blows which had caused them initiating from inside the cargo bay. She walked up slowly to inspect, running her palm over the protruding mounds of metal, chaotically spaced without pattern or purpose, just a vicious struggle to escape by a desperate entity.

"I don't understand," she said, turning to face the crew. Skip sucked in his lips and glanced over at Hurd. Wurther let his eyes fall to the floor. Berlin seemed just as confused as Desna. The serenity in the vault was profound, unmistakable. How long since the last savage outburst? Fifteen minutes? Twenty? Something happened but no one was talking. She shifted her attention to Hurd, who gave her a weak grin.

"What's going on?"

He exhaled roughly, then scratched at his ear.

"Hurd was just trying to calm the damn thing down!" Wurther finally blurted out. "It's not his fault."

"What did you do, Hurd?"

Hurd brought his eyes to Desna's. "I just thought that, well, maybe the entity was frightened, and, um... and that maybe... well, it might feel safer if I... turned the light on."

"You turned on the light in Cargo Hold 4?" she said, unsure why that mattered. "What happened?"

"At first everything fell quiet, and I figured that, well... it worked." Hurd tried to gather himself. "But then, um... all hell broke loose... and the thing, well..." at this Hurd swept his hand toward the large titanium door like a game show host.

Desna walked back to the hatch, giving it a closer inspection. "It's dented. So what? It didn't breach. Maybe the damn thing killed itself, beat itself to death against the door. Problem solved. Unless the stench of its rotting carcass fills the ship."

Everyone was still mute. From her perspective, this seemed like a good thing. "What am I missing here?"

Skip spoke up this time. "Wurther thinks maybe the thing breached the outer cargo door and escaped. And that maybe months and months of irreplaceable research got sucked out with it."

Desna squatted down to think how many different planets had they collected from and stored in Cargo Hold 4? Two? Three? She tried recalling each planet, where its artifacts were stored, once again cataloguing everything in her mind.

"The last three planets," Berlin said. "I checked the records more closely."

Desna rose, feeling the tradeoff was worth it. Maybe they could stop at those planets on the way back, or... the damn *thing* was gone, that was really all that mattered.

"It's just stuff." Desna skidded her eyes between each of them. "We'll find more. What do we do about *Gretel*? Can we fix the breach?"

After regarding each one, she aimed her attention at Wurther. "Well?"

"We're not sure yet if there was a breach," Skip said. "We just figured, you know, with the new peace and quiet, something happened, right?"

"Let's find out," Desna said. "Berlin, is *The Yellow Submarine* ready to go?"

Berlin nodded.

"Well, let's end this mystery so we can figure out this link-up with BC-1, and get back on track!"

CHAPTER SIX

SEATED ON THE BRIDGE, BERLIN GUIDED *THE YELLOW Submarine* out of the airlock hatch and around to the starboard side of the ship, hoping this entire fiasco was over. Spotlights from the CPV-drone etched reliefs of shapes and shadows along *Gretel's* sleek hull. Wurther, Skip and Hurd watched the view from the drone camera, while Desna hung over Berlin's shoulder watching the screen on the remote. Berlin felt her warm breath on her skin. It excited her, imagining slowly peeling off that skintight leotard.

"Whoa, where you going there, Skipper?" Desna said, squeezing the skin at Berlin's waist.

Berlin hadn't noticed she was heading out into deep space, her mind focused elsewhere. She brought the drone around, proceeding down the length of the ship. Cargo Hold 36, 34, 32. Then farther down the hull, 14, 12, 10, passing each hatch, all in perfect condition. 8, 6, 4! Berlin paused the drone several meters out from the hatch to get a good look at it.

"Pull out farther," Desna said, glancing up at the big display. "Whatta you think, Wurther? I don't see anything wrong."

Wurther stepped closer to the big display. Using the remote, he increased the resolution until the image sharpened perceptibly. "Can you pull out, Berlin?"

The drone drew out slowly, framing the door into a wider

view, until the entire hatch filled the screen. Wurther shook his head. "Except for those huge dents, everything looks fine."

Desna eased closer to the big display. "Then the *thing* isn't gone! What the hell...!"

Berlin hurried the drone away from the hull, hoping Desna wouldn't still want to inspect the interior of Cargo Hold 4. So flustered by the events, Berlin accidentally rammed the drone into the hull of *Gretel*. Desna spun around with a worried look.

"It was me," Berlin said. "No big deal."

Desna and the crew members were discussing something, but Berlin couldn't follow the conversation enough to know what they were planning. Berlin figured if she hurried to dock the drone in the airlock, maybe Desna wouldn't entertain any ideas about trying the spacewalk mission today. After all, the entity had been quiet for over an hour. Maybe it was dead, and there was nothing else to be done.

"Berlin, stop," Desna said, rushing back over. "Don't dock the drone. We're gonna try the spacewalk, see if I can figure out what's going on inside Cargo Hold 4."

"But I almost have it docked." She continued guiding the small craft toward the opened hatch."

"Berlin! Turn it around and make it ready while I put on my suit. That's an order."

Desna looked over at Wurther and Hurd, motioning for them to follow her. Skip walked past Berlin and gave her a weak smile, then proceeded up the stairwell behind Desna, Wurther and Hurd.

Berlin brought the drone back around, guiding it down the length of the spacecraft, tempted to spin it out toward deep space and let it rip. It would keep moving away from *Gretel* until it was out of remote range and be impossible to bring back, lost to the ether forever. Maybe that would put an end to this hazardous spacewalk.

Still watching the drone screen, she moved the small craft closer to the exterior hatch of Cargo Hold 4, recalling how she'd placed her palm against the interior hatch that morning during her shift. The titanium had been cold. Very cold. After a moment, she had leaned in closer, until her nose was centimeters away, then shifted her head to press her ear against the frigid metal. At first, she'd heard nothing from the cargo chamber, just the eerie creaking of metal expansion issuing from the darkest parts of the storage vault. When that stopped, she thought she heard something from inside the hold, the memory distracting her.

Berlin took a moment to adhere the drone to the hull so she didn't have to concentrate on maneuvering it, waiting for Desna to appear.

Sitting alone on the bridge, she replayed inspecting the interior hatch that morning, pressing her ear firmly to the door, using one hand like a funnel, the other to cover her exposed ear to shut out ambient noise. She had to stop her breathing for a few seconds. It was odd; she thought she heard voices, like a conversation inside the cargo bay, but speaking too low to make out actual words. Or maybe it was a language she couldn't understand. She'd held her breath, trying to block out the sound of her own heart, pressing her ear tighter to the metal. That's when she heard it, and shot back from the door. She never told anyone about the incident.

Even now, in the stillness of the bridge, she could hear the seethe and whoosh in her head, the unmistakable sound of breathing! Something breathing next to the door, throaty and gruff. Then—but she couldn't be certain—it sounded as if a voice had muttered the word, *drone.*

CHAPTER SEVEN

DESNA WAS ALMOST FINISHED WITH HER ACCLIMATION PERIOD, her space helmet creating an unusual and welcome privacy barrier. Even though Wurther and Hurd were sitting only meters away, talking, they left her out of the conversation as if she weren't even present which was perfect for her. She enjoyed the down time, especially with the *thing* silent. It had to finally be dead, she figured, her mind moving to Berlin and why she'd been acting so strange. Why should Desna care if Berlin entertained Wurther in her quarters. It was as if Berlin wanted her to be jealous. But that was crazy. There was no place to go, even on a ship this size, with those kinds of clingy, childish emotions. They were going to be on this tub for decades, and they all needed to find a way to get through, to make the journey as harmonious as possible.

"Time, Des," Wurther said, looking up from his watch. Hurd checked her gloves, then the aux tank on her back, giving her the thumbs up.

"Can you hear me?" Wurther said into the comm.

"Let's get this show on the road," she responded, chuckling at the corny saying her father always used when he was in a hurry. She clomped toward the exterior airlock door, as Wurther and Hurd exited through the interior airlock, securing it from the inside. A moment later the outer door opened onto a star-studded pure black sky. She hadn't done a spacewalk in months. It seemed risky to have the captain of the ship out on walk detail, but Wurther, or Skip, would be able to take over just fine.

She eased from the hold, grabbing the metal-tube railing to pull herself along.

"How you doing, Des?"

"Hunky-dory."

Easing down *Gretel*'s exterior, she had forgotten this feeling, floating free, and couldn't understand why Berlin was so opposed to it. There was nothing in the world like it; not sex, not booze, not even winning the lottery, which she had almost done once, missing it by two letters and one number. Berlin had laughed at her, telling her she wasn't even close, that winning five meraks was hardly worth playing for. Desna had pinned the credits to her university office wall as a reminder that no one was excluded from great wealth. Of course, it wasn't long before she took down the meraks and bought a latte with them.

"Approaching Cargo Hold 4," Desna said into her helmet comm. "I see the CPV-drone, but it's attached to the hull. Is Berlin there?"

"Negative," Wurther shot back. "Haven't seen her."

"Is the drone remote there?"

"Negative."

Well fuck me all to hell, Desna thought, angry at Berlin for abandoning her on the spacewalk. *Goddamn her, anyway!* "We're going to proceed without her," Desna said. "I'm disconnecting the tether."

"Skip here," Skip said. "Shouldn't we wait for Berlin? I sent Hurd to find her."

"No, let's proceed. Removing umbilical tether, she'd have to rely only on her aux tank for air. After closing the valve on the tether hose connection, she twisted it until it clicked off and came free. She flipped up the connector tab and adhered it to the hull. "Tether secure. Moving to purge vent door."

"Wait. That's a bit dangerous..." Skip's voice betrayed his normal calm.

Without a SAFER, or the drone, Desna was extremely vulnerable; if she became separated from *Gretel*, there'd be no way for her to get back. Under normal circumstances, she'd either wear a SAFER, or a safety harness capable of firing a small emergency harpoon on a 300-meter cord designed to seek out the metal hull and attach itself. Once secure, it could safely hoist her back to the ship, the small projectile designed to "heal" the breach upon impact. Both safety devices, however, were too bulky to enter the purge vent.

"I'll be fine," Desna said. "Let's get that vent open."

"Got you," Wurther said, seemingly unfazed by the potential danger. "Opening the vent door now."

She tilted her head back to see it opening, then reached up to the handle above her, easing slowly toward the dark vent portal. In front of it now, she thought it appeared much narrower than she'd remembered. "Looks like a tight fit," she said. "Entering purge vent conduit."

"Be careful. Inspect it with your lamps first, make sure there're no obstacles."

"Visual inspection in progress." Below her she noticed movement, the CPV-drone sliding up *Gretel's* exterior. "Nice of you to join us, Berlin!" In seconds the drone was floating out from Desna, staying back to illuminate the side of the ship where Desna was working.

"Everything's A-OK." Desna took a deep breath. "Entering tube."

"Your blood pressure rising a little. Everything still go?"

"Everything's go."

"We have eyes on you now, courtesy of *The Yellow Submarine.*"

"Ha! Now all we need is *love, love, love...*" Desna eased into the tube, her aux tank scraping the top. She thought it might be more difficult, but without gravity, she could pull herself deeper into the tube with the slightest movement of her fingertips.

"Approaching interior vent door."

"We're going to shut the exterior vent now. It could get a little claustrophobic."

Desna referred to the tiny side mirror on her helmet, looking past her boots, watching the door go shut. She inadvertently took a deep breath, then another.

"Get your breathing under control, Des. We have you, okay?" Skip said.

She swallowed hard, nodding her head, perplexed by her sudden panic.

"Des, your blood pressure rising again. Do we need to abort?"

"No, I'm fine, for chrissakes! Get the fucking vent open!"

"You only have about twelve minutes of air left. You have to calm down."

She took a deep breath and let it out slowly. After a few more breaths, she felt her heart slowing. "I'm good now."

"Hatch opening."

She tilted her helmet forward to see the opening, but it was dark beyond the breach. She couldn't see anything, the beams from her lamps dying in the cold blackness of the cargo bay. "I'm scooting closer."

"Roger that."

Desna pulled herself forward until her fingertips clung to the lip of the opening. "I'm there. Shining my lamps into the bay now." Her beams fell on nothing, as if the entire cargo hold was empty. She inched closer until she was able to push her helmet through the breach, giving her the ability to rotate the lamps, cover more area.

"Are you getting this?" Desna couldn't see anything herself, and wondered if they had better visuals from the feed of her helmet camera.

"Not much to see so far. Pretty dark."

Just then the beams fell on something moving near the floor. "I've got movement!"

"Okay. Relax. Is there danger?"

Desna had no idea if it was *dangerous*, but there was no way anything should be *moving* in the damn cargo bay. She shifted the lamps to the left, hoping to find traction, when something shot past the beams. A loud screech blasted up from the hold, chilling her. "Did you hear that?"

"Roger!"

Before she could calm her heart, something raced up toward

her, coming within a meter of her face. She quickly pushed back from the opening. "Shut the interior vent! Quick! Get me the fuck outta here!"

She pushed backward away from the interior door, which hadn't completely closed yet. Another piercing screech echoed through the vent tube. "Come on! Get me outta this fucking tube!"

She pushed back until her boots hit the exterior door. She couldn't believe it wasn't open yet. She checked her side mirror, the area too dark behind her to see anything. "What's taking so long? Christ! Let's go!" Just then something started hammering on the purge duct, then the vent door, trying to pull it open, scratching down the length of the vent right beneath where she was prone.

"I'm under attack. Get me outta here!"

"The door is malfunctioning. You have to relax. You have less than three minutes of air. Regulate your breathing."

She kicked at the door, trying to open it, her body heat rising inside the suit, perspiration fogging her shield.

"We think your boots are stuck on the door somehow. Move forward a little."

Desna tried to inch forward, but her boots *were* stuck, and with little room to bend her knee, it was going to be hard to free them. She tried to grab onto something inside the tube, but it was so smooth, with no way to grip the surface. *How can I do this? Think, Desna. Dammit!* She figured if she reached forward and pressed her palms to both sides of the vent, she might be able to pry herself forward. With her hands set, she exerted as much pressure as she could muster, then pulled her elbows back slightly, easing herself forward until her boots came free. The door immediately started to open, the banging on the tube coming again, followed by a horrible shriek that nearly made her lose her bowels.

When the breach was clear, she hastily pushed herself free, then climbed down the side of the hull. She grabbed the tether hose and hooked it to her suit, twisting it until it locked, then released the valve and gulped at the fresh air.

"You okay, Desna?"

"I am now." She still felt a bit breathless.

"Your aux tank's on empty."

"Yeah, I know. Meet me at the airlock." She shot a glance at the CPV-drone camera, then pulled herself quickly along the hull, making sure she didn't lose her grip on the metal tube railing.

CHAPTER EIGHT

SHE HURRIED TO HER QUARTERS AFTER TELLING WURTHER AND Hurd she couldn't discuss anything until she changed clothes. After a quick shower, she wrapped herself in a towel and sat on the edge of the bed. "What the fuck was that?" She studied her hands, which were still shaking. She sniffled and tried to clean up her mind, which was a chaotic mess. Maybe she had imagined it, some kind of chimera her mind tossed out because she was under duress? Or maybe oxygen deprivation? Or just panic? Her chest was tight, her thoughts in disarray.

Hurrying to her bureau, she rummaged through the drawer until she found a joint and lighter. Flicking it on, she held the flame to the tip, then drew hard, holding the smoke in her lungs until they felt they would burst. She sat on the bed and took a few more hits before she put it out. A warm calm started in her abdomen, spreading to her chest, then her arms and legs. She could never un-see what she'd witnessed in the cargo hold.

A knock came at her door. "Who is it?"

"Me! Can I come in?"

"This isn't a great time, Berlin. Please, I just need a few moments, okay."

Desna hated sending her away, but was still struggling with what to tell the crew, especially Wurther. How in the world could she look him in the eye and explain what she'd seen? But maybe she hadn't seen anything but a phantasm, some bizarre illusion forged by misfiring synapses and stress. Maybe she should go to sickbay, get checked out. Just then, Chelsey jumped in her head. Is that what Chelsey had seen? Is that what induced her shock, put her into a coma?

The pot was taking over, quieting her mind, smoothing out the rough spots, filling in the gaps with vacant space. Soon she was drifting, her mind trying to pull her into dreams, until she saw Wurther again, rushing up from the dark to meet her, arms outstretched, his face a tangled mess of pain and anguish, his eyes red, pleading.

She shot up in bed, sweat pebbling her face, her mind spinning. Gasping for air, she glanced down at her hands, which were shaking again. She clasped them together to make them stop.

"Des? You in there?"

"Yeah, Skip, I'm still getting dressed."

"Okay. See you in ten?"

"I'll be there." She wiped her eyes, unaware she'd been crying. The memories from the cargo hold were starting to crystalize, more details surfacing. Others had been there, people she didn't recognize, floating below Wurther, indistinct, their faces hidden in shadow, vague, or maybe malformed. But the one thing they all had in common, what she could sense immediately; they were all horrified. And trapped. Their faces ravaged, suffering, as if they were being tortured, or burned alive.

She checked the mirror, rubbed the puffiness beneath her eyes, then headed from her living space. They planned to meet in the conference room. When she arrived, Wurther, Hurd, Skip and Doc Karl were seated, talking. Wurther was laughing about something, but all conversation ceased when she entered the room. Wurther half stood, prompted most likely by some outmoded chivalrous inclination. Desna shook her head and took her seat. Berlin was noticeably missing.

"Anyone seen Berlin?" Desna sipped the coffee someone had brought for her.

"She said she'd be here," Doc Karl said. "She was kind of upset about something, though." Doc glanced over at Hurd. "I told Hurd here that she may need to talk with someone." Doc turned to face him. "Did you speak with her?"

Desna waited for Hurd to answer, but the curious man seemed to be more focused on his folded hands resting on the table.

"Hurd?" Desna shouted, pressing him to answer. "What's going on? Did you speak with her—"

"I spoke to her..." he said, cutting Desna off, his features pulled tight. "Of course, I did. That's my job!"

Desna had never seen him react this way, and by the look on the other crew members' faces, neither had they. Stress levels were off the charts, no doubt, but Hurd, because of his hybrid physiology, had always been immune to the tension and pressure. That's what made him the perfect spiritual guru; his unflappable optimism and inner harmony.

"I think..." Hurd began, clearly struggling with something. "I think that I should respect the privacy of each and every crew member by not discussing what they tell me in confidence."

"Christ, Hurd, who asked you to!" Desna was flummoxed by his declaration. "I just want to know if she's coming!"

Hurd tensed suddenly, pulling his hands back to his lap as if he'd been assigned the task of protecting some treacherous cosmic secret, like he'd made a death-pact with truth and honor. His behavior left Desna more than a little perturbed; she was creeped-out by his quirky demeanor.

A heavy silence hung in the room until the moaning and howling started again, rising up through the floor of the conference room, echoing off the walls.

Desna flopped back in her chair, shaking her head. "Ah, sweet Jesus, not again..."

Timed to the event, tortured faces wheeled through her skull, coming at her as they had in the purge vent. She could easily merge the soundless scene playing in her head with the dreadful cries issuing from Cargo Hold 4. It was driving her mad.

"What's wrong, Desna?"

She looked up to see everyone staring at her. "I can't take much more of this horrible wailing! We have to do something!"

The crew members appeared confused by her statement, as if

they didn't understand what she was talking about. "You do hear that, don't you?" she said.

They looked at each other then back at her. "Hear what?" Doc Karl said.

What fresh new hell had she stumbled into? No one else was hearing this? Before, at least, when everyone else witnessed the mewling and banging, it was a shared experience, a reality that they all agreed upon. But now... she knew she couldn't bear up against this alone. She'd go out of her mind. Maybe she already had. *Ignore the sounds,* she told herself. *Block them out or be lost forever.* That was it; she'd just have to block it out, at least try. Or go insane. Just then, the wailing stopped so suddenly she thought she'd lost her hearing, until Wurther spoke.

"You don't look good. Let's postpone this meeting."

She cut her eyes toward him. Wurther was reaching out to her with both arms, pleading with burnished eyes, his flesh ruined with anguish and fear... and then he was just sitting there calmly, arms resting on the table, concern coloring his face.

It took a moment to compose herself. She sniffled, and cleared her throat. "I'm okay." She felt certain this was just residual trauma from what she'd experienced in the purge vent, imagery living on her retinas, which would fade over time. She looked over at Doc.

"What's going on with Chelsey?" She wondered if Chelsey might be experiencing these same kinds of phantasms. Maybe that's why the vibrant young woman was having difficulty extricating herself from the coma, if it even was one. Desna couldn't be sure of anything anymore, as if she and the crew had drifted into a new paradigm, one where the rules were not yet clearly defined.

"No change," Doc said. "Her vitals are fine. Everything's fine with her... she's just not shaking out of it."

"Is it possible it's not a coma?" Desna asked, wanting to ease into this discussion. She didn't want to cause alarm, or put them on edge—no matter what was going on in Cargo Hold 4, the crew still had to function. They had to have a successful merger with BC-1, or this entire mission was going down the crapper in a hurry. The whole crew would be in peril.

"Truthfully, anything's possible. I can't say for sure she's in a coma, but whatever it is, she's *offline,* so to speak."

Desna nodded, really wishing she could get Chelsey's take on this aberration; she was the only other person to have a direct experience with it.

Desna took a deep breath to calm herself. "What did you get off my helmet cam?"

No one spoke, which seemed odd. Desna was becoming agitated with their silence. "Did anyone check the damn footage?"

"There was nothing to see." Skip shrugged apologetically. "A blurry smudge of light before you backed away from the vent portal. We went frame by frame. Even sharpened the three frames the smudged light appeared on... but nothing..."

Desna witnessed more than a blurry smudge of light, but contesting the video was pointless. "Okay, so... this is not an easy conversation to start." Desna was still unsure how to proceed. Everyone settled into their seats, the room silent except for the gentle whoosh of the ceiling air exchanger, scrubbing and enhancing the atmosphere so they could breathe it again.

"I experienced something which is very hard to describe," Desna started. "So, please, process what I'm about to tell you with the necessary detachment of scientists, or we'll get nowhere." She filtered her description through an academic lens, presenting the raw facts, avoiding hysterical overtones, tamping down speculation and hyperbole. It required a sober approach, or the mission would devolve into a chaotic clusterfuck.

When she finished, everyone sat somberly, assimilating her discourse in their own way, in their own time. Wurther was the first to speak.

"You saw *ME!*" he blurted, clearly vexed, his face drained of life.

She hadn't expected such a reaction from an ex-paramilitary type like Wurther. He may have worked as a mercenary for several years, but in order to qualify for this mission, he'd had to take university-level courses on general science and space sciences, had to perform numerous experiments dealing with hypotheticals and theories, ingest massive amounts of scientific data and spit it back out with the dispassionate, analytic mind of an astronaut. Now he was acting like a high school kid who'd found out his girlfriend was cheating on him.

"No, I didn't see *you!*" she screamed back, momentarily losing her cool. "How could I? Were you cavorting around in Cargo Hold 4 when I was squeezed into that goddamn tube!"

He recoiled into his own thoughts, hanging his head like a scolded dog. It was now obvious to Desna that her outburst had managed to muzzle everyone who wanted to ask questions. That was never her intent, but obviously she had not come to a place of acceptance with her own experience. She was afraid. Why did she expect any less of Wurther?

"I'm sorry. Look, I have no clue what's going on down in that damn hold, but—"

Hurd interrupted. "She's terrified!" Hurd blurted out. "That's why she didn't come."

All eyes shifted to Hurd.

Desna said, "Berlin? What's got her so frightened?"

He cleared his throat and sat up straighter, as if he needed to assert some professionalism now, especially after violating his own ethics around confidentiality. "I only tell you this as it now seems germane to this discussion."

He said no more and was getting on Desna's last nerve.

"Goddamn it, Hurd. Don't make me keep dragging this out of you! It's exhausting!"

He hesitated, massaging the knuckles on his left hand with his right, as if he were trying to polish them to a reflective sheen. More throat clearing, until he finally spoke, unable to make eye contact with Desna.

"This morning, during her shift, Berlin was curious about the dents in the interior hatch door." Here he shifted his eyes quickly toward Desna, then back to his lap. "So, she went down to check on it. She placed her ear against the hatch to listen..." He stopped, as if he couldn't go on and Desna was just about to shout at him again.

"She heard breathing," he said, inhaling suddenly.

"Breathing?" Skip said, visibly perplexed.

Doc Karl, like a true scientist, scrunched up his face in

concentration, stroking the small beard on his chin with his fore-finger and thumb, apparently pondering the bizarre turn of events. Wurther, seemingly unable to recover from Desna's experience in the purge tube, was most likely stuck there himself. It was impossible to read Hurd's emotional landscape, but Desna was trying to gauge everyone's reaction, wondering if she'd have a reliable crew after all this. She had to snap them out if it.

"Questions? Suggestions? This is not the time to retreat to your own fantasy islands and private hells," she said. "We have obligations moving forward. The merger with BC-1. Crucial. We need to focus or we're done for! Come on, now. We are a team and we need to act like one."

Wurther stood up and left without a word.

"Ah, fuck no!" she said, angry. But mostly afraid. Even so, she couldn't let it show or it would spread like a virus. "Anyone else want to mutiny?"

Skip spoke first. "Nobody's quitting, Captain. Wurther just needs a minute, okay? He's solid. Everyone here is. The team is solid. We're all solid..."

Desna prayed Skip, was right, and that he truly believed what he insisted was true. What made her nervous was that he kept repeating it over and over, as if attempting to convince himself. She was hanging by a very sketchy thread and wasn't sure how long she could do this alone. If everyone succumbed to their fears, the whole crew, including herself, might as well just eject themselves into outer space.

CHAPTER NINE

BEFORE THE MEETING ENDED, THEY ALL AGREED THAT THE most important objective now was to focus on the merger with BC-1. If Cargo Hold 4 became an issue again, they'd have to formulate a strategy to deal with it. Hurd floated the idea of purging Cargo Hold 4, all its contents, claiming that they had basically just begun their expedition, and there were plenty of other samples and artifacts they'd be gathering.

Desna wasn't wild about that idea. They were scientists, after all; you didn't just throw everything out because a new wrinkle in the research presented itself. The occurrence in Cargo Hold 4 needed to be studied, but how?

"We could flood Cargo hold 4 with poisonous gas," Skip said, seemingly content with his suggestion.

"That's a great idea, Skip!" Desna said, so perturbed with the ex-navy guy she couldn't contain her sarcasm. "Now all we need to do is buy some poisonous gas!"

Skip retreated back into his chair, folding his arms over his belly.

"Sorry, Skip, but whatever this *thing* is," she said, softening her bitchy tone, "it doesn't seem to need air, so I don't think any kind of poison is going to phase it. We'd probably just end up killing ourselves."

Apparently, Skip approved of her hypothesis, unfolding his

arms and sitting forward again, nodding his agreement, then: "But Berlin said she heard breathing..."

Desna was exasperated. "We can't be sure what she heard."

Desna met everyone's eyes, trying to pool their attention again. "Okay, so, let's allow our better angels and subconscious brains to forge a solution to the problem of Cargo Hold 4. For now, let's concentrate all our focus on a successful merger with BC-1."

After the men left the room, Desna sat a moment, finishing her coffee, wondering if everyone else was lying to themselves about focusing on the merger and ignoring Cargo Hold 4. That's what they needed to do, but Desna couldn't flush the damn images from her brain, Wurther racing up toward her, arms outstretched, the distorted faces floating below him like a convocation of the damned. She downed the last of her coffee and was heading out when Doc Karl came back in.

Desna looked up at him, hoping he didn't have bad news he felt uncomfortable sharing in the group. He sat next to Desna and swiveled to face her. She waited.

"I have concerns, Captain."

Desna wasn't sure she wanted to hear them.

"Chelsey isn't in a coma," he said. "I know that. But the problem is, I don't know what *is* going on with her. She's perfectly normal... except for not being responsive. I'm going to run more tests, but I'm limited on this ship. I'm sorry to have to admit this, but I'm kind of out of ideas... is there any way we can contact Mission Command?"

Desna knew they'd lost contact with MC a month earlier. She had played it down so the crew wouldn't panic, but the entire team was briefed on this before they signed on, that this could happen at some point during their voyage. It was possible that the messages had just not reached MC yet, or the responses were taking a long time to return. Either way, *Gretel* was no longer in contact with anyone. The crew had only themselves to depend on now.

"Sure, I'll send something out. Can't hurt, right?" Desna hoped to lend some encouragement to the doctor. Nevertheless, he'd most likely read her feeble attempt at placating him. "Is that it?"

"No, not exactly," he said, in a grave tone. "I am really worried about Fawn. I can't crack her virus. I've exhausted all the tests I can run. I see the damn thing on my microscope, but I don't know how to counteract it. It's impervious to all the normal countermeasures I know. It would take a team of scientists months, even years, working with state-of-the-art equipment, to find a suitable treatment." Doc paused, visibly perplexed, then added: "I'm afraid she won't make it, and..."

Desna waited but was getting antsy. "And...?"

"I think it's related to whatever's happening in Cargo Hold 4. It was after our exploration on J-78 that she started getting sick... Fawn's young, Desna. She should have bounced back by now..."

Desna knew all of that was true, but had never wanted to connect their last exploration to Fawn's condition. She had conveniently attributed the illness to Fawn's weakened immune system. Fawn had been experiencing complications acclimating to space travel for some reason, finding it difficult getting proper rest. Being in space seemed to throw off the young child's circadian rhythms and REM sleep. But Fawn marshaled through, her tenacious personality pushing her beyond her biological limits. No one scored higher on the physical and psychological evals than Fawn. On paper, at least, Fawn was the consummate astronaut.

"If you're right," Desna said. "It would seem we need to study this phenomenon in Cargo Hold 4 closer, don't you think?"

Doc Karl seemed to buck at this notion. "I don't know, Des. I hear what you're saying, and it makes sense... but... that seems so risky. At least from what I've heard so far." Doc Karl studied on something for a moment, then: "I wouldn't know where to start."

Desna nodded. "Let's sleep on it."

"Together?" Doc Karl said, smiling.

"Funny."

CHAPTER TEN

THE MERGER WAS ONLY HOURS AWAY. SKIP ASSURED HER everything was set. He adjusted *Gretel's* speed so they would creep up on the supply vessel nice and easy, like a rattlesnake on a mouse.

Desna wasn't sure she liked the analogy, but she appreciated his confidence and enthusiasm. Over the past several days Cargo Hold 4 had remained pretty quiet, at least for the rest of the crew. For her, however, the cargo hold was like a scorned lover, stalking her at bedtime, serenading her with mournful cries and painful sobbing. Occasionally she'd hear scratching along the ceiling, or the walls, or tapping along the floor of her personal quarters. It took a few nights before she successfully managed to shut out the anguished pleas and incessant scraping, and woke refreshed.

Berlin had made herself scarce over the past few days, and while Desna was upset with her First mate, and on-again-off-again lover, for being absent when they needed her, she also respected the space Berlin needed right now. Desna checked in with Hurd several times to see if Berlin was okay, Hurd assuring her that she was, but repeated ad nauseam that he couldn't discuss "details."

Desna took a seat on the bridge and asked for an update.

"Right on target," Skip said, his tone so familiar and calm it was hard at times for Desna to remember they had a *monster* in the cargo storage, at least that's how she was responding within her own mind. What she'd seen, which came back in fragments, was an anomaly, and much more than the sum of its parts, an unexplainable, indescribable beast that came in her dreams. Enormous and unwieldy, and beyond her rudimentary comprehension, which is why she chose not to discuss it with any of the crew. What good would that do? Maybe, if the images started eroding away at her well-being, she'd entertain a session or two with Hurd... especially given his new, hardline relationship to ethics. She chuckled to herself about Hurd's steadfast insistence on secrecy.

"Making our approach, Captain," Skip said, Desna embracing the formality during crucial maneuvers. It was a stark reminder to the crew of how important and serious their work needed to be at times like this; their survival depended on it.

Just then, Berlin plopped down next to Desna and smiled over at her, then took her attention back to the docking procedure unfolding in the huge window at the bow of the bridge. At times it was hard to parse the scene as anything other than a simulation, not unlike the hundreds, thousands, they sat through in training. Witnessing it for real, though, made Desna's knees turn to jelly. *Remarkable!* she thought, hoping the rest of the crew was experiencing this as the magnificent moment it was.

"We are nearing the cargo bay doors of *Gretel,*" Skip stated, unable to keep his mingled anxiety and excitement from his voice. "We... have... link-up, people!"

Applause and cheers filled the bridge, people leaving their stations to land happy-slaps on the nearest backs, hugging each other when that wasn't enough.

Berlin wore a broad smile. Without taking her eyes from the window, she rested her hand softly on Desna's and squeezed. "Nice job, babe," Berlin said in a whisper, the pride in her voice unmistakable.

Desna allowed the celebration to continue for a few minutes before she stood and addressed the room. "Listen up, people. If they could have witnessed this perfect merger today, I know your instructors back at the academy on Earth would be dripping with pride at your accomplishment. I know I am. The Bread-crumb Program will crush the limits of space travel, opening it to future voyagers like you. The universe will no longer have boundaries, except for those we impose upon ourselves!" She paused, allowing everyone to feel the exhilaration she was experiencing in the moment. "The first moonwalk!" she said. "The International Space Station! The very first colonies on Mars! And now this! You just made the history books today, folks!" Desna was proud, but knew, that while they may very well make the history books, none of them would probably live to see it. All except for Fawn, and maybe Chelsey.

When the celebration subsided, Desna announced that they had much work to do and needed to get to it. She was glad to see Wurther celebrate with everyone, like his old self. He'd been glum since their meeting, avoiding Desna and not making much of a secret of it.

When she turned to leave, she was so excited, not to mention surprised, to see Fawn and Chelsey standing together at the back. Doc Karl hadn't said anything about Chelsey *waking up.*

"Fawn! Chelsey! I'm so glad you got to see out first merger!" Desna reached out to take their hands.

"Wouldn't miss it, Chief!" Chelsey said, full of life.

Fawn, wearing a mask over her nose and mouth, still didn't look good, but she nodded, appearing truly happy to have witnessed the link-up. Doc Karl walked over to stand by the two women.

"Miraculous, huh?" Doc said, then shrugged, letting Desna know he had no clue what happened.

Fawn's eyes were smiling, as if she felt it necessary to sport a brave face. But her expression sagged when she looked over at Doc Karl, who nodded, then escorted her off the bridge. Chelsey watched them leave, before bringing her attention back to Desna.

"Are you going down to help transfer provisions?" Chelsey asked Desna, her manner absolutely bubbly.

"I am... but *you* need to rest," Desna said.

"Thanks, but I've had my fill of rest! See you down there,"

Chelsey said, bounding from the bridge, merging seamlessly into the crew members headed for the hold, as if she'd never been incapacitated.

Desna stood dumbstruck, and slightly askew. It had almost been a direct order, but Chelsey treated it as a suggestion. Desna had hoped to speak with Doc Karl, and then Chelsey, to learn more about her experience with Cargo Hold 4, but everything had happened so fast her thoughts became jumbled, lost cohesion. Now she stood on the bridge alone, looking out at BC_1 synched with *Gretel*. It *was* miraculous.

CHAPTER ELEVEN

DESNA COULD NOT HAVE HOPED FOR A BETTER OUTCOME, THE crew moving supplies with two forklifts from BC-1 into cargo holds 40, 39 and 38. If they had to, they'd use cargo hold 37, too. The lower numbers were reserved for artifacts, samples and articles of interest they gathered during expeditions. All digital data —video, photographic and holographic—was stored on the computer system, as well backed up on external memory cubes stored in a shock-proof sealed vault on deck two. Supposedly it could withstand a major crash and fire. She didn't plan to test that theory.

Hurd stood by, videotaping the entire process. If they could transmit any of this back to Earth, she was sure the masterminds of the BreadCrumb system would be elated! It was a total success, except for arriving at the cache nearly eight months early. But given the magnitude of the accomplishment, the time discrepancy seemed like a small issue, which could be solved through better planning, or more precise speed regulation. Regardless, it was a sight to see.

Desna smiled at Hurd as she walked past, toward the darker end of the storage area, down toward Cargo Hold 4. Even while Desna appreciated the new solemnity, she didn't trust the calm. Cargo Hold 4 came in a like a lion, and, so far, went out like a flea. Something wasn't right.

Standing before the huge titanium door, she let her gaze investigate each of the enormous random welts protruding from the otherwise smooth metal. She recalled what Hurd had said about Berlin, that she had put her ear to the door. Desna stepped closer, leaning in, turning her head to the side. She caught herself swallowing hard, could feel her heart ramping up. What was she afraid of? Nothing could get through this enormous door. At least the thing behind it couldn't, as evidenced by the myriad attempts.

The titanium was cold against her ear. She waited, trying to quell her breath so she could hear better. The crew at the other end of the hold was laughing and talking, making it hard to hear. She put her hand over her free ear and tried again.

"Desna..."

"Holy fuck," Desna whispered to herself.

"Desna..."

Desna shot back from the door, her heart galloping.

"Des? I didn't mean to startle you..."

Desna shot around to see Berlin standing there, her eyes apologetic. Exhaling slowly, Desna worked to compose herself.

"Hey, you okay?" Berlin said, drawing closer, reaching out to take Desna's hands. "I'm sorry for being absent lately."

Desna's chest was a hornet's nest, making it hard to calm her breath, as if her lungs were spasming. She forced a deep breath to get things under control.

"Berlin, how's the transfer going?"

"That's what I wanted to talk to you about."

Berlin wasted no time relaying her plan. Desna listened, unsure if it was even possible. She suggested that they could merge *Gretel* with the supply vessel, but instead of where they were currently connected, they could create the link-up with Cargo Bay 4, then open both hatches and maybe the *thing* would move into the supply vessel.

"Then we lock it in there," Berlin said.

Desna liked the simplicity of it, but wasn't sure it was feasible. Could *Gretel* move backwards? Were all the cargo bays compatible with BC-1? How would they coax the thing into the supply vessel? There were a lot of questions, but the plan had merit. Skip would have to weigh in. He'd know if it was worth a try.

"Did you hear it?" Berlin said.

Desna was about to ask what she was referring to, but didn't. She already knew. "No, I didn't hear anything."

Berlin scoffed, with a sour look. "Good. It was creepy."

By the sound of the forklifts and laughter, it was obvious the crew hadn't finished with the supplies. Berlin and Desna walked down to speak with Skip. He was taking a break, studying the new manifest, typing notes into the spreadsheet about where each box and bag and fuel canister was being stored.

"Skip, how's it going?" Desna asked.

He nodded, obviously pleased. "Great, actually. This was brilliant, being able to link like this. Makes this so easy."

"Good.... Berlin has an idea, and I want to know if it will work." She turned to Berlin. "Tell him."

Berlin went through the entire plan, Skip nodding as she went. At certain points his eyes narrowed, and he'd look off into some void obviously seeking the correct answer. When Berlin finished, Skip started nodding, a satisfied smile breaking across his face.

"I like it. Physics, mechanics and math," Skip said. "Nobody crawling into purge vents! I just have to check the schematics to see if all the cargo doors are compatible with BC-1. They seem to be, but until I check I won't know."

"How about *Gretel* moving backward?" Desna said.

Skip cleared his throat a couple times. "Yeah, well, if Fawn wasn't laid up in sick bay, she could easily crunch the numbers to make it work. Have to figure out how much we need to slow *Gretel* once we're disconnected, so we can ease back just a little and not miss our opportunity. Don't forget, we're traveling at just a skosh over 24,400 mph right now. So, that's the tricky part. Getting the math right."

"So it could work?"

"Sure. Let me get on those schematics as soon as I'm done here." He nodded at Desna, then smiled over at Berlin. "Good thinking, girl. We can't be losing our captain in a goddamn purge vent! How would that look on a casualty report?" As soon as his

words echoed back inside his head, Skip's pleasant demeanor
darkened. "That was a stupid thing to say, bringing up casualty
reports!"

"Don't worry about it," Desna said. "Just get me the info as
soon as you can."

Skip walked away with his portable pad, still shaking his head
over his comment.

Berlin spun toward Desna. "I've been scared of losing you
lately." Berlin's eyes were filling up. "I told Wurther our conjugal
visits were over. I just want to be with you."

Desna was about to tell her she didn't have to do that, end
her time with Wurther, but she knew Berlin would take it the
wrong way. Or maybe the right way. Either way, Desna didn't care
who the young woman had sex with. They were going to be out
here a long time, and it was wise to find a way to make it work,
no matter what that entailed.

"Want some company later?" Berlin asked.

As great as that sounded, Desna knew she wanted, *needed*, to
be alone. Until this *thing* was off *Gretel*, she could never fully
relax.

CHAPTER TWELVE

THE PLAN HAD MORE THAN *MERIT*. ACCORDING TO SKIP, IT was brilliant! *Gretel* could use any of its cargo hold doors to dock with BC-1. The schematics didn't lie, and the designers of both ships seemingly had planned for any and all contingencies. It had taken thirty-six hours for Skip to make sure it was possible, and he was convinced it was. That was enough for Desna to move forward with the plan.

When she walked into Skip's office, he was at the computer checking more schematics.

"We still good to go?" Desna said, walking to his terminal.

He nodded without turning around, his fingers banging out commands.

"I'm not feeling the same confidence you had this morning." Desna regarded him with a new queasiness sitting in her gut.

"No... no, I know it will work. I can't get the math right..."

"How do you know it's not right?"

Skip pushed away from his terminal, sending his office chair across the room to his simulator. "Watch."

Desna studied the monitor, watching *Gretel* being slowly overtaken by BC-1, as if *Gretel* was slowly losing a very close race. She continued staring at the screen, trying to figure out the problem, when *Gretel* began the link-up procedure with BC-1, causing an explosion which sent both damaged vessels spinning off into space.

"This happens every time and I can't figure it out."

"What are the variables?"

Skip scratched his ear, gazing at the screen. *"Gretel's* speed is the biggest factor. But there's also the angle of BC-1 in relation to *Gretel,* which is crucial. When we approach from behind, as we did the other day for our maiden merger, BC-1was a constant, and it was easy to adjust... well, not *easy,* but easier to adjust the angle and pitch of *Gretel* to match BC-1. I mean, we ran over that kind of simulation thousands of times at the training center. *Gretel* was designed for that kind of operation, approaching from behind, matching pitch and angle..."

"But not designed for approaching from the front, backwards," Desna reasoned.

"When you put it like that, it sounds impossible..."

"Do we need to scrap this plan?" Desna was now feeling it was too risky.

"I don't know... it's a great plan, and it could just work... but..."

"But?"

Skip exhaled audibly, clearly frustrated. "I can't do the damn math! I feel like such a fucking idiot! I've run these numbers so many times I can't remember where I started or where I'm at..."

"Take a break, Skip." Desna squeezed his shoulder. "Get some sleep. If you can't figure it out after you've had a full eight, we'll blow it off and figure out something else." Desna came around to face him. "Cargo Hold 4's been pretty quiet lately. Maybe the problem solved itself, you know. Maybe the damn thing died." If that were true, Desna wouldn't still be treated every night to hours of wailing and screeching and clawing at the walls. She'd found a pair of sound-cancelling headphones in the supply room and wore those to sleep. The sound was obviously not just in her head, because the headphones actually worked. But that created a new problem; being vulnerable to intruders, as she'd never hear them enter her quarters. The crew wasn't her concern, but she'd questioned herself numerous times about what her concern was.

"You don't believe that..." Skip said. "That it's dead..."

"No. But for now, I pretend it is. Get some sleep. We'll touch base later."

There was nothing more to discuss. She knew Skip was disgusted with himself, but he wasn't picked for this mission because of his math skills. She wanted him to understand that, but she could see he was so tired he'd never hear it. Sleep was what he needed most.

Heading back to the bridge, she decided to take a short detour. When she entered sick bay, she didn't see Doc Karl at first. Looking around, she thought she heard crying, but it wasn't the resonant, otherworldly wailing she'd become accustomed to from Cargo Hold 4. This was human sobbing. Sadness. When she entered Doc Karl's office, he was seated at his desk, his head in his hands, his back heaving.

She decided to knock on the jamb.

"Yes," he said, drying his eyes before he got up from his chair and turned toward her. "Captain Desna. How can I help you?"

Judging by the redness of his eyes, this had been going on for a while.

"By telling me what happened." She took a seat by the door.

Doc Karl sat down abruptly, as if all the air had rushed out of him. "Nothing happened. Please, Captain, tell me what I can do for you." He slipped his glasses off the desk and fixed them on his nose. "I'm just tired. I was getting ready to go back to my quarters."

"Then I won't keep you." Desna hesitated. "I need to know if you think Fawn is strong enough to crunch some numbers for Skip?"

Doc Karl appeared stunned, his eyes bright as light bulbs. Soon he was sobbing into his palms, his body quaking. Desna rushed over, levering his head up gently with her fingers beneath his chin. He jerked away, his face damp.

She squatted down in front of him, placing her palms on his knees. "Karl, what is going on?"

"Fawn..." He seemed to struggle with the next part. "She's dying."

"What? That can't be..."

Doc Karl sniffled and shook his head. He cleared his throat, then wiped his mouth and cheeks. "I don't know how I missed it, Desna. All this time I thought she had some kind of viral infection... I ran a new battery of tests, and... she has congenital heart disease, and I have no way to treat it. I ruled it out because she passed all the physical exams at the academy. Surely it should have shown up. Somehow we all missed it."

"Can you do anything?"

"Not here, not on this ship! And she's at great risk of congestive heart failure."

Desna was dumbstruck. Fawn was the lynchpin of this entire mission. Without her, there was little chance *Gretel* could ever return to Earth. And she was so young, coming up on her seventeenth birthday in two months. "How long does she have?"

Doc Karl shook his head. "Impossible to know. Could be two years, or two weeks. Two days. She's young, a fighter, but... she's just getting weaker and weaker."

Desna pulled a chair up next to Karl and put her arm around him. "You can't blame yourself. The best medical facility on Earth missed it. She would never been approved for this mission if they'd known. You know that. This isn't your fault."

"It just isn't right. Sixteen, dying of heart disease...? It isn't right!"

"Karl, turn off the lights and go get some rest. We've all been burning the candle at both ends these past couple weeks, with BC-1... and... everything..."

He nodded, sniffling, still trying to compose himself. "I'm gonna lock up for the night. Sorry I can't help you with your calculations. I don't think Fawn would be—"

"Stop. Karl. Go get some sleep. We'll figure it out, okay?"

When she felt he had himself under control, she told him goodnight and headed back to her own quarters. It felt like everything was spinning out of control. The merger had gone so well, but now things were coming apart. How could Fawn be dying? She was just a child, and she wondered if Karl had told her yet, or if he would. What was the point of her knowing if he couldn't do anything about it? She was almost to her door when someone called to her. She was pleasantly surprised at Chelsey coming down the corridor.

"Headed to the bridge?"

"No, not for another hour," Chelsey said. "I saw you come out of sick bay and thought we could talk if you're not too tired."

"Sure. I've been wanting to."

Inside her compartment, Desna offered her a seat and something to drink.

"Vodka, if you have it."

Desna drew the bottle out of cold storage and poured her a small glass.

"You feeling okay?" Chelsey asked, taking the glass from Desna's hand.

"Yeah, I'm fine. Just gabbing with Doc Karl." Desna sat across from the young woman, who seemed surprisingly spry for someone just coming out of a coma. "So... do you recall much about your spacewalk that day? Do you remember what freaked you out?"

"Oh, sure! Like it was yesterday. Of course on this ship it's hard to tell yesterday from today, isn't it!" Chelsey chuckled, then sipped the vodka.

"Can you tell me more about—"

"I saw you," Chelsey blurted out, interrupting Desna's equilibrium. "I saw your face through the glass." Chelsey wore a grave expression, the memory obviously still very raw. "You were in agony, terrified. I could hardly stand to look at you." Chelsey paused, her expression blank. She took a long draw from the glass, finishing her vodka.

Desna, feeling a gnawing emptiness from Chelsey's disclosure, stood, a bit shakily, to pour her another drink but Chelsey refused. "I'm good."

Desna sat back down, a bit lightheaded.

"Do you hear them before you go to sleep?" Chelsey asked matter-of-factly. "Crying? Scratching at the walls and ceiling? Knocking on the floor?"

Desna was struggling to regain her footing in the conversation, her mind tilting off center. She could only regard the young woman as if she were studying a rare chemical compound.

"Judging by your expression, I'll take that as a yes?" Chelsey smiled and crossed her legs. "Have you been called yet?"

"Called?"

"Yes, summoned. You will be." Chelsey made her claim with such conviction, Desna felt her insides tumbling.

"Have you? Been *summoned?*" Desna asked, unsure what she was really asking. It all sounded too bizarre.

"I have. But they didn't say much. Actually... I guess, they didn't really say anything at all." Chelsey laughed briefly, as if she'd just remembered that there had never been a conversation.

Desna was confused, and frightened. She wasn't sure what she expected to hear from Chelsey, but it certainly wasn't this.

"You look really tired," Chelsey said, standing. "And my shift is about to start." Chelsey walked over and hugged Desna. "This was fun... and thanks for the vodka. I promise I'm not high or anything. No need to worry. Goodnight!"

Desna eased the door shut behind Chelsey, trying to restore order to her ravaged mind. She ambled through her compartment, shutting off lights, then sat on the edge of the bed in the dark and removed her shoes and socks. For a long while she just stared out the window across her room. The stars were unmoving, frozen in a pure black sky, like ice crystals. With her mind still whirling, as if she'd been the one drinking vodka, she reached the conclusion that their current situation was untenable. No matter the risk, they had to rid *Gretel* of this aberration.

CHAPTER THIRTEEN

ANXIOUS AND UNNATURALLY QUIET, THE CREW SAT AT THEIR stations preparing for this tricky gambit with BC-1. Skip was performing last-minute simulations, adjusting the calculations to achieve just the right pitch and speed for *Gretel's* unorthodox reverse approach. Wurther stood next to him, helping to adjust the computations, offering suggestions. Hurd never looked up from his screen, his fingers tapping out a detailed report outlining the procedures. Eventually, once Skip settled on the correct math and equations, Hurd would add them in. Desna felt it best not to inform the crew of the potential peril of their undertaking. *Undertaking,* Desna thought. What a terrible word for her mind to have chosen at this time.

Across the bridge, Chelsey worked at her computer with unsettling detachment, as if nothing had happened to her, while Desna struggled to dismiss their recent conversation, which occupied every spare moment in Desna's fragmented mind. Doc Karl entered the bridge and came over where Desna was working. When she spotted him, her first thoughts went to Fawn, that something had happened to her. But Karl's demeanor was too relaxed.

"How's it going?" he said to her in a soft voice. "Almost ready?"

Desna was shaky, no longer believing Skip was capable of

pulling this off. If she had to, she'd put an end to the whole operation before it spun out of control. Desna smiled up at Doc,
then went back to her screen. Doc Karl meandered around the
bridge, looking over shoulders, checking displays, probably
needing a break from sick bay and his own feelings of powerless-
ness. She knew Fawn's condition weighed heavily on him.

Berlin hurried into the bridge and slid into her chair next to
Desna. "We all set?"

"Not sure," Desna said under her breath. "Keep an eye on
Skip and Wurther, and let me know what you think."

Berlin got up, checking in at everyone's work station, pausing
to strike up a casual conversation with the two men who held
the fate of *Gretel* in their fingertips. Wurther smiled and joked
with Berlin, while Skip was all business, his face pulled tighter
than a snare drum. His fingers never stopped typing. From
across the bridge, Desna couldn't tell if his brow was beaded
with sweat, but that was always a dead giveaway he was under
duress.

Hurd came over to Desna to tell her he had to check in at
the sanitation plant, but assured her he'd be back before the
merger attempt with Cargo Hold 4.

"Thanks for the heads up." She watched him hurrying off to
his next assignment. It was unfortunate that no crew member
had only one job they were responsible for. The planners of the
mission decided that every member would be required to multi-
task, trained in different disciplines, to reduce the crew size,
thereby reducing food and resource consumption, and limit
waste production. *Gretel* functioned around the clock on a
skeleton crew, everyone tasked with no less than three jobs, most
with more. Everyone worked sixteen to eighteen hours on, the
rest of their time off, that time primarily used for sleep. Recre-
ation was intertwined in the course of each crew member's day.
If you were in charge of the gymnasium, you were expected to
stay fit through exercise, while at the same time making sure
there were always clean towels and the equipment functioned
properly. The same in the kitchen, making sure to eat between
cleaning dishes and restocking refrigerators. There could be no
wasted efforts if the mission was to succeed. And so far, four

months past the four-year mark, Desna was proud of the crew's efficiency and diligence, as well as their ability to keep morale at peak level.

Berlin came back over and seated herself at Desna's side.

"Find out anything I should know?" Desna asked.

"Wurther has some kind of STD I should be concerned about..."

"What!"

"Just kidding...This whole place feels like it's about to implode, everybody's so uptight."

"How's Skip?"

"Working like a gerbil in a square wheel. He'll probably be all right."

Desna sighed, shaking her head. "That doesn't help much..."

"Relax. It'll be fine... I think." She swiveled toward Desna, leaning in close, trapping Desna with her big, moon-pie eyes. "Anything will be better than you crawling into that damn purge vent again!" Berlin appeared genuinely concerned, but more than that, fearful, cupping Desna's fingers in her palm.

"Hey, you're my First mate," Desna said. "You're supposed to be supporting *me*."

Berlin turned all gooey, leaning into Desna. "I'd like to be your *only* mate," she whispered breathlessly.

"Jesus, Berlin, I hope to hell you're messing with me."

"Oh, come on. Lighten up!"

Desna ignored her and went over to talk to Skip. He was clearly immersed in running his final trials, but she had to know. "Where are we?"

A second or two passed before he responded. "I feel good about it." He directed her toward the screen. "Watch."

A graphical, three-dimensional representation of *Gretel* creeped slowly backward, lining up with BC-1, which appeared to be sitting still. She did notice a slight glitch just before *Gretel* stopped moving. "What was that?" Desna asked.

"Not sure... just a glitch in the software, I think."

The graphical animation was deceiving, giving the impression this would be a simple procedure. And it would be if they weren't presently traveling at 24,000 miles per hour in a nearly perfect vacuum where the slightest mishap could spell disaster. Tiny dots of perspiration speckled Skip's forehead. And she wasn't sure she bought his software-glitch theory. Something felt off.

"Is there a way to get sure... about the *glitch?*"

Skip nodded, frustration coloring his face. He stared a moment, then turned to Desna. "If Fawn could just give my math a quick once over, maybe... Never mind. I'll run another sim."

"Thanks, Skip. Think we can go in an hour?"

Stunned for a moment, he recovered and asked for two.

Desna clapped to get the attention of the crew. "People, can I have your attention, please? As you know, we are going to execute a very tricky maneuver. Our pilot, Skip, has mapped out a very precise plan. We are going in two hours, and I need everyone back here, alert and ready to go."

Desna went over and sat next to Berlin, whispering toward her, "I hope this works."

CHAPTER FOURTEEN

WHEN CHELSEY ROSE TO LEAVE THE BRIDGE, DESNA TAPPED Berlin on the knee and told her she had something she had to do. She hurried after Chelsey, hoping to catch her in the corridor.

"Hey, wait up."

The young woman spun toward her, smiling. "This is exciting!"

Desna only nodded, coming up beside her. "Do you have a minute to walk and talk?"

"Sure."

Desna motioned forward and walked beside her. "You've changed since the incident in Cargo Hold 4..." She hadn't wanted to sound dramatic, though it still came out that way.

"Really? Maybe it's because I'm not afraid anymore."

Desna could only nod, hoping she wouldn't have to prod the young woman for more information, because she didn't know what to ask, or how to ask it to learn what she needed to know. And worse yet, she didn't even know what she needed to know.

"I was afraid at first, I guess, after the Cargo Hold 4 debacle... but lying in sick bay, I realized I could hear everyone talking. I could even feel my body lying there... but... it was like... I don't know, like, I was there but I wasn't... like I existed in two places at once. I mean... I could hear conversations. Even Doc singing as he worked, or cursing something that didn't go his way. Then he'd laugh to himself. And sometimes I'd laugh with him, but not out loud that he could hear me. I even saw movement, but not with my eyes. With some other part of me..." She stopped and twisted toward Desna. "I know it must sound like I've been drinking vodka all night, but... this is just hard to explain."

They started walking again.

"I knew I wasn't dead," Chelsey said, but I felt nothing. It was really weird..." She gave Desna a broad smile. "That's when *they* summoned me. Now, before you start conjuring images of God-only-knows-what, let me explain that I never saw *them*. I never went anywhere, and *they* never spoke one word to me. I just *sensed* them all around me, some kind of presence, but not a singular one. A *multiple* presence, if that makes any sense. After that, I found that I could leave sick bay and—"

"Leave sick bay? That's when you came out of your—"

"Coma?" Chelsey said, interrupting her. "No, my body was still in sick bay, but..." Chelsey grinned at Desna. "But the *other* me could go anywhere on *Gretel,* even into Cargo Hold 4. But I didn't see anything except the big sealed cases holding all the artifacts and samples we'd collected on our expeditions. But moving through the ship I saw you, and Wurther, all the crew, everyone working at their stations, eating... normal stuff... I felt like a ghost or something... it was kind of weird, but not really..."

Just then Chelsey brightened and stopped in the corridor as if she recalled something she was excited to share. "I even traveled to BC-1 and had a look around at all the cool supplies headed our way. I only had to think of a place and I was instantly there."

The young woman started walking again and Desna was thoroughly confused.

"You know... when I saw myself in Cargo Hold 4—"

"Wait!" Desna grabbed Chelsey's arm." You never told me that. You said you saw me..."

"Yeah, sorry. I did see you. First." Chelsey flinched, suddenly looking very uncomfortable. "It's very personal, but I don't mind telling you now." They began walking again. "I saw you, then... I saw myself, kind of behind you, I guess. But just like you, I appeared terrified, so miserable and afraid. After *they* summoned me, I had the most profound revelation about what I'd seen in Cargo Hold 4... seeing my own face... well, sort of... I mean, it was me, yes... but the *prior* me, the one who was always afraid of everything! I realized that's why I always pushed the limits— rock climbing, hang gliding, skydiving. I even tried BASE jumping..."

"BASE jumping?"

"You don't want to know... Anyway, it was even the reason I signed up for this mission! But all that risky business, I finally understood, was me trying to outrun my fears. On the outside, I was bold, intrepid. But inside... deep at my core..." She shook her head. "...a petrified young child terrorized by her own fears; that was the me I saw in Cargo Hold 4...

"But now, Desna..." she continued, beaming. "I'm free! I'm totally free! And I know this operation we're about to perform is dangerous, and we could all be killed... but I'm not afraid."

She paused, tears streaming down her cheeks. She looked at Desna. "I love you so much, Desna! I love everyone on this ship! And I have never in my life felt this kind of peace..."

She hugged Desna, then walked down the corridor to her quarters, smiling back before disappearing inside.

Desna had to stand a few moments until she recovered. Once she gathered her wits, she continued her trek toward the mess hall, unable to remember why she was going there in the first place. Berlin was seated at one of the tables. Desna grabbed a parfait from the refrigeration unit and peeled away the protective covering. After grabbing a spoon, she sat across from Berlin, who was nursing a coffee.

"How are you feeling about this *scheme?*" Berlin asked with a degree of sarcasm.

"Scared shitless." Desna exaggerated to hide her true anxiety. "Skip's got it figured out."

Berlin chortled, then reached over and placed her hand on Desna's thigh. "Skip was sweating like a whore on dollar day."

"Oh, that's just lovely." Desna had almost forgotten how crass she could be.

A few minutes later, someone across the dining room caught Desna's attention. "That's the one I'm concerned about," Desna whispered to Berlin, spying Wurther sliding a sandwich onto his tray.

"Wurther? What's wrong with him?"

"He's been avoiding me."

"Talk to him, Des..."

"What am I going to say? 'Hey, Wurther, why've you been giving me the cold shoulder? Boohoo!' It's not affecting his work, so what do I care."

"I could talk to him." Berlin glided her palm along Desna's thigh.

"Yeah, I don't think so, sweetie. This isn't high school." Desna hated to admit she was enjoying Berlin's attention. "If we live through this deal today, why don't we hang out later..."

"Sounds good. Want the rest of my coffee? I have to hit the can."

Desna closed her eyes, declining with a shake of her head. How could such an intelligent, sophisticated woman be so coarse and petty and clueless at times? Desna watched Berlin drop her cup in the recycler, then sashay from the room, shooting a mock-sultry glance—puckered-kissing lips and all—over her shoulder at Desna.

"Can we talk a moment?"

Desna looked up. "Have a seat."

Wurther set his tray on the table and pulled out a chair.

He arranged his napkin, then hesitated, as if waiting for the precise right moment to start the conversation. "I know that you know that I've been avoiding you."

"What's up?"

Wurther's features hardened, as if he were secretly battling demons. "It's about your experience with Cargo Hold 4... you seeing me there..."

"Hey... let that go. It was a phantasm, nothing more." Desna tried to assure him, hoping that was true, though after her talk with Chelsey she couldn't be sure. "I have no clue what's going on in Cargo Hold 4, but you have to know that—"

"Please don't treat me like a child, Captain," Wurther said, his jaw tightening, angry but obviously still trying to maintain some shred of decorum. Desna appreciated that, an indication that things between them hadn't deteriorated too far yet.

"I'm sorry." Desna was about to reach over to touch his hand but caught herself.

Wurther pushed his plate back to fold his hands on the table. He leaned forward, contrite, as if imprisoned in some dark memory. "I don't talk much about my time in the paramilitary, because... well, it wasn't my proudest moment. And there are things I'd just as soon no one on this crew ever learned about my past."

He started twisting his large hands together, like he was trying to wring out some horrible stain. Desna saw a tear escape his left eye. He was trembling, frightened, this brawny rough and tumble soldier. Desna felt bad for him, but remained quiet.

"When you told me what you saw... I knew in that instant I was going to hell..."

Desna bit back the urge to negate his assumption, watching tears rolling down his cheeks, his stern visage beginning to crumble. Wurther was fighting back the slow dissolution of his composure, the flesh of his face juddering under the strain, a skill he most likely honed in the military. His inner struggle with fear and damnation was palpable, Desna an inadvertent witness to his unspoken confession.

He stared straight ahead, unable to meet Desna's gaze. In the gathering silence he brought his hand to his face and gently erased the trail of his tears.

She wanted to express some profound words of wisdom, but she had nothing. In the span of a few short minutes, he had completely renovated himself. He finally gave her his eyes, and managed a weak smile. "I'm glad we figured that out," he said.

"Me too."

He slid the plate forward and was preparing to eat.

"I'll let you eat in peace." She stood to leave, excusing herself, wishing she could have offered him something other than *hell*.

"Are you okay with the plan?" he asked, bringing the sandwich to his mouth.

"I think it's brilliant."

"I guess I meant... are you okay with Skip's calculations?"

She sat back down. "Aren't you?"

Wurther's brow rose and fell, rippled with doubt. "Skip's a brilliant guy, don't get me wrong... but the math on this move is... well... damned complicated. I'm no mathematician, but I'm not sure he's up to the task."

Desna was bleeding off confidence by the millisecond, anxiety chewing at her gut. The wheels were in motion. Even so, there was still time to pull the plug. But that would mean resigning their fate to the life form in Cargo Hold 4. Was that even a workable option? She didn't think so. And if her conversation with Chelsey was any indication, it was already affecting the crew members in unpredictable and disturbing ways. And what would the future look like moving forward if they didn't eradicate this threat now? And to Desna, it was certainly a threat. She couldn't see it any other way.

"Any thoughts?" she said. "Don't hold back. I trust your opinion."

"I don't mean to be overly dramatic here. Like, I don't think we're all going to die, or anything silly like that, but... we could end up damaging *Gretel*..."

"We have to address this situation in Cargo Hold 4, don't you think?"

He nodded. "You're right. No doubt... I'm just glad I don't have to make the call. But I'll support your decision to the end of the universe and back... that's why I'm here..."

Desna was uncomfortable pursuing this any longer with Wurther. Every time he spoke, she felt herself dropping down another notch into a very a dark chasm.

"How's the hydroponics lab?" she said, trying to switch into a brighter lane. "I haven't been down there in a while."

He nodded, giving her something that at least wasn't a frown. At times Desna had a hard time imagining what Wurther and Berlin were like together in bed; him so serious, her so flighty. But people showed different sides to different people. Who knew what their particular chemistry created.

"It's doing great," Wurther said. "You should drop in. I'm there on and off for the next seventy-two hours, then Hurd's in for his shift. He's had some stunning ideas down there. Things I would never have thought of. Quite an asset, that peculiar man."

Desna decided to end on a high note. She told Wurther she'd see him shortly, then headed for the exit, her insides twisted with indecision.

CHAPTER FIFTEEN

Everyone was at their stations, awaiting Skip's command. Skip would do all the heavy lifting on this venture, while the crew monitored all crucial systems to ensure that *Gretel's* mechanical and computerized components stayed within safety limits established by academy protocols.

The first order of business was decoupling from BC-1, while maintaining *Gretel's* speed to match BC-1's, then slowing to allow BC-1 to gradually overtake *Gretel,* which was the trickiest part, since there were no brakes or drag on either vessel; no natural entropy existed in a vacuum. Skip would have to create it, by reversing thrusters just enough, like tapping the brakes for a millisecond, but not so much as to push the ship askew, or change its pitch or angle.

When the full impact of what they were attempting finally hit Desna, she suffered an awful panic attack. Desna was just about to throw the off switch on the op when Skip announced across the bridge: "We have separation."

Gretel was disconnected from BC-1.

Desna trained her eyes on the large display on the far wall. The two ships seemed to be moving independent of one another, but everything was happening so slowly it was hard to tell. She glanced toward Skip, who was focused on his screen, typing into his console. Hurd updated Skip every five seconds, reading off a string of numbers and coordinates. Chelsey only added to the conversation when something began to stray beyond acceptable limits. Wurther sat at the console next to Skip, studying the data streaming across his screen.

Time elongated intolerably for Desna. She wanted more progress updates. Skip had fallen silent, so had Hurd. Chelsey started screaming out numbers in degrees until *Gretel* was jolted, tossing Desna off balance. "What the hell is going on?"

Gretel bumped again, setting off alarms and flashing lights. Chelsey shouted, "We're losing her. Correct for yaw."

Hurd followed. "Three degrees starboard."

Others added to the corrections. Wurther typed frantically on his keyboard. The next collision sent Desna to the floor, jostling others from their terminals.

"Come on... come on, dammit!" Skip cried. "Almost there..."

Hurd and Chelsey shouted more corrections, Wurther shifting his attention between Skip's monitor and his own. A second later *Gretel* screeched and clunked, then shuddered. The metal groaned torturously, as if losing integrity. Suddenly, as if sparked by the calamity, hideous cries and wailing rushed up from the cargo area below the bridge, drowning out *Gretel's* distress.

"For the love of everything sane!" Desna gripped the deck railing, then swung her attention toward Hurd, then Skip. "Get this vessel under control!" she screamed, her command lost in the uproar coming from Cargo Hold 4.

After several minutes, *Gretel* settled into its normal steady demeanor, while the amplified shrieks and bleating still echoed from the hold. Desna's heart collapsed when she glanced back at the large display on the far wall, BC-1 mangled, releasing almost four and a half years of refuse and debris into space. The waste had been moved to BC-1 to make room for more research and provisions. That was always the plan. Efficient and hygienic, but now it floated around both ships like a toxic, menacing cloud.

When Skip saw the damage, he shrieked. "This spacecraft was never meant for such a foolish maneuver!" He glared across the bridge at Berlin, as if she'd personally crashed the ship.

"Hey, pal, I didn't cock up the math on this," Berlin screeched. "You did, asshole!"

"Why isn't Fawn contributing anything to this mission!" Skip shouted, his face read, his hands shaking.

"Because she's dying, Skip..." Berlin held the man's eyes as if trying to crush them with her stare.

Skip froze, losing his color, until Berlin hurled another insult his way, calling him an insensitive *fuckwad*. The two volleyed insults back and forth across the bridge, shouting, finger pointing, fist shaking, until Desna broke it up.

"First mate Berlin, you're relieved of duty. Leave the bridge! Ship's pilot, in my day room, now! Quartermaster Wurther, take over the helm!"

Berlin lingered near the exit glowering at Skip until Desna swung around and pointed toward the door. After she left, Skip shambled across the bridge and entered Desna's day room, his face ruddy and dark.

"Dr. Hurd, damage report, please..." Desna stared at the large screen in disbelief. She wanted the wreckage to be just another simulation, the reality of it sending a crippling chill down her legs. She felt weak, a million regrets circling her gut. It was Hurd who delivered the crushing blow.

"Cargo hold doors 8, 6, 4 and 2, all inoperative or malfunctioning." He continued on without looking up from his screen. "BC-1 immobilized. Minor damage to *Gretel's* hull, no breaches. No injuries reported yet."

Desna pulled her eyes from the large screen, pointing them at the huge window looking out onto space, the flotsam floating eerily in *Gretel's* lights, a massive metal hatch door tumbling slowly amidst the mess. "What is that, Hurd?"

Hurd checked his data, then performed a digital-scan inventory of the debris. "It appears to be the hatch to Cargo Hold 4, Ma'am."

"Anything else show up on your scan?"

"Only what you'd expect. Nothing anomalous."

Desna's fear was realized. All the sealed containers floating nearby were months of work and research, artifacts and samples they'd painstakingly collected over the past year. But not the entity from Cargo Hold 4. Why wasn't its dead carcass drifting out there with the rest of the jetsam?

"More damage reports are coming in, Ma'am," Hurd announced. "We have electrical failures and a minor breach on the port side of *Gretel.*"

"The port side?" That was odd, Desna thought, since the attempted merger had transpired on *Gretel's* starboard. There shouldn't be any damage on port.

"How bad is the breach?"

"Outer skin only. The hull has already self-repaired."

"Mr. Wurther, can you get us out of here without further damage?" She wanted distance between *Gretel* and the rubble.

"Yes, Ma'am."

"Dr. Hurd, you have the bridge." Desna left for her day room. When she entered, Skip's head was cradled in his hands, his shoulders shuddering. She took her seat behind the desk. "Skip?"

He looked up, his eyes wet. "I'm so sorry... I... I should have known I couldn't pull it off... I just..."

"It was *my* call, Skip! Not yours! This is on me... but we can't have outbursts like that on the bridge, or anywhere else on this ship. I know this isn't a military vessel like you're used to, but we must maintain some semblance of order, or this whole mission is going right down the shitter."

Skip sniffled and nodded his agreement. "Is Fawn really dying?"

"Yes. I'm not sure there's anything we can do. Doc is working on it... right now, though, I need you to pull it together. *Gretel* suffered a lot of damage, and I need to know if this mission is in jeopardy."

Skip hung his head, on the verge of tears again, his features caving.

"Drop the guilt, goddamn it! I can't have it! I need you now. Because if we can't go on, I'm aborting this entire mission and we're heading back to Earth."

Skip cleared his throat, sliding his damp eyes up to meet hers. "Did we lose any research?"

"That's not your concern. What I need from you is to assess

Gretel's damage as quickly as possible. I need you to get Berlin on the CPV-drone and scan this ship from stem to stern."

"She may not even speak to me..."

"Dammit, Skip, you *make* her speak to you! You're not a couple of grade schoolers. Fix the riff and get your asses on this damage assessment! I need to know if it's safe to go on."

He stood slowly. "Yes, Captain. I'll get you something in the next hour."

"You have thirty minutes."

As Skip opened the door to Desna's day room, Hurd was poised to knock.

"What is it, Hurd?"

"Another damage report just came in. The CPV-drone is inoperable."

CHAPTER SIXTEEN

CHELSEY AND DESNA WERE SUITED UP, BREATHING PURE oxygen in the airlock, acclimating for the spacewalk. Wurther performed last-minute checks on their suits, made sure their helmet-cams were functioning properly, tested their LED lamps and comms.

Berlin stood by, worried, fuming. Why did Desna volunteer for these risky missions? She should be on the bridge; she was the captain, not some fucking interstellar repairman. They had gone back and forth in Desna's day room, Berlin arguing that Skip should do the goddamn spacewalk. "It was his fucking fault!" "Jesus, Berlin. You just don't get it, do you?" Desna's statement had pissed off Berlin even more. What didn't she get? To Berlin, it was Desna who didn't *get it,* didn't get how much she loved her, how much she needed her.

Unable to watch Desna depart the airlock, she hurried to the bridge, where Hurd would be recording their walk, making sure the audio was intelligible, the video transmission sharp and clear. Entering the bridge, her gut was a boiling stew. She went into Desna's day room looking for something to settle her stomach, but could find nothing in the medicine cabinet or in Desna's desk drawer.

Shutting the door behind her, she called over to Hurd, who was concentrating at his terminal. "Have they started?"

He looked over at her. "Not yet. A problem with Chelsey's helmet-cam. It will be a few more minutes."

"Great, everything's going to crap on this ship," Berlin said under her breath, rushing down the hallway toward her quarters. At the end of the corridor, she saw someone walk past on the intersecting walkway, then disappear past the corner. It had to be Fawn, because Chelsey and Desna were in the airlock. The woman was nude, from what Berlin could tell. Maybe Fawn was delirious from painkillers, and had wandered out of sick bay. Where was Doc Karl? Surely, he would have seen her leave. Unless he was on duty in the science lab doing research.

Berlin dashed toward the intersection, hoping to catch Fawn and take her back to sick bay before she hurt herself. By the time she reached the junction, Fawn was gone. Berlin ran to the science lab hoping to find Doc Karl. The lights were off in the huge library. She touched the pad on the wall, bringing up the ceiling lights. When her eyes adjusted, she saw movement near the back stacks.

"Dr. Karl, is that you?"

Obviously, he hadn't heard her. She eased deeper into the room, past several large bookshelves. "Dr. Karl!" she called again. He seemed to be present one minute, then gone again. She weaved in and out between the stacks, feeling a little disoriented by the maze of physical books, as well as digital publications, laser orbs, and holosport bricks. Someone moved just beyond the last row of shelves, near the audio booths and terminal stations.

She ran toward the back, calling his name. "Dr. Karl! Wait up! Doc Karl!"

He was gone.

"Where the fuck'd he go?" She peered through the darkened windows of the audio booths. The computer terminals were empty. She surveyed the lab again, trying to detect movement between the stacks. The lights started snapping off, like a rolling blackout, the room thrown into total darkness. A smudge of light shown through the bookshelves, coming from the front of the lab library. She had just started heading toward it, when the light slowly squeezed to a sliver, then gone, followed by the sound of the lab doors sliding shut.

"Oh, this is just great!" She snapped on the aux-light on her belt and walked toward the entrance. Once in the hallway, she glimpsed someone rounding the corner. "Dr. Karl! Hey, wait a second!"

When she reached the intersection—after looking both ways —the hallway was empty. The running and intrigue did nothing to settle her jumpy stomach, so she headed for sick bay.

Entering the medical facility, she went straight to Doc Karl's office. It was vacant but the light was on. She walked down the hall to Fawn's room. The young girl looked pitiful, like a different person, feeble and gaunt, tethered to monitors, a machine helping her breathe. Way worse than Berlin had imagined when Desna told her she was dying. "Doc doesn't think we can save her," Desna had said.

How could somebody so vibrant and young be at death's door? Berlin recalled the girl she'd seen in the corridor a few minutes earlier; that young woman's gait certainly not the one of someone lingering near death's veil. Berlin's eyes traced the labyrinth of tubes and wires cocooning Fawn and knew the woman she'd seen in the hallway couldn't have been her. The realization was like a chilly palm against her chest.

Turning away from Fawn, Berlin hurried from sick bay to get back to the bridge. Hurd was listening to chatter coming from his terminal, watching the video of the spacewalk.

"They just started about ten minutes ago," Hurd said, updating Berlin. She plopped down in her chair, watching the walk on the large screen.

"Hey, Berlin," a voice whispered from behind her. She hadn't noticed Doc Karl sitting at the back of the bridge when she'd rushed in.

"Doc!" she said, an uncomfortable sensation squirming through her gut. "Were you just in the science lab?"

"Holy Christ!" Doc Karl screeched, his eyes wired open, fixed on the big screen beyond her. She wheeled around, spying what Doc Karl had reacted to. They all knew the hatch for Cargo Hold 4 had been knocked off in the collision between *Gretel* and

BC-1, but actually seeing that huge empty bay exposed to outer space was mind boggling, like some unhealed wound in *Gretel's* side. Berlin shot up to walk closer to the screen.

"Hurd, can you crank up the resolution?" In seconds the image sharpened, Berlin letting her eyes inch across every detail in the bay. Everything was gone. Months of research, all the samples they'd gathered, everything lost to the cold vacuum of space. Up near the ceiling something glistened oddly. She eased closer, pointing her finger at the upper corner of the screen. "Zoom on this area."

He tapped in commands on his keyboard, the area of the image growing larger.

"Can you get me closer?"

Hurd pecked repeatedly, the image expanding but losing resolution. Berlin hurried to his workstation and spoke into the comm. "Desna, can you hear me?"

"Roger that."

"Can you enter the hold."

"Moving in."

"Up in the upper right-hand corner... do you see that... something shimmering?"

A brief patch of static interrupted the conversation, then: "I don't see what you're talking about."

"In the back, up near the purge vent duct..." As soon as her words echoed back in her head, Berlin felt a moment's shock, like a jolt to her heart, recalling the panic in Desna's voice when she was stuck in that vent.

"I see it," Chelsey said. "Going up to inspect."

Berlin experienced a sudden relief watching Desna hang back. Chelsey drifted up toward the unusual glinting coming from the surface of the duct. She studied the substance a moment, easing around it to view it from different angles. She pulled a sample vial from her suit. Using a small brush, she scraped some of the substance into it, then sealed the container and gave the camera a thumbs up and a smile.

The two women moved to the next cargo holds, the doors present, though creased badly, the metal buckled in numerous places. When they finished their inspection, Desna's voice came through the bridge speakers. "Moving to port."

"Why is she moving to the port side?" Berlin said, confused. "There shouldn't be any damage on port..."

"There is," Hurd said. "A minor breach and electrical issues."

Berlin shook her head, perplexed over that development. It made no sense. Wurther entered the bridge and went directly to his terminal. Desna and Chelsey pulled themselves along the hull by the tubular railing. They chose to go beneath *Gretel*'s belly to check for damage, though none had been reported by the ship's systems.

Berlin went over to speak with Wurther. "Were you in the science lab earlier?"

"No." He continued typing, distracted at first, then: "I know you called a timeout, but... you want to hook up later?"

"I'll let you know, okay." She thought it might be nice; they hadn't *hooked up* in a while. She went back to the large screen, then glanced over her shoulder toward Doc Karl, but he was gone. Hurd zoomed the image on the large display back to normal. Berlin watched, her attention fragmented between Wurther's offer, the person in the science lab, Fawn so sickly... and the nude woman in the corridor.

CHAPTER SEVENTEEN

THE SPACE WALKERS HAD REACHED THE PORT SIDE OF *GRETEL*. Berlin sat behind him at the helm, quiet as a snowflake. Wurther knew she was worried about Desna, that they were lovers. He didn't care. There was no room for possessiveness. The journey demanded directness, honesty, a fresh approach to social mores.

He expected Skip would've visited the bridge by now. His friend was obviously wracked with guilt over the unfortunate incident, but no one could have predicted what would happen. They'd spoken before he'd gone to the gym, and Skip admitted he hadn't figured in the weight of the new supplies in his calculations, yet couldn't bring himself to admitting the mistake to Desna. "I just can't," he'd told Wurther, tears coming to his eyes. "She'll never trust me again!"

Wurther believed Skip was completely off base in his assessment of Desna, but the man was too overwrought to hear reason. Another time, maybe.

"Go back, Hurd!" Berlin screamed, jumping from her chair. "Run the video back!"

Hurd typed frantically, until the video was running backward. "Slow it down!"

Wurther's nerves were on full tilt by the urgency in Berlin's voice. What in the hell did she think she saw?

"There! Stop!" Berlin ran up to the screen, studying something near the top edge of *Gretel.* "Here!" She circled her finger over the screen. Hurd zoomed in.

"Stop!" She leaned in closer. Wurther went over and stood next to her.

"What are you seeing?" he asked.

"Can you run it back a frame at a time?" she asked Hurd, then turned to Wurther, pointing to a specific place on the screen. "Watch right here..."

He trained his eyes and squinted for more focus. The video rolled backward a frame at a time.

"There! There it was!"

Wurther never took his attention from the screen. "I didn't see anything!"

She rushed over to Hurd's keyboard, nudging him aside. She poked the arrow key once, then again, then one more time, and went back to the screen. She leaned in and poked the screen with her forefinger. "There! Right the fuck there! What the hell is that?"

Wurther still couldn't see what she was going on about. "Can you zoom in, Hurd?" he said. The picture grew larger, the area in question nearly filling the screen.

"Sharpen, please," Wurther said, never taking his eyes off the image. The spot Berlin had pointed to was at the top edge of *Gretel,* but even at maximum resolution, it looked to Wurther like nothing more than the sun glinting off *Gretel's* reflective surface.

"I know what you're thinking, Wurth, but that's no solar anomaly!"

Wurther was flummoxed. He leaned in closer, but could see nothing that betrayed his assumption. He sighed, shaking his head. "I don't see what you're seeing." He was sorry to disappoint her.

"Oh, you're fucking blind!" She moved Hurd out of his chair and started typing instructions. In seconds the video was looping ten frames. She went back to the screen and told Wurther to watch only this one spot.

"Well move your finger and maybe I'll see something." He

wanted to see something, but couldn't. All he saw was an instance of sun glare off *Gretel*'s skin. It was there, and then gone. A couple of frames.

"Oh, for shit's sake!" Berlin said, shaking her head.

"I saw it," Hurd said. "I saw what you were looking at."

Wurther whirled toward him, knowing the weird man was not above sucking up to anyone who was one-hundred percent human.

"It appeared as if something had slinked down the port side of the ship as Officer Chelsey and Captain Desna started inspecting the starboard side," Hurd stated with academic certainty.

"Yes! Yes! That's exactly what I saw!" she screamed. "Something *slinked*... Oh I like that word, *slinked* over the edge just as Chelsey and Desna looked up!"

Wurther wasn't sure who was crazier, Berlin or Hurd, but the explanation they had settled on was a stretch at best. He was about to inject some sanity into the discussion when he noticed Berlin's expression darken, panic etched into her features. "What's wrong?"

"Get them back in the ship!" Berlin was frantic. "Hurd, get them back in the ship!"

Skip entered the bridge.

"Tell Hurd to get Desna back in the ship!" she screamed at Skip, her eyes puckered with fear. "Fuck it!" She shoved Hurd aside with her hip, then screamed into the comm. "Get back to the airlock, Desna. Get in the ship! Now!"

Nothing came back. Skip looked at Wurther. "What's going on?" he said calmly, Berlin still shouting into the comm. Wurther had no idea what was happening. He shrugged at Skip. It was like Berlin had come under a demonic possession, shouting like a lunatic, tears rolling down her cheeks.

"Goddammit, answer me, Desna!" Berlin was frenzied, trembling, falling back into Hurd's chair weeping into her palms.

Skip walked over and squatted down next to her. "Desna and Chelsey are in the airlock. They're reacclimatizing," he said softly. She threw her arms around him and wouldn't let go.

Wurther went back to his terminal, uneasy with the trajectory of crew morale; things were destabilizing at the speed of light.

CHAPTER EIGHTEEN

DESNA WAS IN HER QUARTERS RELAXING, STILL PROCESSING THE damage to *Gretel.* Berlin had stopped by earlier, so worked up Desna could hardly calm her down. They had sex, and that seemed to help, but soon after Berlin became so sullen and detached Desna had to send her away.

"I'll be better, I promise! Please don't make me leave," she begged, blubbering.

Desna assured her she needed time to process the damage to *Gretel,* that it had nothing to do with her, which was a lie. It had everything to do with Berlin's morbid rant about something she thought she saw on the video from the spacewalk. Desna couldn't take anymore. When Berlin finally left, Desna contacted Wurther on the comm, telling him that Berlin was in a state, that she may need a *bunkmate* for the night. "I'm not talking about sex, just look after her. I can't deal with her right now."

After they'd talked a short while, Wurther agreed to check on her. Desna ate a light meal, then concentrated on Skip's assessment of *Gretel's* damage based on numerous viewings of the spacewalk video. They had met for several hours earlier, going over his long list of necessary repairs, and the order they needed to be implemented. Skip and Wurther checked out the electrical failures on the port side of *Gretel* and concluded that they were design flaws which failed due to the collision with BC-1. "They would have malfunctioned anyway at some point during our journey," Skip had told her. There was no reason to distrust Skip's suspicions, but it did seem he was still trying to minimize his part in the damage. She assured him several times during their meeting that the decision to move forward with the BC-1 plan was hers and hers alone, that he really needed to move on.

Studying the report Skip and Wurther had prepared was giving her a headache. She closed her eyes and sat back on the couch, wondering about the entity. Where had it gone? Clearly it was no longer in Cargo Hold 4. Maybe it had been ejected during the mishap with BC-1 and they just hadn't been able to see it amid the debris cloud. If so, that collision would prove to be the most advantageous event of the journey so far. She and Chelsey had discussed that possibility when they arrived back on *Gretel*, but Chelsey only smiled noncommittally. Wurther, Skip and Hurd agreed with Desna, that the damn thing was probably gone, though their commitment to her theory was suspect. Berlin refused to talk about it at all, wanting only to be held and pampered.

Desna's mind went to the gel they'd discovered. It covered portions of *Gretel's* hull in one section, and Desna couldn't help but believe it was some residue from the entity. Chelsey wasn't so sure about that. Regardless, they had secured numerous samples and gave them to Hurd for testing, along with the one Chelsey had gathered from inside Cargo Hold 4. They also gave samples to Doc Karl, so they'd have two different perspectives. Desna laughed to herself imagining Doc Karl coming back with the results, telling her it was nothing but KY Jelly left over from the calamity with BC-1.

Sitting up, almost ready to tackle Skip's report again, she decided to grab that bottle of Vodka and have a drink. Maybe two. Taking it from the freezer, she held it against her forehead first, Berlin suddenly in her mind. Now she wished she hadn't shooed her away so quickly. It would be nice having a little company tonight. She couldn't fight back the image of Wurther's large frame plowing away at Berlin, the movie playing in her mind almost comical. Even after her divorce, Desna tried male companionship at different times, never quite able to find the connection she had with women, especially Berlin, which she could never understand; they were different in every way, and yet, against all odds, they worked.

Desna stood at the counter and poured a drink, knocking it back in one gulp, then poured a second. She carried it back to the couch and picked up the report. She was reading the fourth page when she heard something out in the hallway. At first she ignored it, until the sound came again. Setting the report on the sofa table, she got up and slid open the hatch. No one was there. That's when she heard the scratching. First beneath the floor, then the walls. One side, then the other, then the floor, followed by thumping and tapping.

"Not tonight. I can't deal with this shit." She downed the drink, then went back for the bottle. She poured another to the rim and tipped it back, letting the cold liquid slip slowly down her throat. The scratching at the walls continued, then soft moaning, muffled sobbing. She could almost picture a small child tucked into a ball sitting in a corner, knees to her chest, her hands covering her face. A memory eased forward from some dark cavern of her mind, a little girl, seven years old, crying after her mother died. She had somehow blocked that out for years.

The scraping was fainter, now. The thumping more like light knocking. Until everything fell silent. She finished her drink and poured another, succumbing to the pleasing void, a gentle swaying in her legs that moved into her abdomen.

The knocking started again, but this time it was different, sounding as if it were coming from the door. She took another draw on the vodka, the sound becoming a gentle continuous rapping. She put the glass down and went to the door to listen. She heard breathing.

"Is someone there?"

No one answered.

Cautiously, she slid the door only a few inches and saw a woman— *Berlin!* — excited she'd decided to come back. Sliding the door fully open, she saw Berlin was completely naked. But it wasn't her after all, but Chelsey. She was gorgeous. Desna thought she was imagining her, hallucination born of stress, lack of sleep and too much vodka. She eased forward, edging Desna backward into the room. The naked young woman slid the door shut, then pressed her lips to Desna's, beginning to undress her. The moment was so tender, so needed, Desna closed her eyes and allowed it to happen. Chelsey guided her back to the couch, Desna welcoming the intimacy, giving in to the advance. Afraid it would end if she opened her eyes, Desna kept them closed, surrendering to the warmth of Chelsey's palms sliding along her flesh, to her breasts. Kneeling before Desna, Chelsey leaned closer, pressing her lips to hers, before tracing her tongue around her nipples, into her naval, slipping down between her legs.

They made love for hours it seemed, resting for short periods in each other's arms, before growing intimate again. And again. Until Desna led her to the bed and asked her to spend the night. Chelsey kissed her, then went to the main door of Desna's compartment, giving her one last glance before leaving and easing the door closed. A warm hush filled the room, a peace Desna had never experienced in her entire life. She was exhausted, yet energized at the same time, some wild inexplicable current buzzing in her abdomen. Falling back against her pillow, she stared at the ceiling only a short time, never noticing the room fade to black.

CHAPTER NINETEEN

THE ENGINEERS WHO DESIGNED *GRETEL* CREATED AN ingenious, autonomous lighting system for the ship, which mimicked a normal twenty-four-hour cycle on Earth. This helped to align human biorhythms and aided in REM sleep, as well as create a faux-but-effective designation between day and night, making it easier to schedule work, sleep and meals. They called it RVW, short for *Rip Van Winkle*. Crew members could plan their days along normal parameters experienced on Earth, eliminating the need for a bothersome and unnatural adaptation to space, where time was chaotic at best.

On this morning, though, Desna would have welcomed twenty-four-hours of space blackness, instead waking to the glaring, sunny warm light in her room, and a blaring headache.

She, Wurther and Skip planned to meet on the bridge early that morning to hammer out a repair schedule. Before she even pulled herself from the covers, she knew she was late. If being Captain had any perks, it was that no one could yell at her for missing an appointment. She dressed, brushed her teeth, and walked to the mess hall to grab a cup of coffee. Hurd was eating breakfast and told her he'd have a report to her later that afternoon on the gel she and Chelsey collected. *Chelsey!* Desna hadn't thought about her at all. Had that really happened? She sipped her coffee, glancing in Hurd's direction.

"Thanks," she said, trying to mentally prepare herself for the meeting.

When she entered the bridge, Chelsey was at her terminal. Desna didn't want the clumsy smiles and awkward glances, so she kept her head down and entered her day room, relieved when she saw Skip and Wurther weren't there. She was about to shut the door and enjoy her coffee in peace, when Wurther came onto the bridge, then walked directly toward her.

"Morning," he said. "Did you sleep well?"

What the fuck was this? she thought. The crew had pretty much dispensed with these ridiculous pleasantries. It was tiresome, seeing each other at all hours of the day, yet trying to maintain the illusion that it had been a while since seeing one another, or that anyone really cared how their lunch had been, or if they had a good night's sleep. It had to be that Wurther got laid and was feeling much more relaxed, upbeat and ready to engage in moronic banter.

"Seen Skip?" she said.

"Yeah, earlier. He'll be back. I saw you come down the hall and called him on his comm to let him know you were ready.

"How'd it go with Berlin last night?"

"It didn't. She wouldn't even open her door."

That seemed odd, given how distraught she was when she left Desna's quarters. "Have you seen her this morning?"

Wurther shook his head.

Desna peeked into the bridge to see if Berlin had shown up, unable to remember her schedule. Chelsey was headed her way.

"Did Hurd post any results on that goo we found?" Chelsey said, smiling. Desna was proud of how well she was handling what could've been a very thorny situation.

"I saw him in the mess," Desna said. "He thought he'd have something after lunch."

"I hope it's not something stupid like thruster lube... or silicon rotor grease," she said, then turned and went back to her station.

Desna didn't know what either of those things were.

Skip showed up a few minutes later to discuss repairs. They talked about the CPV-drone first, Desna curious if he thought it was salvageable; it could help in making the other repairs. Wurther told her he thought it was and planned to rummage through the manifest for the new supplies to see what parts were aboard. Desna never discussed with the crew the major flaw in the BreadCrumb system, though some of them had probably already figured it out. The provisions from BC-1 were the most up-to-date stockpile they would receive. All provisions in the future would become increasingly older and less useful technologically, with the last BC vessel carrying the most outmoded of all. It had been launched into space nearly ten years earlier, before some of the technology they currently used was available.

Desna welcomed the discussion of repairs and schedules, but knew she needed to address the biggest issue; Cargo Hold 4.

"It sounds like we have a repair plan," she said, ready to broach the more difficult discussion. "What about our friend in Cargo Hold 4? Is that still a problem, or do you believe it's gone?"

The men regarded each other, neither wanting to field the question.

"I have a theory," Skip said. "It may sound crazy, but we don't know what's out here. I think we may have passed through some kind of *zone* in space that threw off the telemetry in *Gretel's* systems that caused the weird sounds. To our ears they sounded like screams and all that, but maybe it was *Gretel* titanium hull stretching and groaning. Nothing more."

He looked at Wurther, then brought his attention back to Desna and shrugged. "It's possible, right?"

"Yeah, it's possible, Skip," Desna said, unable to contain her snarkiness. "If we can ignore the huge dents in Cargo Hold 4's massive door... How does that comport with your theory?"

Skip raised his eyebrows and said nothing.

"Wurther?" she said.

"I don't know. Why don't we wait until Hurd and Doc have something on those samples."

"That's not going to tell us the status of that *thing* now, though. If the gel and it are even related. We need to know if it's still with us. Don't you think?"

"I don't." Wurther shook his head in disagreement. "Look, if we can't see it, and can't hear it anymore, and it's not affecting our daily routines, what difference does it make? Let's get on with our work and forget it. I mean, I can't explain the huge dents, but maybe Skip's right. Maybe it was just some kind of space anomaly and it's done."

Wurther sat quietly a few moments, then: "To be honest, I think we're all freaking out too much over this. I mean, look what happened—" Wurther cut his thought short and looked down at the floor.

"You mean, what happened to BC-1 and *Gretel,* is because we were chasing phantoms? Is that what you're saying? That we fucked everything up?"

Wurther shook his head, his attention pinned to the floor, then: "I don't know what I'm saying. Can I be excused?"

"You can both go." Desna was disgusted. "Get the repairs underway. Suspend your other duties for now. I and the rest of the crew will take up the slack. If you need more hands, let me know. We need to get on track again."

She tipped her coffee cup back, ignoring them as they left her day room.

CHAPTER TWENTY

"*Captain Desna's presence is required in sick bay.*"

Desna finished her coffee, the image of Fawn's haggard body hooked to tubes and wires rising behind her eyes. Sadness overtook her, figuring the child had lost the long battle. She walked past Chelsey, about to speak to her on her way out, but decided it wasn't necessary; Chelsey obviously was keeping things in their proper perspective. She would as well. Perspective was the very thing she had tried to stress to Berlin, but her part-time lover never grasped the importance of keeping things separate and discreet, of erecting workable barriers, keeping emotions in check. *Gretel* was a massive spacecraft, but where human emotions were concerned, it was no bigger than a tea cup.

Gretel seemed unnaturally quiet, which should have been soothing, but a frisson of foreboding hung in the air. Desna felt it in every cell of her body. She knew it was about Fawn. How would she contact the child's parents, tell them their youngest daughter had passed? Desna tried to push away insensitive thoughts about the fate of the mission. Fawn had been chosen to complete it, the planners figuring the youngest of the crew could very well be the only one left alive to bring *Gretel* home to Earth. The ultimate irony. The youngest dies first.

Desna expected to encounter the perplexing redolence of death when she entered sick bay. Instead, she smelled mint tea and a toasted bagel. She walked past the three rooms, spying Fawn in the last one, wires and tubes growing out of her like mechanical roots, the machines steady sentries, their lights and readouts telling a different story than the one she had braced herself for.

"Glad you came," Doc Karl said, coming up behind Desna.

"She's okay...?"

"Fawn's stable. Oh... I guess you thought... no. I'm so sorry... There's another matter we need to discuss. I didn't think it appropriate to address it on the bridge."

Doc Karl turned to go back to his office, obviously assuming she would follow. She took a seat across from his desk when he slid the door closed.

"This is difficult to talk about, Captain... We had a very serious incident last night," Doc Karl said.

"Spit it out, Karl." Desna couldn't think anything could possibly be as grave as he was painting it.

Doc gave his ear a tug, then pushed his glasses up on his nose. "Berlin was attacked last night. In her quarters."

"Attacked? What kind of attack are we talking about? Who attacked her?"

"Wurther. Sexual assault, but Berlin was able to fight him off. She stabbed him with a screwdriver..."

"Wurther! That doesn't seem possible... Where's Berlin? I want to talk to her."

"She's pretty shook up. I have her in my personal quarters... she's really afraid."

Desna couldn't believe it. Wurther seemed very upbeat when she'd seen him earlier; not at all the disposition of a sexual preda- tor. Desna knew Wurther had a history of violence, but he never seemed like a danger to the crew, or was haunted by sick sexual proclivities. And he hadn't seemed hurt, or in pain, and certainly didn't act as if he'd been stabbed with a screwdriver.

"Thanks, Doc. I'll check on her. This shouldn't need saying, but not a word to anyone."

"Of course not. How are the repairs coming?"

"Slowly."

Desna had barely made it from Doc's office when the impossibilities of this situation overtook her. If it was true, what would they do? Arrest Wurther? Have some kind of trial? Then what? Convert a cargo hold into a cell? Keep him locked up? It was insane. Then the notion took a darker turn. Maybe Doc could induce a coma and keep him in sick bay. Or maybe they'd execute him, eliminate any future risks. "Holy Christ, Desna! Stop!" she said to herself, lacking the fortitude to wrangle with such nefarious thoughts.

Standing outside Doc's quarters, she hesitated before knocking, feeling a slither of guilt over sending Berlin away the night before. She rapped several times, then spoke softly to the door. "It's me, Berlin. Desna. Open the door, sweetie."

Desna heard the locks click, unaware the doors even had locks. She'd never used hers before. There were only seven other people aboard *Gretel* beside herself. This all seemed crazy. A random statement seized her thoughts: "*To be honest, I think we're all freaking out too much over this...*" The words Wurther had spoken to her less than an hour ago.

The door opened slowly, Berlin's pasty face staring out, her eyes like red-hot coals stuck in dough. After Desna entered, Berlin quickly latched the door and ambled over to the couch, where she'd made a nest from comforters and pillows, then buried herself to the neck.

"Tell me what happened." Desna took the chair near Berlin's makeshift fortress.

Berlin's teary recounting of events seemed so out of character for any of the crew, much less Wurther. If she hadn't known Berlin for over fifteen years, she'd have Doc fit her with a straightjacket and keep her sedated until the mission was over. Tales of Wurther showing up naked at her compartment, forcing his way in, tossing her around, ripping her pajamas, trying to force her to the floor, were daunting to say the least. The only reason she'd escaped was because she'd been trying to tighten the screws on her bed frame and had had the screwdriver lying nearby.

"I hated stabbing him, Desna, but he was a monster!"

It took several minutes for Berlin to compose herself, which

Desna used to make them a cup of tea and retrieve a vac-sealed container of cookies from Doc's larder.

Berlin sipped her tea and fumbled over some of the more salacious details, the memory of the previous evening distorting her face in heart-rending ways. With every disclosure, Desna felt worse and worse, wishing she'd never sent Berlin away, then felt even more loathsome recalling the amazing evening she'd spent with Chelsey. It would crush Berlin if she ever found out.

"Didn't Wurther call you last night?"

Berlin sniffled, bringing a tissue to her nose. "How did you know?"

"He said he was going to."

Berlin's eyes sharpened. "No... you *told* him to, didn't you!"

"What happened when he called?"

"I told him I didn't want company..."

"How did he take it?"

"The way he always does. 'Maybe another night, then?' he always says... and that was that... He was always a gentleman..."

"How about when he came back later that night?"

"I was finishing up with my bed, and getting ready for sleep, when he just walks in naked. I was shocked at first, then started laughing. I thought he'd say something funny the way he always does, like, 'Is this where the luau is?' But he said nothing... then, a second later he's all over me. Pawing me, pushing me down, hitting me..." Her tears came in torrents. "He was such a bastard!" she screamed. "I wanted to kill that fucker, and I almost did. I stabbed him three times until he finally got the message..." She rubbed her cheeks roughly, residual anger tightening her features. "Then he ran out."

"Did he say anything when you stabbed him?"

"Not a word the whole time. It was creepy... like he was possessed or something!"

Desna could only nod, trying to carve out a new place in her mind for this kind of behavior, especially from one of her crew.

"You gonna talk to him?" Berlin asked, swabbing the tissue beneath her nose.

"Of course I'm gonna talk to him! I'm just not sure what I'm going to do with him... don't you worry about that, though. Get some rest, and if you don't want to stay here tonight, you can stay with me..." Desna didn't really want Berlin staying in her quarters, but also didn't want her to feel so afraid. She went over and kissed Berlin on the forehead.

"Come lock up after I leave, sweetie. I'll be back for you later, okay?"

Desna stood in the corridor, listening to the locks latch, then heard Berlin pad away from the door.

CHAPTER TWENTY-ONE

DESNA HATED CRAWLING THROUGH CONDUIT TUNNELS, BUT they were the quickest way to the main power supply on the port side of *Gretel,* much faster than traversing the myriad corridors and stairwells. Skip and Wurther were repairing the electrical systems that failed during the BC-1 debacle. Skip didn't believe the failures caused the catastrophe, but theorized it could have gone smoother if they hadn't malfunctioned at such a critical time. Maybe that was true, or maybe it was his way of making it right in his mind. Either way, Desna didn't care. The episode was over, and whatever Skip needed to tell himself to be able to carry on was fine with her.

Exiting the conduit, she took the catwalk across the reactor bay and down the stairwell on the other side. Already she could hear the men's voices echoing through the ship, talking and laughing. Up until now, this conversation with Wurther had been theoretical, transpiring in the safe haven of her mind. Now the rehearsal was about to go live, and everything she'd planned to say was gone. Everything felt surreal. A conversation with her Quartermaster about sexually assaulting her First mate? That was the stuff of movies and books, not life on a spacecraft millions of miles from Earth where their very survival depended on each other.

"Captain Desna!" Skip looked up from a massive tangle of

wires and circuits. "Another two days and we'll have her fixed up better than new. Literally!"

"Unbelievable how those DESG boys installed these Remote Bus Isolators," Wurther stated with pride, finding flaw where the space-ace engineers had slipped up. "Luckily there were a few crates of them in the new supply shipment. Have to make 'em last though. I doubt we'll receive any more in the future... because they'll really be coming from the past..."

Both men chuckled at this twisted logic, as if they'd discussed it at length over shots of bourbon.

Desna wanted to laugh with them, do shots and celebrate their competency, bask confidently in the knowledge that her engineers could probably handle anything that arose on *Gretel*. But dread over her impending discussion with Wurther had her stomach in knots.

"Wurther? Can I have a word in private?" The statement landed like a sledge hammer on steel, sounding far more ominous than she'd planned.

Wurther stood up slowly, as if he'd been working in the cramped space for too long.

"He's coming back, isn't he?" Skip asked in a downhearted tone.

Desna said nothing, leading Wurther away to an isolated cubby off the main corridor.

"This sounds serious, Captain." Wurther wiped his hands into a shop towel. "What's going on?"

Wurther was such a huge man, it felt to Desna like one of those David and Goliath moments, wondering if she'd be forced to bring the big man down with nothing more than a slingshot. She wasn't sure what her *slingshot* was, or if she even had one. Yet, Berlin's account of the previous evening was extremely damning.

"Wurther, this is the most difficult conversation I've ever had in my entire life, but we have to have it."

Wurther looked like he'd been punched, his eyes unfocused, confused. "What's going on?"

"I just came from speaking with Berlin, and... she claimed you attacked her last night..."

"Attacked her? I went by her quarters like you asked me to do. She said she wasn't in the mood for company. I left, and Skip and I played gin rummy on the bridge during his shift until all hours. Ask Skip! Why would I attack her? I really like that crazy girl..."

His eyes shifted back and forth of their own accord, it seemed, as if they were trying to erase some unthinkable notion. "What'd she say I did?"

"Said you tried to rape her..."

"*Rape her!* That's insane! In my worst life I've never done anything like that to a woman! I could never do that!" Wurther's face turned bright red, sweat beading along his brow. It was obvious he was in disbelief and extremely upset.

Skip appeared, wearing an awful expression. "I'm sorry, but I couldn't help overhearing your discussion. Wurther and me played cards till nearly four this morning. There's no way he did that to First mate Berlin. Even if he hadn't been with me, Wurther just doesn't have that kind of evil in him, Captain. I don't know why Berlin would make that claim. And I'm not insinuating anything, but I'll tell you sure as I'm standing here, Wurther did no such thing."

Desna believed both of them with the same ferocity she believed Berlin, but something had to be done. The situation couldn't stand in limbo, not if she was going to maintain harmony among the crew.

"Mr. Wurther, I need you to return to your quarters and remain there until I can sort this out." Desna was crushed by her own proclamation. It felt as if solidarity and morale were disintegrating rapidly, and she didn't know how to prevent the situation from devolving into chaos.

"Skip, I need you to finish these repairs best you can." She felt the bottom fall out. "I can send Chelsey over if you think that will help..."

Skip gave her a hard look, then glanced at Wurther with empathy, pressing his lips to a hard line. "This is all bullshit," he said under his breath as he walked away, but Desna heard him.

"You gonna escort me to my room?" Wurther's tone landed somewhere between indignant and embarrassed.

"I'll walk with you. Maybe we can figure this out."

Wurther proceeded with the torpor of a man going to his execution. Desna asked about details, Wurther supplying answers with a flat affect, as if he'd lost all purpose and direction. Desna could hardly stand to see him this way. Then she recalled something Berlin had told her.

"Lift up your shirt," Desna said, stopping Wurther.

"What?"

"Lift up your shirt."

Wurther grabbed the bottom seam of the material and slid it to his belly button.

"No, all the way up. Over your chest."

Wurther hoisted it up to his chin. "Find what you're looking for?"

"Turn around."

Wurther twirled slowly until he faced her again.

"Okay," Desna said, bewildered.

Wurther dropped his shirt, pulling at the lower edge to straighten it.

Desna had no idea what was going on, but had to make room for the possibility that Berlin was delusional. Maybe the stress of the journey had finally taken its toll. If Berlin had stabbed Wurther three times like she said, it would be impossible for Wurther to hide it. There wasn't a mark on him.

Wurther had just started walking again when she stopped him. "Go back and help Skip."

Wurther regarded her with a crosswise look.

"Go on. Not a word about this to anyone. Make sure Skip understands that, too." Desna couldn't help but wonder if she was making the right call. "And don't go see Berlin for any reason. Not until I figure this out."

Wurther was tucking in his shirt as he idled away.

Desna needed to see Hurd and Doc Karl, find out if they'd made any progress on the gel samples. Something was off, Desna could feel it, nothing lining up quite right. She suspected *Gretel* and the crew were not yet free of the entity that had taken up residence in Cargo Hold 4.

CHAPTER TWENTY-TWO

DESPITE THE INGENIOUS RVW DAYTIME TRACKING SYSTEM aboard *Gretel,* Desna had lost all sense of time since Berlin's alleged assault. She could find no proof that anything happened except for Berlin's hysterical testimony, and her ripped pajamas. So upset that Wurther wasn't *put in chains* for his crime, Berlin wanted nothing to do with him, or her. She hadn't reported for duty since the incident, and as far as Desna knew, she was still staying with Doc Karl.

Desna caught herself losing traction in her discussion with Hurd about the curious gel. He blathered on about empirical formulae, then gave a detailed description of moles—a mole equal to the exact number of atoms in 12 grams of pure carbon—and on and on until Desna glazed over. She didn't rejoin the conversation until he finally said, "...and that's why this is taking so long."

Hurd mentioned further testing they planned to perform; high-performance liquid chromatography, NMR spectroscopy and myriad diffraction techniques. He explained that these were highly-sensitive methods that would take time, but between Dr. Karl and himself he felt they would yield positive results.

"Dr. Karl is going to load the gel into his centrifuge, see if we can separate the substance into its components."

Hurd didn't stop there. Desna heard terms like isolation and purification, recrystallization, acid/base separation until she eventually stopped him, telling him to contact her when they had something other than a detailed and very long laundry list of scientific procedures.

"I don't mean to be curt," she said, trying to ease her nasty tone. "But I need answers, not a bunch of nomenclature that does nothing to move the ball down the court."

"What ball?"

"Look... just come get me when you know what that crap is, okay?" Desna planned to go to Doc Karl's office to get a different perspective on the gel. Doc was every bit the scientist Hurd was, but with a much better bedside manner. He'd break it down so even she, with her Ph.D. in Space Sciences and Planetary Exploration, could understand.

On her way to his office, Desna's insides collapsed when she spotted Chelsey walking toward her in the corridor. Over the past several days, they had done nothing more than exchange innocuous smiles on the bridge, or in the mess hall, yet she felt the young woman was aching to talk. Secretly, Desna was relieved Berlin had chosen to stay with Doc Karl. She would've loved to have spent another night of lovemaking with Chelsey, absent the cloying chatter that usually accompanied her time with Berlin. Nevertheless, in this moment, she didn't want to rehash the fantastic sex she and Chelsey had shared.

"Hey, I've been meaning to talk to you," Chelsey said to her.

Here it comes, she thought, then: "I suppose we should..."

"No, it's nothing *heavy* or anything... I just wanted to tell you how much I enjoyed our evening. That's all. It was special. I'd never been with another woman before, and... it was... really nice."

Chelsey brushed Desna's hand and smiled as she passed before continuing down the hall. Desna wheeled around, befuddled, watching Chelsey walking away. The young woman hadn't seemed at all like a newcomer.

Without further contemplation, Desna headed for sick bay. Doc Karl was seated at his desk studying data on his palm-pad. She flopped down in the empty chair opposite his desk, about to say something when he spoke first.

"You must be reading my mind," he said, placing the pad on his desk. "Somebody disconnected Fawn from her IV and all the monitors last night. I think someone was trying to kill her... If I hadn't come back for the test results I'd been waiting on... she'd be dead."

"What? Why would anyone want to kill Fawn?" The doctor's disclosure flipped open a trapdoor in her mind, all her thoughts suddenly sucking down into it. "That makes no sense." She couldn't formulate any other response beside outrage... and fear. Believing the gelatinous substance they'd discovered on the hull would somehow illuminate what was happening on *Gretel* seemed irrational, but that was the only clue she had to hold onto.

"Are you any closer to learning anything about the gel we found?"

He sat back, his face registering shock, or disgust, she couldn't be sure. "Why would you ask about that after what I just told you?" He didn't bother trying to disguise his revulsion over her insensitivity. A breath later, his features softened, then: "You think this is somehow related to that Cargo Hold 4 business, don't you? And Berlin and Wurther... you think that's related, too?"

They sat in the awkward new silence for several long seconds. "I'll make it a priority, Captain," he said with fresh vigor.

"Thank you, but let's keep this between us. I have nothing so far but suppositions and nightmares..."

"I can give you something for the nightmares..." He pulled out his desk drawer and began rummaging around.

"Not necessary... so far, anyway." She stood to leave, then inquired about Berlin. "She go back home yet?"

Doc Karl went a little flush, and dug his finger into his ear.

"Relax, Karl. She's a very sexual woman, and you're... well... we're all making the best of this long journey. Let me know as soon as you learn what that gel is."

She hadn't been to the cargo area for quite some time, and didn't relish the idea of going down alone. Stopping at her sleeping quarters, she went to the bureau and pulled out the bottom drawer, withdrawing the D-mobilizer from beneath her long-sleeve shirts. Turning it over in her hands, she recalled her training, then flipped the switch on the side to disable the safety. At the base of the handle stock was the power setting knob. She twisted it all the way to High, then pulled out the holster harness and strapped it on, hoping none of the crew saw her with the weapon. She'd only ever used one at the academy, and only on inanimate objects to get the hang of how close one needed to be for the weapon to be effective, and to practice discharging it. Never had she believed she might actually need to use it. Lately, it seemed, she had to remind herself she was still a *scientist,* though much of her space science skills were being supplanted by sleuthing, policing and investigation.

She saw no one on the trip to the cargo area, which had been what she'd hoped for. At the same time, it gave her pause. If something happened to her down there, no one would find her for days. *Gretel* was huge, and with only eight people aboard— one of which was bedridden on life-support in sick bay—it wasn't likely anyone would come across her by accident. They'd have to miss her, then search for her, then... Desna stopped the mental what-if list.

Before she traversed the staircase down into the cargo hold, she stood holding the hatch open, listening, waiting for the lights to come up to full intensity. Once the dark area was washed in a pseudo-welcoming glow, she took the steps carefully, cautiously, her hand resting on the D-mobe. Her eyes went first to Cargo Hold 4, the large metal blisters, the distressed metal, still in awe of how powerful something would have to be to make such impressions. She took her eyes down the length of the vault, trying to dig out detail at the far end. Except for normal ship noises, what Skip referred to as *Gretel's* "digestive system at work," the area seemed to have fallen under an oppressive hush. It wasn't hard to breathe, exactly... it just felt dangerous to.

Desna came closer to Cargo Hold 4, placing her ear to the metal. She was unable to tell if the sound she was hearing was breathing, or something to do with the outer hatch being gone, like a gentle shushing of air past an opened window. But that made no sense; there would be no shushing, no sound whatsoever. Then the breathing stopped. Maybe she imagined it.

Maybe she wanted to hear something, anything that would point her toward a solution to the puzzle. She listened a while longer. More nothing, except for a sound coming from the far end of the cargo area.

Using her quietest gait, she crept down the long vault, the sound growing louder. Moaning. Someone or something was mewling softly. Maybe in pain, injured. When she'd gone about thirty meters, she heard the sound coming from one of the fork-lift bays. A double-doored garage enclosure housing a single forklift. As she approached, the moaning grew louder, as if the person, or thing, behind the double doors had attempted to get out, but couldn't get them open.

CHAPTER TWENTY-THREE

DESNA HELD A HEATED DEBATE WITH HERSELF OVER THE wisdom of this decision. Maybe this matter would be better handled by someone more intrepid than an academic professor with a D-mobe strapped to her hip; a weapon, that for all intents and purposes, may not even function properly.

She listened before she touched the doors. No sound at first, then a muffled whimpering, as if something was trying desperately to remain undetected. Get some help, she told herself. But it would take too long. She withdrew the D-mobe and held it forward, pointed at the doors. It was a simple entryway; slide open one door and the other would open at the same time, only in the opposite direction. With her weapon in her right hand, she planned to use her left to open them. But when she tried, the doors seemed stuck. She pulled harder to her left, using her body for leverage, always with her eyes fixed on the space between the doors. The crack was now a few centimeters wide, but the doors still felt jammed.

Using her weight, she gave the left door a hearty tug and both doors shot open. When they did, a naked body spilled out through the opening, pouring onto the floor on its side, its face angled down and away from her. She gasped, jumping back, her weapon pointed at what appeared to be a corpse. It was most likely a man by the hair on his back and shoulders. Even though he wasn't moving, she edged closer carefully, the D-mobe pointed at his head. With her free hand, she grabbed his upright shoulder and pulled him onto his back. *Wurther!*

Fucking Wurther? Her mind scrambling, slipping backward down into a deep tangled mess, replaying Wurther pulling up his shirt so she could look for stab wounds. That wasn't necessary here; the ruddy gashes were obvious and on display, and exactly where Berlin had described them in great detail. A pool of dried blood lay on the floor just inside the entrance.

Wurther! When was that the last time she'd seen him? In the power plant with Skip? She couldn't think. No, that was wrong. She saw him this morning in the mess hall. They didn't speak, but she saw him. He was fixing a bowl of cereal, carrying it to a table to sit by himself. What the fuck was going on? She was in full meltdown mode, taking her eyes from Wurther, then to the forklift, then back to Wurther, as if she had to keep her eyes busy so she could think.

It was obvious he was dead, and had been for some time, the blood dried, dark brown. Who made the noises, then? That's when she saw them, two eyes, peering out from the dark end of the garage behind the forklift. The owner of the eyes was partially hidden by the large piece of machinery. They stared as she pointed her D-mobe at them.

For a moment Desna froze, her mind unspooling, her legs going limp, her thoughts stuck in some deadening loop. The movement of the eyes shifting behind the forklift and out of sight jolted her back to the moment. She turned and bolted for the stairwell, stumbling up the steps, falling and banging her shin, stealing quick glances toward the forklift garage. Yanking on the railing to pull herself up, she clawed her way back to the top landing. She swung the hatch closed and secured it, rushing back to the main stairwell that would take her up to A-Deck.

Straining for breath, she stopped to settle herself when she reached the main floor, her heart flapping like a flag. She clutched her chest, certain she was in the grips of cardiac arrest. A few minutes later, she looked down at her shin, blood blossoming through the material of her pants. *What the hell is going on?*

she thought. But she already knew, or at least had a really strong hunch. Yet, the notion was so disturbing she found it hard to take herself seriously. Most of all, though, she prayed she was wrong.

Outside the bridge, she steadied herself with a stern reminder: You're the captain of this ship, and the fate of the crew rests in your hands. She erupted into the bridge and marched directly to Wurther's work station, pointing the D-mobe at the back of his head. Watching the drama unfold, Skip spun around, shocked. "What are you doing!"

Wurther turned more cautiously, stopping when Desna shouted at him. "Don't move!"

Chelsey remained at her station, her eyes darting between Skip, Wurther and Desna.

"What's going on?" Skip shot out of his chair. "What's gotten into you?"

"Tie him up!" Desna yelled, her D-mobe fixed on Wurther's head.

"Tie him up?" Skip asked. "Why? For what? And where would I even find rope?"

"I don't know, Skip... maybe some wire. We have wire, don't we?"

Skip scoffed, obviously bewildered. "This is insane..."

Desna threw a quick glance over her shoulder. "Chelsey! Get over here. Do you know where we have wire? Or rope?"

"Maybe in the cargo hold, but..."

"No! You can't go down there... Why don't we have any goddamn rope on this ship?

"If I could just turn around, we could straighten this out..." Wurther said.

"Don't you move!" Desna said. "Chelse, go into my day room and get a roll of duct tape out of that box. There's a whole case in there... in the closet..."

Chelsey returned shortly with the tape. "What now?"

Desna reached forward, grabbing the back of Wurther's chair, pulling him and his chair away from the console.

"Tape his wrists to the armrests," Desna said.

Chelsey regarded her, then with her eyes, pleaded with Skip

for direction. He could only shrug, his head rocking side to side in disapproval.

Chelsey taped Wurther's wrists to the chair. When she finished, she brought her eyes to Desna.

"Now his feet. Tape his ankles together," Desna said.

She squatted in front of Wurther, gently securing his ankles, looking up at him with forlorn eyes. This time Chelsey set the tape on the console.

Desna relaxed, sliding the D-mobe into the holster.

"What's this all about, Captain?" Skip asked, obviously vexed by her display.

"This isn't Wurther. I don't know *what* he is, but *it* isn't our Quartermaster! Wurther's dead in the cargo hold."

Skip and Chelsey were silent, clearly dumbstruck by Desna's pronouncement.

Wurther started to protest. "That's crazy! What the hell is she talking about? Skip? Chelsey? It's me! Wurther! Skip, you have to—"

Desna shut him up with more duct tape.

"This isn't right, Captain," Skip said. "I'm not sure what's going on, but this... this is insane..."

"You won't think so in a few minutes." Desna instructed them both to go back to their quarters and retrieve their D-mobes. While they were gone, Desna used the ship's comm system to summon Doc Karl. "Dr. Karl, secure sick bay and meet me at the hatch leading to the cargo vault now. Bring a weapon!"

Desna pushed Wurther into the center of her day room, then locked the door from the outside. In the hallway she caught up to Skip who was coming back toward the bridge. He had his weapon, though wasn't yet convinced he needed it, evidenced by the incredulous look on his face. On their way to the cargo hold, they met up with Chelsey, who seemed confused but attentive.

They only had to wait a minute or two before Doc Karl showed up, carrying a scalpel.

"This was all I could think of..."

Desna unlocked the hatch, then led the crew down the stairs. They followed her along the length of the cargo area. Before they arrived at the forklift hold, she could see Wurther's body lying on the floor.

Skip and Chelsey slowed their pace, with Doc Karl hurriedly squatting next to the body. He felt Wurther's neck for a pulse. "He's dead." He squinted at the wounds, then lifted Wurther's arm; it moved easily. "Rigor's passed, most likely. His body's ice cold... and by the look of the wounds, he's been dead a while... at least thirty-six hours, maybe more..."

Skip stepped forward to inspect the body, his face twisted in horror. "Wurther's duct-taped to a damn chair in the bridge! This makes no sense..."

"That's not Wurther in the bridge, Skip..." Desna said, noticing the terrified look on Chelsey's face. Doc Karl appeared equally upset.

"I'll explain it when we get upstairs. We have some serious decisions to make. But first, we need to get Wurther to sick bay." She shifted her attention to Doc Karl. "I need an autopsy."

Doc nodded.

Using a gurney from the medical center, they hauled Wurther's body from the cargo vault on the freight elevator, then reconvened in the conference room. Desna had asked Doc Karl to bring Berlin with him, so that every active crew member would be in on the discussion. Berlin walked in wearing pajamas, looking like she'd spent the past week of her life at a frat party, shuffling by in bare feet. Hurd finally showed up, remarkably alert for someone who had started his eight-hour rest cycle only two hours earlier. Desna apologized, asking him to please have a seat.

Skip sat like a zombie; all signs of life siphoned from his face. The first thing he'd done when they got back to the main deck was demand to see Wurther. Desna had unlocked the door to her day room, and Skip had slowly circled his shipmate, his eyes big as portholes.

Desna started the discussion. "I'm not *certain* what is happening on *Gretel*, but I have a theory. The entity from Cargo Hold 4 is still aboard the ship... and is duplicating our crew..."

Doc Karl was the first to speak. "Cloning? That's just not possible."

"Out here," Desna said, spreading her arms wide to suggest the full breadth of outer space, "we have no idea what is possible. Chelsey and I both witnessed this phenomenon in its infant stages, no pun intended. We both saw crew members in Cargo Hold 4 in some tortured stage of incubation, but as adults. Now it would seem they have reached maturation and are interacting with us on the ship. Living, breathing simulations. They are affecting our actions, our thinking, even how we relate with one another."

There was an interlude of quiet before Berlin spoke. "What's going on here, Des?"

"We found Wurther."

"Is he okay?"

"He's dead."

"No! He can't be!" She squealed as if she'd been cut. "I killed him? I never meant to..." Berlin was shaking, her eyes red.

"Wurther's not dead!" Skip shouted. "That thing we found in the cargo bay wasn't Wurther! He's duct-taped to a damn chair in the captain's day room!"

Why hadn't Desna considered that possibility, that the actual *imposter* was the dead body in the hold, not the man she'd imprisoned in her day room? That made sense, given that the dead body was naked. That would mean that it was a duplicate that had attacked Berlin.

"Skip, please go set Wurther free and bring him back here," Desna said.

Skip came alive, hurrying from the conference room. Berlin was infuriated, screaming at Desna. "You said Wurther was dead! How could you be so cruel!"

"Not now!" Desna's energy was draining off. "It's a very confusing situation."

Berlin stood, pounding the table, demanding answers, when Desna looked over at Doc Karl, asking for help with her eyes. Speaking in a calming tone to Berlin, Doc Karl wrapped his arm around her shoulders, escorting her from the room. Hurd had yet to say anything, and Chelsey was her dependably composed self, taking it all in.

Skip and Wurther entered, taking seats next to one another.

"I'm sorry, Wurther," Desna said, truly horrified by how she'd acted.

"Skip kind of explained what's going on, but..."

"We're all having difficulty understanding this," Desna said.

"Everything makes sense now," Chelsey said, smiling over at Desna. "When you showed up naked at my quarters that night, I was shocked. It seemed so out of character for—"

"What!" Desna shouted, appalled. "I never went to your quarters. You came to mine! You were the one—" Desna stopped, aghast at her revelation, the events of that tryst playing back in her mind, but with a new wrinkle... it hadn't been Chelsey after all.

Chelsey smiled, shrugging. "We couldn't know, Desna," she said, as if this little escape clause made everything right again. Desna was repulsed by the thought of it, then terrified at the possibility of being infected with some kind of alien virus. Was that what was happening to Fawn? Had she been contacted by one of these dupes? But Doc Karl said it was her heart. Her mind was spinning out of control, traveling a long, unmanageable tunnel.

CHAPTER TWENTY-FOUR

Before the meeting broke, everyone had agreed that the first order of business was to find this entity that was duplicating crew members. And exterminate it. The only dupe they'd found so far was Wurther's. And it was dead. They knew at least two more skulked about somewhere, Desna's and Chelsey's. Desna told everyone that when she'd found Wurther's dupe, another one had been hiding behind the forklift.

It was decided that everyone's quarters would remain locked at all times to prevent unwanted visitors. And no one was to approach a dupe for any reason. Just report its location and give it wide berth.

After a DNA test, Wurther was fully vindicated—proven to be who he was—and relieved, as if he'd started doubting his own identity. And sanity. Doc Karl was doing further testing on the dead dupe, trying to determine if it had any of the properties of the curious gel they'd found, which still remained a mystery.

They chose to begin the search in Cargo Hold 4, all agreeing it was the most likely habitat, even though Cargo Hold 4 was now open to outer space. For that reason, the crew couldn't just open the interior hatch. Even if they could, how would they destroy the entity, armed with nothing more powerful than D-mobes? In order to secure funding for the mission, and to be taken seriously, no one at DESG lent any credence to the possibility of aliens and deep space monsters. Hence the lack of any real firepower. Potentially dangerous microbes, exotic cyanobacteria and pesky invasive spores topped the list of most likely encounters, with the tiny predacious insect finding itself a spot near the bottom. But even that was a stretch. How could an insect be present unless an entire ecosystem was in place? And no one at DESG considered that likelihood as plausible, at least never openly.

"Another spacewalk," Desna said, after they'd exhausted all other possibilities. She wasn't wild about it either, but if they could at least establish that the life form still maintained its residence in Cargo Hold 4, they could at least formulate a strategy to eliminate it. However, with speculation as their only guide, it was impossible to hatch a plan that made any sense. They had to know what they were dealing with.

Since finding Wurther's dead dupe, only Skip had spotted another one traversing the catwalk a few days earlier near the power plant. He'd gone to the port side to finish up repairs to the electrical system. "Naked as a newborn," he'd said. "With hair like yours, Captain."

Desna could have done without that detail, especially given that Skip had now seen her naked. Even so, Desna and the crew had not yet addressed the biggest dilemma they faced. There was no debate over eliminating the entity in Cargo Hold 4. That was a given. But what would they do with the dupes once they rounded them up? They looked and functioned like humans, and were created in the likenesses of the crew. Would they just be able eject them into space? Or set their D-mobes on max and zap them? Who on the ship was capable of such barbarism? As far as Desna knew, Wurther was the only person aboard *Gretel* who had actually taken a human life in his mercenary days. Was it fair to ask him to take care of that nasty bit of business on his own? It was unthinkable.

"What would we accomplish with another spacewalk?" Hurd asked.

"Eliminating Cargo Hold 4's inhabitant," Desna said. "Once that's done, we'll widen our search to find the remaining dupes."

There was accord among the crew that the spacewalk was in

order. Chelsey volunteered. Desna waited to see if anyone else would step up. When they didn't, Desna said, "It's me and Chelsey again, then."

A few grumbles rustled through the group, which quickly faded into the ambient hush of *Gretel*. The plan paralleled that of the one they formulated around dupe sightings; verify and report. If she and Chelsey witnessed the thing, they were to verify and report. Take no action whatsoever.

"What's the status on the CPV-drone?" Desna switched her eyes between Wurther and Skip.

"It's good to go," Skip said.

"Is Berlin up for operating *The Yellow Submarine?*" Desna posed her question toward Doc Karl. Apparently, Berlin now spent every minute with him, feeling a comforting security with the middle-aged physician. She shirked her duties and avoided all contact with the crew, having him bring her meals to his quarters. He had become the worst enabler, and he knew it; he just didn't know how to break the cycle, though he had no real incentive, reaping the fringe benefits of her company. Hurd had tried to advise him, but Karl could only reply by saying, "Oh, I could never do that to her. She's too fragile."

Doc Karl seemed to be floating in some other universe, so Desna asked again.

He shook his head sadly. "I don't think so. She's still a mess." Then, after an obvious moment of panic, he added, "Don't tell her I said that."

"You're safe, Doc... nobody even sees her, much less talks to her." Desna knew when this dupe business was concluded, an intervention was in order.

"I know how to operate it," Wurther said. "What are you thinking?"

This part of Desna's plan was sketchy, but she felt she needed to share it with the crew. "I thought Chelsey and I could hide on the hidden side of *The Yellow Submarine* as you guided it in front of Cargo Hold 4. That way we could search undetected..."

"That makes sense, but I get the feeling there's more..." Wurther said, reading her perfectly.

After nibbling around the edges of her idea, Desna finally spit it out. "We hit the thing with the drone's spotlights!"

Wurther studied on the concept, then said, "What happened to 'verify and report?'"

"We need action! Remember when Hurd flicked on the lights in Cargo Hold 4? The damn thing went crazy! Maybe it'll jump off the fucking ship and we'll be done with it..."

Wurther took his eyes to Skip, who nodded at first, then seemed to give it more thought, and shrugged.

"Wait," Hurd said. "If we're going to use the CPV, then there is no reason to risk you and Chelsey. We can do everything from the drone."

Heads nodded, everyone agreeing with Hurd. Desna was relieved, though a little annoyed she hadn't thought of it. What kind of leadership relied on unnecessary risk and crazy schemes? She pushed away her narcissism to focus on pivotal details.

"Is the drone fit for service?" she asked.

"Wurther and I will test her out, but I'm pretty sure she's ready."

The plan was set, and now they just had to get through the next few hours until they sent the CPV-drone to Cargo Hold 4.

CHAPTER TWENTY-FIVE

No one complained that Berlin was absent for this latest maneuver. Maybe everyone believed she was a little off and it was safer if she wasn't involved. Desna certainly felt that way. Wurther, holding the remote for *The Yellow Submarine*, said it worked perfectly on the trial run. Doc Karl apologized, saying he couldn't make it, that he was running tests, and doing research. He assured Desna it was very important, that he might have discovered a plan to save Fawn's life. Desna didn't need him to prove anything, elated he'd come up with an idea to cure the young girl. Even though he hadn't used the word *cure,* it was still uplifting news; she needed that more than ever.

"We ready?" Desna asked the crew. Skip gave her the nod. Wurther guided the drone toward Cargo Hold 4, its progress detailed on the large screen in the bridge. Eerily, the drone illuminated a bright patch of light that crawled along the shadow side of *Gretel* like a huge amoeba under a microscope. Glints of light created by hull imperfections sparked back to the camera, giving the impression that *Gretel* was sprinkled with glitter.

The drone came upon the damage to the other cargo hold doors, which they had not yet been able to address. Cargo Hold 4 was coming into view, revealing a gaping square black hole in the ship's hull where the door had been. The drone's LED lamps could barely penetrate the dark space, the vessel still too far out from the hull. Even in the meager light, Desna thought she'd seen movement.

"Can you bring it closer?" she asked softly.

Wurther worked the lever on the remote, the light from the drone digging into the black void. There it was again; movement at the back. "Did anyone see that?" Desna said

"I did," Chelsey said, almost in a whisper.

Hurd was nodding, mesmerized by the big screen.

Burrowing deeper, the spotlights caught on something enormous in the darkest corner of the hold, the beams reflecting oddly off the object.

"Can you get closer?" Desna asked, afraid to make too much noise, as if that could spook the undulating dark shape on the screen. The light cut deeper, until the shape came into view, the crew letting out a collective gasp. Just then, a deafening, sonic surge, like a bolt of pure energy, blasted the drone, sending it tumbling into outer space, Wurther unable to corral it. The high-pitched din continued eating into the normally quiet bridge, everyone holding their ears. With hers still ringing, Desna watched from the view window, the drone spinning away like a toy. In seconds the CPV was gone. She glanced at the large screen. It was dark.

"What the fuck?" Desna said, the ear-splitting whine making it difficult to hear. She was trying to parse what she'd witnessed before the big blast, wondering if anyone else had seen it the way she did. It was nauseating, an immense gelatinous blob reaching the ceiling of the hold, humans haphazardly encased inside it, floating and struggling in its mass. She saw them moving, could tell they were alive, their mouths open, arms outstretched, reaching.

CHAPTER TWENTY-SIX

DESNA ASKED CHELSEY TO BRING UP THE DRONE FOOTAGE AND fast-forward to the end. No one was discussing what they'd seen, or what had happened. If they were of the same mind as Desna, they were aghast and couldn't believe what they'd witnessed; an abomination beyond comprehension.

Soon the video was speeding past, the frames an indecipherable blur until Chelsey slowed it down, the lights of the drone notching a path into Cargo Hold 4.

"Stop!" Desna called to Chelsey. The picture froze, the single frame etching onto the crew's retinas. Groans and utterances of disgust rippled through the bridge. Desna stepped closer, Chelsey refining the image until the details were too agonizingly sharp to refute. She couldn't count the beings suspended in the curious glop, but they certainly outnumbered the crew. Some of them were in embryonic stages of adult life, not fully formed, yet fully grown, while others had features which were tortured and frightened.

Some crew members turned away in revulsion, holding their mouths, when they recognized themselves in the gelatinous soup.

"It's not possible…" Desna backed away from the screen shaking her head.

"It assimilated our DNA," Hurd said with scientific detachment.

"Where would it get our DNA?" Chelsey said.

"It was on everything in that cargo hold. All the research and sample containment units. The doors, the light switches. Everywhere." Hurd paused a moment, as if contemplating the source of the anomaly. "We must have inadvertently brought the life form in with our research... and now it's doing what it does... create life..."

"No! That's not possible, Hurd!" Spittle flew from Skip's mouth. "J-78 was uninhabitable!"

Desna quickly countered. "Uninhabitable by what measure, Skip?" She knew the only metric they had for reaching such conclusions were biased at best, constructed around science based on humans and life on Earth. To her, it was much more probable that the universe didn't share such a limited yardstick. "And it's not creating life, Mr. Hurd... It's merely copying us... mimicking what's already been created..."

Hurd was unmoved, not reacting to Desna's accusation. The bridge fell silent, the loud whine finally gone. Wurther was the next to speak up. "What it is and what it's doing don't amount to a hill of beans... the question is, how do we get rid of it?" Wurther's face was stolid, his eyes sharpened on the video image of the curious creature. "It's obviously not done making copies."

Desna, with her hand covering her mouth, had yet to make peace with her own alarm over the situation, her muddled mind chewing through the infinite list of untenable pitfalls they were facing. With her mind trapped and fettered, she threw the problem into the ring.

"We need solutions. Anything. No matter how off the wall."

The hush that followed was exasperating. Desna couldn't do this alone. She needed someone to step up, toss out a workable resolution; her ideas were juvenile and dangerous, and unacceptable.

No one said a thing.

"Skip," Desna said. "When do we come to our next research planet?"

Skip went to his terminal and brought up his screen. He typed, then: "Roughly 173 days."

"That's nearly six months!"

"What are you thinking, Captain?" Hurd asked.

"That if we landed... maybe it would get off the ship." The idea sounded so naïve to her own ears, she was embarrassed she'd even thought it, much less said it out loud.

"There's an asteroid large enough to put down on...let's see... in roughly 23 days," Skip said.

"Asteroid? That sounds tricky..."

"Trickier than a monster cranking out new crew members by the dozens?" Wurther said, dead serious.

Desna pondered Wurther's support of the idea, surprised, and a little dismayed that no one had challenged it more vociferously, or at all.

"Everyone in agreement, then?" Desna said, feeling as if she were losing control of her ship and crew. Leaders weren't supposed to put mission decisions up to a vote. But given the unusual circumstances, she felt she had no other choice.

All heads nodded their accord, maybe a bit more timidly than Desna would have preferred. Nevertheless, they had a plan, even if it was sketchy. Hurd and Wurther got up and left.

Desna conferred with Skip about the upcoming challenges of landing this enormous ship on an asteroid, Skip working to ameliorate her trepidation. He went over all the procedures. Assured her that protocols were in place for just such a tactic. "There are asteroids in our research agenda," Skip explained to her. "It's not as rogue an operation as you might think."

Desna nodded her agreement, but only to end the discussion with Skip. His assurances hadn't lessened the gnawing dread in her gut. Chelsey was at her station when Desna walked past.

"Can we talk a sec?" Chelsey said in a quiet voice, obviously not wanting Skip to hear.

"What's up?" Desna was edgy, losing patience, and just wanted to get off the bridge.

"Would you like to have some wine later, when my shift ends?"

"Your place or mine?" Desna wasn't sure where the joke came from, yet it had no effect on lessening her own discomfort.

"I guess mine."

Desna nodded and left, the invite lifting her spirits. She'd been wanting to speak with Doc Karl, but everything was happening so fast, she hadn't made time.

When she entered sick bay, he was near Fawn's bed, tending the monitors, checking them against data on his palm-pad.

"You have a moment?" she asked.

"I bet you're here about those gel results." He looked a bit harried. "Hurd and I are collaborating now. You just missed him."

After witnessing the entity from the CPV-drone footage, she was convinced the gel was some kind of residual slime left behind from the organism, like the trail from a snail. Even so, some insight into its makeup might be helpful before they tried the risky asteroid landing. What if it could be destroyed by something as simple as *water*, and they failed to discover that in time?

"I was wondering about the DNA results from the Wurther dupe. Anything on that yet?"

"No, sorry. Not yet." The doctor scurried around her, as if she were an unmovable obstacle.

Was this his way of avoiding this conversation, buzzing around like an annoying house fly? He must realize the implications of the DNA and gel results.

"Hurd filled me in on the drone video," he said, heading toward his office. Desna hurried to keep up. "Very disturbing, to say the least. But you have a plan, Captain... that's all that matters."

By his flighty tone, she could tell he was absorbed in other matters, peacefully disengaged from the situation aboard *Gretel*, mindlessly carving out little slivers of concern from his distracted mind, passing them off as attentiveness.

"What's going on, Karl?"

He stopped abruptly, like a child caught stealing a candy bar. "It's Fawn..." His face lit up briefly before it was instantly eclipsed, it seemed, by some shadow of doubt. "I can save her now."

"How? What's changed?"

"The dupes!"

Desna waited a moment, thinking this should make sense to her, but it didn't.

Apparently reading her confusion, he clarified his statement. "Fawn needs a heart transplant... now I can give her one!"

Desna didn't believe he could possibly have the skills or equipment to perform such a surgery aboard *Gretel*, but even if he could, where would he get the...

"You have to be kidding, right? You're gonna stick a dupe heart in Fawn?"

"Not any *dupe* heart...The heart from Fawn's dupe! A perfect match!"

The possibilities for this being a terrible idea seemed to be infinite, and Desna hardly knew where to start.

"Once she shows up, I can begin. I've been studying nonstop for days, brushing up on the procedure—"

Desna interrupted. "Brushing up? You've done these before?"

"No... but, I am a doctor, Captain. I can do this. Hurd has already agreed to assist me. Besides, this is Fawn's only chance to survive..."

Desna couldn't believe this. "And Fawn's dupe, if there is one...what do we tell her?"

"I don't get your meaning?"

"Do we just kill her and take her heart?"

The man's face twisted with disgust. "Oh, please... you don't have to be so coarse!"

"Then what is the ethic here?"

Doc Karl grimaced, busying himself again, shaking his head like a prude upon hearing an off-color joke. She waited, but he had no response, his face reddening.

Then, like an explosive device detonating, he shouted, "You of all people should understand... these things aren't human! They're monsters... clones! Look what one of them tried to do to Berlin. And the one that seduced you... and Chelsey! They have no morals, no sense of right and wrong..."

"They die like humans, like the one in cold storage."

"That doesn't make then human! Lots of organisms die that aren't human... your argument is ludicrous!"

"When I found the dead Wurther dupe in the cargo area, I spotted another one hiding behind the forklift. It was whimpering... obviously afraid..."

"That's your thesis? That it was whimpering! Afraid! So what! Mice have fear! Dogs whimper! That doesn't make them human!"

"So, if it's not human, we can do what we want to it? That's *your* thesis?"

He wasn't cornered, she knew that, and could have pushed his proposition further, but obviously wasn't wild about the trajectory of the discussion, and chose a different tact. "You care more about *them* than Fawn! She's not even seventeen! She deserves to live... more than any goddamn clone!"

Desna didn't disagree with the doctor—Fawn definitely didn't deserve her fate—but if they managed to justify killing a dupe for her heart, what future atrocities would that open the door to? Would there be consensus among the crew that aligned with Doc Karl's premise, that saving Fawn's life was justification enough for any action? That possibility was scarier still. She could imagine the fabric of solidarity evaporating quickly among the crew over this issue. She tried to guess which members might sympathize with Doc's treatise. It wasn't that Desna was vehemently opposed to his idea, on the contrary, she was encouraged by the prospect of saving Fawn, but it did seem necessary for them to stake out some ethical territory to guide the rest of the mission.

CHAPTER TWENTY-SEVEN

DESNA HAD ONLY BEEN TO CHELSEY'S QUARTERS ONCE SINCE the inception of the journey. It was not much different than anyone else's, a few personal items which made it her own. Chelsey handed her a glass of wine and sat down across from her.

"This is awkward, isn't it?" Chelsey said, smiling. "It feels like we've been intimate, and yet, we're like complete strangers." She chuckled nervously and sipped her wine.

Desna knew exactly what she meant. She had thought they would embrace and kiss and hold each other when she arrived, but it felt more like a visit to her accountant than a lovers' reunion.

"It's nice, though, just sitting and sharing a glass of wine." Desna hated that the evening was already veering off into a ditch of small talk and pleasantries.

Chelsey was telling her about her time at the academy, while she wanted to roll the conversation toward dupes and ethics, and her earlier debate with Doc Karl, wondering where Chelsey would come down on that front. Chelsey droned on about classes and testing and how challenging the physical training for the mission had been. "I always thought I was in pretty great shape, you know... but wow, some of that stuff we had to do... well, I'm not telling you anything..."

Desna was about to call it a night when she noticed a slow change washing over Chelsey, the young woman's normally genial mien transforming into a roadmap of anguish and terror. Tears poured down her cheeks as she bent forward, burying her face in her palms. Desna walked over and sat, placing her arm around the young woman's shoulders.

"Hey, now. What's going on, here?" Desna was rattled by the woman's curious change, finding herself suspicious of everything and everyone. This was new, this barrier of distrust she was erecting.

Chelsey twisted into Desna's embrace, sobbing against her chest. Desna waited, gently rubbing her back, trying to calm her. After a few minutes, Chelsey managed to compose herself. With ruddy, ruined eyes, she drew back from Desna, her face wrecked with sadness, fear.

"I'm so scared!" she said. "I had that revelation I told you about, then all that crap about being *summoned,* and now, I'm a mess! I thought I had truly experienced some kind of spiritual awakening... had come to grips with my fears... It was all bullshit! Seeing that fucking monster in Cargo Hold 4 destroyed me! What the hell was that? And these fucking dupes... are they, like... demons or something? Nothing at the academy prepared me for this!"

Crying uncontrollably again, she fell forward, back into Desna's embrace.

"I'm afraid too, sweetie. Everyone is..."

When Chelsey got herself under control, Desna told her they should probably call it an evening. Chelsey darkened, her eyes pleading. "Please don't go! I'm going out of my mind! We don't have to have sex or anything... I just... I can't be alone tonight."

Desna agreed, taking the extra pajamas Chelsey offered. They shared a toothbrush, then cleaned up the dishes in silence, and headed off to bed.

It wasn't long after they'd retired, when Desna thought she heard someone enter the quarters. "Did you lock the door?" Desna whispered to Chelsey.

"What?" Chelsey seemed a bit groggy. She'd obviously dozed off.

Desna got up and walked slowly toward the foyer. Someone was standing there, unmoving, like a shadow. Switching on the lights, she was shocked to see Berlin standing there... completely naked. Berlin approached her when Chelsey came from the bedroom. "What the hell?"

Berlin turned her attention on Chelsey.

"What are you doing here?" Chelsey said.

Berlin approached Chelsey and slapped her across the face.

"You bitch!" Chelsey lashed out, throwing a weak-fisted assault at Berlin. Berlin elbowed her in the face, knocking her to the floor, then jumped on top and started strangling her.

Desna pushed Berlin off. "Get up, Chelsey!" Desna guarded her from another attack while she struggled to her feet.

"It's one of them, isn't it!" Chelsey screamed, rubbing her cheek as she got to her feet.

The dupe came closer to Desna, her eyes dispirited, begging for acknowledgement, as if she expected Desna to recognize her. The dupe's miserable expression baffled Desna, the idea that they, she and the dupe, should be familiar. Yet the dupe displayed all of Berlin's most irritating traits, her possessiveness and jealousy, her tempestuous nature.

"Can you speak?" Desna said to the dupe.

It opened its mouth, muttering unintelligible, raspy grunts.

"It's repulsive!" Chelsey shouted.

"It's trying to learn, Chelsey."

"I don't care if it's trying to *fly!* It's depraved!"

"Sit down," Desna said to the dupe, motioning toward the chair. The dupe stepped closer and put its hand on her breast. It leaned in and pressed its lips to hers, then embraced her. She didn't thwart the advance at first, but instead, began drawing away gently. The dupe held her tighter, pushing down on her pajama bottoms, Desna pushing her away.

"Stop!" Desna slapped the dupe's hands away.

The dupe paused its advance, its eyes gloomy, then gently tried to pull Desna's pajama top off.

"Stop!" Desna screamed again, knocking the dupe's hand away.

A moment later, the dupe's eyes hardened. It advanced on

Desna, mauling her, grabbing at her, trying to wrestle her to the floor, when suddenly the dupe went limp in her arms, blood streaming down her naked hip and leg. She released the dupe, its limp body sinking to a heap at her feet. Chelsey stood resolute, a bloody kitchen knife clutched in her hand, tears streaming down her cheeks. On the dupe's lower back was a stab wound oozing bright red blood.

"Why'd you do that?" Desna wished Chelsey had allowed the experiment to play out.

Dismal and unresponsive, Chelsey squatted down next to the dupe, tears dripping onto its flesh, then plunged the knife repeatedly into its back until Desna yanked her away, wrenching the knife from her hand. "Jesus, Chelsey!"

Chelsey got up slowly, shuddering as though she were freezing. "I can't deal with this," she said flatly, shuffling back to bed.

Obviously, Chelsey was checking out for the remainder of the evening, leaving her to clean up the mess. She used the ship's comm to find out who was on the bridge.

"Hurd... and Berlin just walked in," Skip said.

"Is she wearing clothes?"

"What? Of course, she is!"

"Okay, put Hurd on." Desna stared down at the dupe lying on the floor. She looked so natural, human, and so dead.

"Yes, Captain?" Hurd said.

"Don't ask questions, just do exactly as I tell you, understand?"

"Yes."

"Do you have the code to get into sick bay?"

"Yes."

"Get a gurney and come to Chelsey's quarters."

Desna waited for Hurd to respond. "Hurd?"

"Yes... leaving now, Captain."

By the time Hurd arrived with the gurney, Chelsey was snoring and snorting, waking herself up and falling back to sleep. Chelsey must have taken a sleeping pill, she figured, the young woman zonking out so quickly.

After they wrestled the dupe onto the gurney, Hurd rolled it into the corridor. Desna made sure Chelsey's door was locked when she closed it.

"Are you coming with me?" Hurd asked.

"Yes."

On the way to sick bay, she explained what had happened, how the dupe had attacked Chelsey, then acted submissive with Desna at first, soon turning aggressive, trying to sexually molest her. She hoped Hurd might have some insights into the dupe's behavior.

"Based on encounters with crew members so far," Hurd started to explain, "I would suggest that these dupes are currently governed by the amygdala, the reptilian brain. It is responsible for survival, hunger and mating."

Desna hadn't considered that these creatures could be driven by the oldest and most primitive part of the brain. She wondered if they were capable of learning, growing intellectually, psychologically, emotionally. Wanting another opinion, she posed her question to Hurd. He pondered it, saying that he wasn't sure.

"The question of nature or nurture has never been adequately answered, making it nearly impossible to gauge," Hurd said. To her, it appeared that he was doing everything in his power to keep his eyes from looking at the dupe, not necessarily due to her nudity, but more likely because she looked exactly like Berlin, and was dead. Maybe he had not yet formed a satisfactory concept around death.

"A century or more ago, there was promising research about the effects of positive and negative experiences on the epigenome, which purportedly could cause humans to exhibit differing behaviors in the way of health, skills and social interaction." Hurd eased the rattling gurney down the hallway. "But for me, I suppose, it still comes down to nature or nurture; ultimately, development was still guided by good or bad circumstances, which can occur in both arenas. So, it's both, I believe, and we can never know which is more influential."

"You're saying they could remain primitive?"

Hurd stopped pushing the gurney, bringing his attention to Desna, his eyes aimed at the center of her face. "Are you trying to determine if these life forms can be exterminated, or need to be trained?"

Hurd's blunt assessment of her inquiry flattened her. She truly wasn't aware of her agenda. Maybe she *was* trying to determine if the dupes could just be eliminated, if they were merely hopeless anomalies that could quickly put a strain on *Gretel's* resources, as well as the crew's sanity, clearly in evidence by Chelsey's behavior.

"I appreciate your struggle..." Hurd started pushing the gurney forward again. "Dr. Karl asked me the same question in regards to Fawn's heart transplant."

"And?"

"No one can answer that responsibly without further clarification. It's a matter of degrees. Here's what I mean. Humans eat cows and chickens and pigs. These are all mammals, the same as humans. But most humans find it repugnant to eat a cat, or a dog —though some cultures do—or a hamster, or especially another human. Yet, given the right circumstances, even civilized humans will eat other humans. Everything in degrees. Believe it or not, it's actually situational. Every life form is rated or judged by humans based upon situational factors and current norms, then placed on a particular rung of the hierarchical ladder that determines the significance of that life form. When factors and norms change, so goes the ladder."

They arrived at sick bay, Desna ready to end this disturbing discussion. He unlocked the entrance, then pushed the cart in. She followed him to the cryovaults where the Wurther dupe was stored.

When they finished, he escorted her to the entrance, and told her he was going to stay and do research. He had some things he wanted to check out. Leaving sick bay, she heard the latch snap shut, the lock engage. The situation on *Gretel* was changing quickly.

CHAPTER TWENTY-EIGHT

OVER THE FOLLOWING TWO WEEKS, CREW MEMBERS SPOTTED more and more dupes, all of them strolling around *Gretel* like naked zombies. Most of them kept to themselves, or remained hidden in the darkest corners of the spacecraft, making it hard to determine their current numbers. The crew was expected to carry D-mobes at all times, and were ordered to use them if accosted by a dupe. For the most part, they just passed in the corridors without incident. Occasionally though, one would accost a crew member and had to be put down. They could no longer store them in cryovaults, and instead, ejected the dead into outer space.

Doc Karl's DNA assessment of the dupes determined that they were 94% similar in DNA to humans, so about the same as dogs. But the dupes had genetic material that was foreign to him, not present in any of his texts. This rendered his proposed heart transplant for Fawn a little suspect. Regardless, he tried to convince Desna it was worth the risk; Fawn would die otherwise. No one as yet had come across a Fawn dupe, which seemed odd, especially since the young girl had been on the past several missions before she took ill, and would have left her DNA in Cargo Hold 4 like the rest of the crew.

Desna passed two dupes on her way to the bridge to speak with Skip—a Doc Karl dupe and another Berlin one. She had never seen herself as a prude, but treated to these daily *buff* sightings of her crew mates was becoming surreal and beyond disturbing.

When she entered the bridge, she asked Skip if he would join her in her day room. He followed her in, then closed the door as she'd requested.

"The gestation period for these dupes is unworkable, Skip." She had seated herself on the edge of her desk. "I know we have the asteroid landing in about nine days—"

Skip interrupted. "More like seventeen. It's traveling faster than the computer originally calculated."

"Great..." She was more exasperated than ever. "I don't think we can wait nineteen days."

Skip raised his eyebrows in place of a shrug.

"Can we at least get them clothes?" Desna said. "What's the status on our uniforms? Do we have enough in storage to accommodate the current dupe population? At least the ones we know of?"

"I'll check when we're done here."

"Okay, so... we have to do something." Desna was thinking about the entity in Cargo Hold 4. If they could just kill it, they could at least halt the production of new dupes. So far, though, the crew hadn't been able to figure out how the dupes were getting from Cargo Hold 4 into the ship. No one had actually witnessed their entry. Wurther and Berlin installed cameras outside the Cargo Hold 4 interior hatch, but had not captured anything yet.

"Does Wurther, with all his military training have any idea how we can kill this entity creating these dupes?" Desna walked around to sit behind her desk.

"Wurther thinks we could create an explosive that might kill it, but..." Here Skip paused. "He isn't sure if it would damage *Gretel...*"

"Set off a bomb in the cargo bay? That seems a bit dicey, doesn't it? How would we even deliver it, with the CPV-drone gone?"

"Through the purge vent. But it's tricky, because the bomb

has to be substantial enough to kill the thing, but still able to fit through the vent. And if it goes off in the vent, well—"

"Don't go down that road." She wanted to bask in the slight surge of hope over Wurther's plan, though she knew she would probably be the one to administer this bomb. Chelsey was still a wreck, Doc Karl battling her depression with light therapy and lithium. She was responding, but not enough to be effective in her duties, shuffling through the ship with a vacant smile. Wurther and Skip were working round the clock on little sleep, Desna not even sure Wurther could be trusted concocting an incendiary device.

"Let's get Wurther going on the explosives," Desna said. "In the meantime, let's figure out these uniforms for the dupes."

"If you want, we can go down to Cargo Hold 20 right now and rummage through the containers. I'm just about finished with my shift anyway."

"Who comes on?"

"Wurther and Berlin, if she shows."

She didn't have the energy to address Berlin's absenteeism, the crazy woman's approach to her duties sketchy at best. She could no longer be counted on. And Doc Karl was so distracted by his volatile relationship with Berlin, and his obsession with Fawn's heart transplant, he might as well have stayed back on Earth. The full responsibilities of the ship had fallen to Hurd, Wurther, Skip and Desna, with Skip and Wurther carrying way too much of the burden.

"Let's go," Desna said, ready to be proactive in any way possible, even if it only meant getting the dupes clothed.

They walked toward Cargo Hold 20, hearing a commotion at the far end of the storage area. From their vantage point, it appeared that Cargo Hold 34 was open, at least the smaller single entrance hatch that was situated at the bottom right side of each large door. That made it easy to access any hold without opening the massive cargo hatches, which were only used when they docked, or moved supplies between cargo areas with fork-lifts. And since it was temperature-controlled—as were all holds with provisions—it was always accessible.

Desna and Skip walked past Cargo Hold 20 to check on 34. The single access door was opened it appeared. Moaning and soughing spilled out from the dark doorway. Skip withdrew his D-mobe, Desna following suit. Skip was the first to enter, touching the light pad at the entrance. The lights shuddered, yet even in the fractured, stuttering darkness, she saw dupes scattering. A few were fornicating, and didn't bother to stop when the lights came up. Food rations, containers and opened provisions were scattered across the floor, the smell of defecation and urine filling the air.

"Oh my God!" Desna cried "This can't be happening!"

Skip was pale, his eyes big as planets, obviously dumb-founded by the carnality. Desna shouted at them to clean up the mess, as if they were badly behaved children, quickly realizing the futility of her command. About then, the Doc Karl dupe finished humping a female that looked a lot like Desna, and was instantly displaced by a Skip dupe who cared not the least about her and Skip's presence. Another Doc Karl dupe approached Desna with an erection, while munching a mouthful of raw oats, offering her some from his cruddy palm, then moved closer apparently to have sex with her.

Without hesitation, Desna discharged her D-mobe, sending the dupe stumbling backward, eventually falling to the floor. The dead dupe's sudden demise however didn't distract the copu-lating ones, or dampen their enthusiasm in any way, the Desna dupe down on all fours writhing and moaning under the humping Skip dupe. Another one in the back corner was defecating.

"I can't take anymore..." Desna backed from the hold, grab-bing Skip by the sleeve and pulling him along with her, both of them honing their attention on the peripheral dupes milling about. Skip shut the door to the hatch.

"Bolt it," she said.

"But... they'll be trapped in—"

"Bolt that fucking door, Skip!"

Skip latched it and turned to Desna with a peculiar light shifting across his eyes. She moved past him and punched in the code to open the exterior hatch. Yellow and red warning lights flashed, the alarm blaring. *Womp! Womp! Womp! "Warning! Exterior*

Hatch 34 is opening! Warning! Exterior Hatch 34 is opening! Warning! Exterior Hatch..."

"What are you doing!" Skip shouted.

"Making the tough calls." Without further regard for the situation, she walked back toward the stairwell.

"How about the uniforms?" Skip tried to catch up to her.

"That ship has sailed, so to speak." She continued walking, taking the stairs two at a time and was practically breathless when she reached the bridge. She went directly to Wurther's station and tapped him on the shoulder. "In my day room." She turned away, striding toward her private office. "We're gonna talk explosives."

CHAPTER TWENTY-NINE

DESNA WAS READY TO MOVE ON THE PLAN. WHAT WURTHER had laid out sounded much more effective than trying to land *Gretel* on a goddamn asteroid. Plus, there were no guarantees the damn thing would leave even if they were successful with the risky move. And if they weren't, they were all going to die anyway. Desna was relieved to have witnessed what she had in Cargo Hold 34; it made this decision so much easier.

Skip had joined the meeting with her and Wurther, but left after a heated exchange. Skip mentioned what she'd done at Cargo Hold 34, seemingly trying to spark some negative reaction from Wurther, but Wurther sat stone-faced, unmoved one way or the other, which infuriated Skip. But when she announced her plan to issue a "destroy on sight" order to the crew if they found a dupe, Skip came out of his seat.

"That's unconscionable!" he screamed. "You can't just kill them like they're mosquitoes! I won't do it!"

"You don't get it, Skip! If we don't end this now, in a few months all those females are gonna be strolling around *Gretel* pregnant. Followed by another wave the next month, then the next. All the while this damn monster in Cargo Hold 4 keeps cranking out more dupes. The provisions will disappear so quickly none of us will survive to see all these lovely babies crying and shitting themselves. And the fucking adults are so demented, they're probably incapable of taking care of their own offspring." Desna paused to catch her breath. "Then what, Skip! Is that when we march them into a cargo hold, lock the fucking door, and open the outer hatch? If you don't have the stomach for it now, you certainly won't when all those chubby little babies are crawling around crying for food!"

CHAPTER THIRTY

SKIP HAD CHECKED OUT. HE PERFORMED HIS DUTIES AS always, then left the bridge without a word and sequestered himself away in his quarters between his other assignments. The majority of *Gretel's* upkeep and care fell to Wurther, Hurd and Desna, with Wurther busy most of the day building the explosive device. Doc Karl and Hurd both agreed to follow her "destroy on sight" order, realizing that while it wasn't a perfect solution, the alternative was suicide for everyone aboard. Berlin embraced the D.O.S. order with a fervor Desna hadn't expected, taking it to the extreme of actually hunting dupes when she wasn't on duty. Doc Karl, hopelessly in love and searching for a Fawn dupe, went with her on her wild safaris, "bagging" two or three dupes some nights. Doc finally found his Fawn dupe. They managed to capture her after a lengthy chase through *Gretel's* labyrinthian interior.

Desna hadn't bothered to check on the Fawn dupe prisoner Doc was keeping restrained in sick bay, too focused on ships' maintenance, and helping Wurther with the bomb. Doc intimated that within a week or two he'd be able to perform the transplant, with Berlin—when she wasn't hunting dupes—training assiduously to function as his nurse. Hurd would be assisting as well, informing Desna that there was at least a seventy-percent chance of success for the child's heart transplant.

As much as she would have liked to have been more interested, her focus was on the dupes. Over the past week alone, she had come across numerous ones coupling; men with women, men with men, women with women. Once she'd witnessed some kind of deranged orgy combining sex and savagery, fucking and beating one another to death, then copulating with the fresh corpses. In that instance, they scattered as soon as she started zapping them with her D-mobe, except for a few who attacked her, them ending up dead as well.

She, with the help of Wurther, Hurd and Berlin, hauled the corpses to Cargo Hold 34, where they would *purge* them once a day.

Desna could hardly wait; detonation time only forty-eight hours away. Wurther was confident the explosion would be contained within Cargo Hold 4.

"I studied the tensile and yield strength tables on the titanium used for *Gretel.*" Wurther said. "We may get a bit of flex, but no structural damage to the hull or danger to the crew."

This was great news, and she had no choice but to trust Wurther on this; it seemed he'd done his due diligence. Nevertheless, it still made her nervous, setting off a bomb on *Gretel,* though nothing close to the foreboding she felt over the sudden proliferation of dupes.

When she entered the bridge, she went directly to her day room to study the information Doc Karl had given her on the dupe's DNA. Doc was obsessed with performing Fawn's transplant, but the fact the DNA was not an exact match set off alarms for her. What bothered her even more was his blindness to that fact. Understandably, matching DNA was not a factor for a heart transplant. How could it be? It would be a virtual impossibility to find a donor except in the rare case where a twin died and donated her heart to her identical. It wasn't that the DNA didn't match that bothered her, but the fact that the dupe DNA contained material unknown to humans. That was too risky, to her mind, to conduct such an experiment without further study.

Doc Karl would never get away with this on Earth, and she felt the need to step in, place a hold on the transplant until he could provide proof that the unknown DNA material was not an issue.

Hurd knocked on the jamb, sticking his head in, then asked if she had a minute.

"I could use a break." She eased back in her chair. "What's up?"

He entered carrying a book, then came around the desk to her computer terminal. "May I?"

"Here, sit." She started to move out of his way.

"No, I'm fine. Please, stay where you are." Hurd set the book down so he could type on her keyboard. "I've been going over the footage from the camera Berlin and Wurther installed by Cargo Hold 4. See these dark frames..." The video showed long interludes of black video, then abruptly displayed the Cargo Hold 4 door.

"This video goes on like this for hours," Hurd said. "We concluded that the black frames were due to a camera glitch, but they bothered me. So, I did an experiment."

Hurd brought up another video and touched play. Extended sections of the footage were completely blown out, pure white, lacking any detail. "Just a moment. We're coming to it."

She watched, the bright white screen causing her to squint. A few seconds later the screen changed to mostly dark imagery with intensely-saturated, coloration. "It's very grainy because I had to greatly over-expose this."

As she studied the footage, she could just make out the hatch to Cargo Hold 4. She waited, trying to understand what she was supposed to be seeing. "I'm not sure what—" she started to say when Hurd interrupted her.

"Here! Here it is! Watch!"

She focused on the screen, something happening in front of the door it seemed, but it was so degraded it was impossible to tell what it was.

"I took that section of video and enhanced it. Watch." Hurd brought up the next video.

She watched some kind of strange aberration happening to

the main hatch, followed by what seemed to be a body falling onto the cargo area floor. The body eventually got up and walked away and the video ended. "What was that?" Desna was confused by what she'd just witnessed.

"I believe that is how the dupes are getting aboard *Gretel*, Captain."

"Help me out. What was I seeing?"

Hurd rewound the video to the point where the aberration appeared. He pointed at the curious shape in front of the main hatch. "I believe this is the entity, Captain. It is able to penetrate the metal hatch, then..."

He advanced the video to the body falling to the floor. "It delivers the dupe into *Gretel*, then retracts itself back into Cargo Hold 4."

Her head was spinning. "I'm very confused right now, Hurd. Walk me through this. If this entity is capable of just passing through the titanium hatch, why hasn't it entered *Gretel* itself?"

"I pondered that same question for days. That's why I didn't come to you sooner... I believe the creature cannot survive in an oxygenated environment. And because that concept is so contrary to our own belief system, we never even considered it."

She was both shocked and relieved. Several nights she'd fallen asleep wondering if she'd wake one morning to find the entity had taken over the entire ship. One night she even dreamed a scenario similar to that fear, waking up in a cold sweat. "That's brilliant work, Hurd. It really is."

He lingered, then: "There's more, Captain..."

She regarded the curious man with trepidation, hoping this second shoe would still be positive news.

"I wondered about the black sections on the footage. Each time it goes black, a dupe is delivered into *Gretel*..."

"But, wait, Hurd. That's not possible... I mean..."

"Yes, I know. I suffered the same consternation; how could the creature even know if the cargo area was dark, and why would that matter anyway. Then I remembered switching on the lights in Cargo Hold 4 and the thing going crazy. Which led us to the understanding that the organism didn't like light."

"Yes, right, but—"

Hurd cut her off. "The organism can only deliver the dupes in darkness, and must do it quickly, and probably with much discomfort to itself by exposing a part of itself to air. If that's the case, it must control the lights in the storage vault temporarily."

"How can it possibly do that?"

"Electromagnetic pulse. Or at least something like it. That's what we experienced when the CPV-drone tried to enter Cargo Hold 4. The entity blasted it with an electromagnetic pulse. That's how it damaged the interior hatch as well."

"Wow, Hurd, you've been busy. This is amazing—"

"I think we should postpone the detonation..."

"Why! Wurther assured me that—"

"Yes, Mr. Wurther's work on that is comprehensive and sound, but it doesn't alleviate the danger of such a strategy."

Hurd expounded on his theory that the creature could not survive in a light-filled, oxygenated environment for very long. That hypothesis had made sense to him since they most likely, though inadvertently, had brought the creature aboard *Gretel* from their exploration on the sunless side of planet J-78, which was also without a breathable atmosphere. The creature was probably in some spore state when they were collecting samples, and grew inside *Gretel,* maybe due its exposure to the crew's DNA. Regardless, Hurd felt they could use this to their advantage.

"Flood Cargo Hold 4 with oxygen and light?" Desna said.

"Well, if Cargo Hold 4 still had the exterior hatch, then yes, filling it with oxygen would be possible, but not with the hatch gone. By using light, we could disrupt the entity in Cargo Hold 4, but without any way to contain it, as was the case during the second merger with BC-1, the creature will just leave the hatch."

"How did you reach that conclusion, that the creature would leave the hatch?" Desna felt Hurd was making an uncharacteristic leap.

"I think that's where the gel came from that you found on *Gretel's* outer hull. And I think that's what Berlin saw on the video. What looked like a reflective aberration along the top surface of *Gretel's* hull was actually a last glimpse of the entity escaping detection from you and Chelsey during your spacewalk.

Once you and Chelsey came back aboard *Gretel,* the entity returned to Cargo Hold 4. It didn't matter the outer hatch was gone."

Desna was elated and anxious at the same time. "Mind if I get another take on this?" She pressed the comm button. Hurd nodded, agreeing heartily.

CHAPTER THIRTY-ONE

THE RAMIFICATIONS OF WHAT HURD HAD JUST SHARED WAS sucking up every bit of bandwidth in her brain. She was wrestling with all this new information when Wurther knocked on the doorjamb.

"You wanted me?"

"Come in, Wurther. Have a seat. I want you to hear what Hurd has come up with."

Hurd explained everything to Wurther, Desna gaining a greater understanding of his suppositions upon hearing them a second time.

"Great work, Hurd!" Wurther said. "If you're right, this will be simple."

"That's why I wanted you to sit in," Desna said. "We're still working out the—"

"I already have it!" Wurther said. "We roll *Gretel!*"

Desna looked over at Hurd, wondering if he'd made better sense of Wurther's statement than she had. If Hurd's drawn features were any indication, he was as confused as she was.

"Look," Wurther began. "We need the blob to leave Cargo Hold 4 and move to another cargo hold, one with the outer hatch in place so we can swamp it with oxygen. This thing doesn't like light, so we roll *Gretel* upside down, exposing Cargo Hold 4 to sunlight, and the blob is gonna scramble to get back to the dark side. So, if we happen to leave one of the cargo holds open on the dark side of *Gretel*, it'll go right in. We shut the hatch and flood it with O_2. No more blob!"

"How does that sound, Hurd?" she asked.

"Like a much safer plan than detonating a bomb!"

"When do we go?" Wurther said.

"I'm a little vague on this 'rolling' move?" She wasn't sure how that might work. "Is that something *Gretel's* capable of? I don't recall that from my training."

"Absolutely," Wurther said. "I don't know if I could do it, but Skip certainly can."

Hurd added: "*Gretel* is equipped with aileron thrusters. They could certainly be employed for this very purpose."

Now all they had to do was get Skip onboard with the plan, she thought, even though the man kept to himself like a hermit, barely talking to anyone these days.

"Can you speak to Skip, Wurther?" she said.

He dropped his eyes, gently shaking his head. "We don't even talk when we're working a shift together..."

She swiveled toward Hurd, unsure why Skip had become so irascible. She knew it had to do with her stance on the dupes. Until then, though, he'd always been one of her most stalwart supporters on the mission.

"I will speak to him," Hurd said. He seemed a bit cagey, as if he knew something about Skip he didn't want to share, or felt he couldn't. That bothered her, but she didn't want to make heavy weather of it; functioning as ship's spiritual liaison and therapist, he was bound by some tenets of confidentiality.

Wurther asked to be dismissed, saying he would check Cargo Hold 3 to make sure it was empty and ready to go. Though still distracted by Hurd's thesis, Cargo Hold 3 seemed to be the best option, she thought, since it was on the port side directly opposite Cargo Hold 4; the most direct route for the entity to escape to.

As Hurd was about to leave, she asked him to please speak to Skip when he had a moment, so they could implement the plan as soon as possible. Wary of Hurd from the onset of the mission, she hadn't valued his importance. Being a hybridized human, he was certainly not completely human anymore, having been retrofitted with countless enhancements after a terrible accident on one of the numerous ship-building stations orbiting Mars. But neither was he an android. Even so, that gray area had always left her with a small pocket of discomfort, especially given the issues with artificial intelligence seven decades earlier. Nevertheless, she'd been assured by mission creators that while Hurd was not a product of AI, he was highly intelligent and trustworthy. She was beginning to appreciate him more and more, feeling a bristle of shame over her small-mindedness.

"Oh, Hurd! Here, you forgot your book." She jumped up from her desk, extending it toward him. Though the extra weight was a concern, mission planners insisted on *Gretel* having an adequate library of real books, noting that the crew may long for the touch of organic materials, and wish to read and relax with a sensate object on their long journey.

Hurd walked back to her and took it, thanking her, then was about to leave again but stopped, facing her but saying nothing.

"Something else?" she asked.

Hurd nodded, looking down at the book in his hands. "This is very hard for me to tell you. The conundrum has kept me up many nights."

Desna closed the door so they wouldn't be disturbed. Hurd opened the book to a spread he had marked. He showed her a close-up photo in the book. She was struck by how closely it resembled the entity captured on the CPV-drone footage before the vessel was destroyed. She read the caption beneath the photo.

"Frog eggs?" She was somewhat baffled by the resemblance to the entity in Cargo Hold 4, at least what they could make out on the drone video, though she was fairly certain Hurd was not suggesting it was related to this tellurian amphibian.

"The photo depicts the vitelline membrane and the adhesive jelly the female frog coats her spawn with," he stated flatly. "Inside each egg, the tadpole is visible."

She saw exactly what he was referring to, with no idea why he was showing her this. Hurd went back to her desk, bringing up another video. "I performed the weekly hull integrity check yesterday and saw this."

The video was from hull cameras located along the length of *Gretel*. This particular footage was from the camera nearest Cargo Hold 4. It showed a large jelly-like structure—which closely resembled the frog eggs photo—protruding from the hold. Obviously, the protrusion was the entity.

"What's it doing?" she asked.

"Expanding. I believe if we don't do something soon, it will spread outside the hull, clinging to *Gretel,* until it completely encompasses her."

"I'm glad you showed me this, but we have a plan, now. We're moving forward as soon as you speak to Skip."

Hurd darkened, seemingly in a battle with himself. "That is part of the problem. Skip may refuse to help..."

She was powerless if any member of the team refused to follow her orders. The size of the crew was barely adequate as it was, to perform mission duties, especially with Fawn incapacitated. It wasn't as though Desna could threaten to restrict someone to their quarters; there was no way to enforce the order. People aboard *Gretel* knew they depended upon one another for survival, and shared a common affinity for exploration and adventure; that was the glue that held things together. Until the dupes. That's when morale and solidarity took a serious hit, causing everyone to reevaluate their objectives, or just throw them out altogether and stop caring about anything.

"Do you know what's going on with Skip, Mr. Hurd?" She hadn't meant to sound stern, but it came out that way.

For several seconds, he hung his head like an insubordinate schoolboy reporting to the headmaster. "He's involved in... an experiment." Hurd fidgeted, unable to meet her eyes. "One I have sworn not to divulge."

CHAPTER THIRTY-TWO

DESNA POUNDED ON SKIP'S DOOR, HER D-MOBE DANGLING from her waist. Hurd stood nearby, feeling sheepish. He had asked if he could be excused from facing Skip, but Captain Desna wouldn't hear of it, ordering him to accompany her to Skip's quarters. And to have his D-mobe set to medium.

Hurd felt ashamed over not honoring his promise to Skip, who had entrusted him with his secret mission. Part of Hurd's duties were to provide crew members console, a safe haven for personal problems. Who would trust him now?

Desna pounded Skip's door again. "Open up, Skip! Captain Desna."

The hatch opened slowly, the door sliding to the side; Skip filled the opening. "What?" Skip tried to block the captain's sightline into his quarters.

That's when Skip's eyes hardened on Hurd. He felt some component inside slipping, coming loose, as if his system was in jeopardy of complete failure.

Desna pushed the door open, shoving past Skip's huge frame, Hurd reluctantly following the captain in. On a chair in Skip's living quarters was a naked dupe—a Desna dupe—appearing to be reading a book. Skip said nothing as she narrowed her eyes on her dupe double, then glowered over at him.

She scoffed, shaking her head. "What is this, Skip!"

At first, he appeared embarrassed, beginning to crumble. A split second later, he bounced back, his face suddenly fixed and resolute.

"I am teaching them how to read and write. Unlike you, who thinks they're savages, I believe they can thrive intellectually if given the chance..."

"Really!" Desna said, walking over to the dupe. She jerked the book from the dupe's hands and turned it right side up before handing it back. The dupe smiled at her, then at Skip, who reached in his pocket and handed her some kind of treat. The dupe hungrily took it and shoved it into her mouth.

"Oh my God!" Desna exclaimed. "You've got to be kidding, Skip! Pets with benefits! Really! This is sick."

"Look, I don't care what you think, Desna, but they just need attention!"

"Oh, I'll bet she gets plenty of attention! You're twisted, Skip!"

Hurd shook his head, preparing himself for Captain Desna's reaction upon seeing the second dupe coming from Skip's galley. When Desna spotted the Fawn dupe, her eyes grew wide as alien moons. Hurd was trembling all over.

"What the hell! Another one! A Fawn dupe!" There was no mistaking the disgust on the captain's face. "You are one sick, sick fuck, Skip! How did you ever pass the psyche eval!"

The Fawn dupe, naked as the Desna dupe, carried over a cup of hot tea to Skip, then kissed him briefly on the lips. Skip flushed with embarrassment; his gaze downcast. The Fawn dupe took a seat across from the Desna dupe and started painting her toenails.

"Well, I can't wait to meet these two beauties..." Desna walked over to the Desna dupe, extending her hand. "I'm Desna, what's your name?"

The Desna dupe leaned forward and kissed the captain's knuckles, then, with the forefinger on her right hand, poked herself in the chest repeatedly, saying, "Me, Desna! Me, Desna! Me, Desna!"

"Oh, what a lovely name," the captain said to her, the

sarcasm so thick Hurd blenched. She shifted her attention to the Fawn dupe painting her nails, then extended her hand.

"And you must be Fawn," Captain Desna said. Though the captain was smiling, her eyes were like bullets. The Fawn dupe kissed her fingers, then proudly stated her name. "Me, Chelsey! Chelsey!"

Captain Desna shook her head, looking to Hurd as if she were about to explode. Never had Hurd seen her so angry. She glowered at Skip. "I am absolutely speechless, you perverted pig!"

Captain Desna stood in the center of Skip's quarters, shifting her gaze between him and the two dupes, her features glossy. The silence grew heavier by the second, as if at any moment it could crush them all. Hurd was about to say something, then thought better of it, quietly bolstering himself against the toxic hush. After a short while, the dupes continued with their activities, the Fawn dupe painting her toenails, the Desna one pretending to read.

"No matter what you think of me," Skip said, shattering the silence. "These dupes are making progress. You were wrong about them!"

"Oh, yeah," Desna said. "I can see they're ready to start splitting atoms with Dr. Hurd here."

Hurd wanted to remain invisible, orbiting far from the center of this skirmish. But the captain's reference to him, regardless of how silly and inconsequential, managed to draw Skip's ire. He had no capacity for this kind of confrontation, shifting his attention toward the floor.

"You didn't have to kill them!" Skip added.

Captain Desna nodded, her eyes still shifting between the three, her mind hatching some kind of plan. Hurd knew it would be harder to eradicate these dupes now, as Skip had managed to make them appear somewhat domesticated. Regardless, no matter how tame the dupes appeared, or how much he argued they could be habituated to human normal interaction, Hurd held a much darker suspicion about these replicated organisms, one he had not yet been able to share with Captain Desna.

"Seems you've made it more difficult to destroy your little

playmates here," the captain said, her natural color and mien returning. She stepped over to Skip's comm system and pressed the ship announcement button.

"Mr. Wurther. Come to Skip's quarters, stat!"

The dupes seemed inoculated from the charged events transpiring in Skip's living quarters, happily going about their activities. Hurd tried to remain still, not wanting any undue attention from either the captain or Skip. When Skip left the room, Hurd had no idea where he'd gone.

The captain, waiting for Mr. Wurther, turned to Hurd. "How long's this little love-fest been going on?"

He shook his head, as if he weren't really clear on that point, knowing it started within days of the captain issuing her "destroy on sight" directive. The two dupes had visited Skip one night, and he'd allowed them to stay at first primarily to keep them from being killed. But after a few days, he'd confided in Hurd that they had become wonderful companions, and he planned to start working with them, teaching them how to read and write... and talk. Hurd had thought it a terrible idea, but never spoke his mind, suspecting the dupes were not currently who they would soon become.

Mr. Wurther entered Skip's quarters, spotting the naked dupes first, then Captain Desna, shock rippling across his face. Skip returned with some kind of snack chips, handing each of the dupes a handful. They greedily munched them, crumbs falling from their over-packed mouths. Evidently Skip's *Eliza Doolittle* experiment left a lot to be desired.

Captain Desna spun around to face her Quartermaster. "Mr. Wurther, escort these women to Fawn's quarters and make sure they have everything they need, including some damn clothes. Mr. Hurd, accompany them and help get them set up."

"But, Captain—" Hurd started to protest mildly, but was quickly cut off with a wave of her hand.

"Just go, Hurd. And report to my day room once you've changed the code on Fawn's room and locked the dupes into their new quarters."

Skip threw his chips across the room. "You can't do that! Who the fuck do you think you are?"

The two dupe women scrambled along the floor grabbing up the chips and shoving them in their mouths, fighting over the last scraps. "Jesus, Mary and Joseph!" Desna shouted, wrenching them apart. Wurther grabbed one, raising her to her feet.

"For fuck's sake! Get 'em out of here, Wurther! Let's go, Mr. Hurd. Grab one!"

He reluctantly took the hand of the Fawn dupe, the way Wurther had done with the Desna one. Hurd's dupe immediately cuddled up to him, her hand going to his crotch. He pushed it away, following Wurther out.

"Fucking, Judas..." Skip mumbled to him as he walked past.

CHAPTER THIRTY-THREE

WITH SKIP CONFINED TO HIS QUARTERS, THE CREW WAS shrinking. Desna was feeling it, having to take on more responsibilities, barely able to sleep more than a few hours at a time, even with meds. Wurther practiced exhaustively on the *Gretel* simulator, trying to master the aileron thrusters, perform the perfect roll. He told her he was getting closer. "One more day. Maybe two." It had been more than a week since the incident with Skip, and she was becoming anxious.

Berlin dropped by to see how she was doing. When Desna told her what had happened with Skip, Berlin was aghast at what he'd done, and wanted to personally go to his quarters and *deal* with him.

"No one is castrating anyone on *Gretel*," Desna said. "What's going on with the heart transplant?"

"Karl's doing more research but doesn't believe the weird genetic material's gonna be a problem."

"Did he call it *weird?*" She was more than a little worried if that was the word he'd used.

"*Anomalous,* I think was what he said. What does it matter?"

There seemed little point in explaining it to her so she let it drop. Berlin went on to explain about the Fawn dupe they'd captured for the transplant, that Doc Karl no longer had her restrained, but kept her locked in sick bay during the night. "He spends a lot of time down there after I go to bed," Berlin said, showing a bit of anger, scoffing. "He says he's *evaluating* the dupe for the transplant, but I think he's banging her, and has convinced himself it's necessary for scientific reasons..."

"He said that?" Desna worried Doc Karl might be going 'round the bend.

"That he's banging that alien slut for scientific reasons?" Berlin said, picking something from her teeth. "No, he just does stupid shit, then blames it on science, and his 'rigorous study ethic.'" Berlin wore disgust like a familiar emotion, then: "I hope his pecker falls off after *probing* that little space skank!"

Desna wondered if Berlin was still shacked up with Doc.

"I caught him squeezing the dupe's tits the other day." Berlin chuckled, smirking. "Red-faced, that asshole had the gall to tell me he was checking for lumps. The only lump was in his pants!"

Desna laughed quietly, though distressed that the moral fabric on *Gretel* was being stretched to the ripping point. If she lost Doc, after losing Skip, she'd have only two men she could depend upon; Wurther and Hurd. Which was okay, she figured; Wurther had proven to be a rock through all of it. And Hurd, he was loyal, dependable, and by the book—which was crucially important now—plus wickedly smart.

They talked about Chelsey, Desna telling Berlin the ship could really use her back on the crew. Berlin told her Chelsey had been working closely with Doc Karl and was improving, not needing the sleep meds anymore. According to Berlin, Chelsey knew some of the problems on *Gretel,* and was working hard to resume her duties.

"Karl told her the best thing for her was to get some routine back in her life."

Desna asked her if she thought more dupes were aboard *Gretel.* Berlin responded first by saying, "You mean, besides Skip's two sex slaves in Fawn's room?" She told Desna she figured there were, but hadn't seen any in several days. "They're becoming scarcer... or just getting better at hiding...!"

She couldn't share Berlin's lighthearted take on their dupe problem, certain the entity was down in the dark hold churning out more. She could hardly bear to think about it. Berlin excused herself from the bridge, telling Desna she had some work to do in hydroponics.

After a few hours, Desna felt she should check on Doc Karl and the transplant. She'd never been able to quite shake the conversation with Berlin. It was disturbing at best, and downright troublesome if Doc had misplaced his ethical compass.

She was shutting down her computer when Hurd walked in.

"Is it important?" She felt an urgency to get to sick bay.

"It is," Hurd said, his expression pulled with concern. "Skip has fled his quarters. He must have tried his D-mobe first to disrupt the electronics, as the lock was burned black. When that didn't work, he used the emergency fire axe in his room and hacked the lock off his door."

She sat back down, her own inner fabric strained. "I'm not going to waste resources looking for him... I don't have them. Damn! This is so fucked up!" She looked up at Hurd. "Is that it?"

"I'm afraid not..."

She motioned for him to have a seat.

He sat and stared at her, then: "He broke into Fawn's quarters and freed the two dupes..."

"He's lost his mind!" She tried to resign herself to the impossible circumstances. It was like some madness had taken over everyone on board, including herself. As a scientist interested in exploring the universe for unknown life forms, she couldn't believe she'd been so eager to destroy the dupes. And now she and Wurther were plotting to eliminate maybe the most consequential life form they might ever come across on their journey; the entity in Cargo Hold 4. It was miraculous, and at the same time, a mortal threat to the crew's survival. There was no thin line to walk, just horrible decisions to be made, and time wasn't going to wait for her to sort out her feelings.

"Thanks for bringing this to my attention." She expected him to stand and leave. But he didn't, his gaze steady, tangled in hers. "There's more?"

He nodded. "The problem we face, I fear, is far greater than we imagined." He reminded her of the frog egg image from the book, so she'd have a reference point for the speculation he was about to share.

"I remember," she assured him, losing patience and wishing he'd get to the punchline.

"As you recall, the tadpoles in the picture were clearly visible in their tertiary egg membrane." He paused, waiting for her to concur. She nodded her agreement, feeling this conversation growing more tedious by the second.

"Those tadpoles were in the larvae state," he went on to explain, as if a meticulous description were necessary to her understanding of his hypothesis. "In fact, even after they penetrate the vitelline membrane, they remain in their larvae state, swimming about with their large heads and tails..."

"Yes, I understand that life cycle!" Her frustration was beginning to grow fangs.

"I know the dupes appear to us as physically mature adults. However, I suggest that they may actually be in a larvae state... and like the tadpole, might change in unimaginable ways during their later stages of development."

She hadn't considered that the dupes could metamorphose physically. She wasn't even sure they could transform mentally, considering their childish, repugnant behavior, no matter what bullshit Skip had fed himself.

"Are you suggesting they could turn into something else?"

"The frog bears little resemblance to the tadpole," Hurd stated. "I believe it's a possibility we must gravely consider. There is no hint in the tadpole's unthreatening simple structure that even remotely suggests the profoundly effective predator it will become as a frog."

Desna felt a new urgency, a high-amperage current shooting up her spine, down into her legs, as if they couldn't waste another second. Against a formidable foe—which it sounded like Hurd was suggesting—the crew had little chance for success, their weapon stock sorely lacking and inadequate.

"What do you suggest?" She tried to remain calm, her heart flailing and sparking like a severed high-tension wire.

"I think destroying the entity in Cargo Hold 4 is key; cut off the source. Then we must hunt out any remaining dupes and destroy them... and..."

"What?"

"We can't allow Dr. Karl to perform the heart transplant surgery... I know Fawn will not survive without it, but it is too risky, having dupe DNA implanted in her body. We just don't know what could happen..."

She agreed. "Have you mentioned this to Doc?"

Hurd nodded sadly. "He is blinded by his ego's desire to perform this procedure. Not so much for Fawn's sake, but his own craving. He believes now, after countless hours of study, that he is capable of performing the transplant surgery. And he most likely is, though I'm not sure he even considers Fawn's health, or the Fawn dupe, anymore. He is possessed by a gnawing desire to succeed, no matter the threat or cost... at least that's what I've observed."

Desna knew what she had to do. "See if Wurther needs any help with the simulations. We need to get this done pronto..."

Once Hurd left, she contacted Berlin and Chelsey on the ship comm, telling them to report immediately to her day room.

CHAPTER THIRTY-FOUR

CHELSEY CARRIED THE NEW SURVEILLANCE CAMERAS TO CARGO Holds 1, 3 and 5, while Berlin wrestled the huge multi-task ladder from the utility closet in the hold area. Desna had explained in detail the plan to rid *Gretel* of the entity in Cargo Hold 4, and Chelsey was so glad she felt strong enough to pitch in. The plan sounded a little wild to her ears, but she knew Wurther, Hurd and the captain could pull it off if anyone could. The news about Skip was disturbing, though; she'd always liked him and couldn't believe he'd be capable of co-opting two female dupes as roommates.

Berlin hit the button to open the massive interior hatch, revealing supplies inside the hold. Desna had instructed them to remove any provisions they might find. All three holds needed to be empty, so if the entity decided to go into a neighboring hold, it wouldn't be able to, as they would open 1 and 5 as soon as the thing was securely captured in hold 3.

"How can it get into the neighboring holds," Chelsey had asked, a bit confused how it could travel through the titanium dividers. When Desna explained what Hurd had discovered about the life form, Chelsey felt a bristle of renewed fear. This wasn't an organism like anything she'd ever heard of, and quietly questioned the potential success of the plan. Desna assured them both that it would work, that they needed the cameras installed in those three holds so they could monitor the creature's movements.

They loaded the provisions onto skids that Berlin then moved by forklift to an empty hold on the starboard side. They strapped everything down to keep things from being destroyed by the roll. Once they had it emptied, they installed the camera. Chelsey was amazed by Berlin's electrical skills; the energetic young woman knew exactly what buses to tap into, which wires to connect, where *Gretel's* main camera fiberlaz-cable was located, extending it into each hold, feeding it though a small diameter conduit seemingly made for housing wires, though it didn't currently hold any.

"I can't believe the ship's architects didn't think to have cameras installed in each hold when they built this thing..." Berlin said, standing on the top platform of the multi-task ladder, over five meters above the floor, her fingers nimbly locating, separating, then connecting wires, a wire connector nut held between her teeth, a wire-stripper in her left.

Chelsey was about to hand Berlin the voltage tester when she heard something out in the main cargo area.

"What's wrong?" Berlin looked down at Chelsey from her perch atop the ladder.

"Did you hear that?" Chelsey listened more closely to see if she could hear it again. Nothing came.

"What'd it sound like?" Berlin reached down to Chelsey who was bringing the voltage tester up the ladder to her.

"Like someone moaning," Chelsey said, clinging to the ladder, halfway up, slowly making her way back down.

"Not the moaning again. I'll be glad when this shit is over with!"

A moment later they heard a torturous scream; someone in hellish pain.

"Holy shit!" Berlin scrambled down the ladder. Chelsey rushed toward the hold entrance to see what all the commotion was about. Berlin joined her, both of them alert, listening. About then a strange noise flooded the cargo area, a loud chittering that echoed off the steel cargo hold hatches. It stopped, then started again, reminding Chelsey of a recording she'd heard in school of Australian Behemoth Cicadas, an invasive predatory species not native to that continent. Another scream cut the silence, then moaning. It sounded like a man in agony some distance off. The two women regarded each other.

"Should we check?" Chelsey said, frightened, not really wanting to explore the cries.

"Let's finish these last two cameras and get back to the bridge," Berlin said, her expression stern. "The quicker we get this entity off *Gretel,* the quicker we get back to normal."

Chelsey agreed with finishing the cameras and getting back to the bridge, but was fairly certain *normal* would never be an option again.

Berlin shoved the tools she needed into the pockets of her work belt, while Chelsey stood guard at the hold entrance with her D-mobe. Occasionally she glanced into the hold, Berlin high up the ladder in the metal rafters, her hands busy stripping and connecting wires, dropping cutoffs and debris to the floor. The cargo area was quiet, no screams or moaning, just the normal low groan and periodic sputter of *Gretel's* internal systems keeping them hurtling through space.

When Berlin finished the camera in Cargo Hold 3, Chelsey helped her move the ladder and tools to the last hold. While Berlin climbed the ladder, Chelsey took her station at the entrance to Cargo Hold 5. Berlin started whistling some tune while she worked, seemingly oblivious to the screams they'd heard earlier, while Chelsey couldn't erase them from her mind, a chilling fear sitting at her core.

"Almost done!" Berlin shouted from the top of the ladder, then resumed whistling her bouncy tune. Chelsey felt a second's relief until she took her eyes down the length of the storage area. Roughly ninety meters away, a figure crawled forward, moving painfully slow through the shadow areas on the floor between ceiling lights. From that distance, it was impossible for Chelsey to see who, or what, it was.

"How long?" Chelsey called to Berlin, anxious to leave.

"Just a few minutes."

She wanted to tell her to hurry, when something darted into

view, grabbed the figure on the floor, effortlessly dragging it back into the shadows at the farthest end. Several cries escaped the darkness of the storage vault.

"What'd you say, Chelsey?"

"I didn't say anything. Just finish up, okay!"

CHAPTER THIRTY-FIVE

THE NEXT AFTERNOON, AFTER BERLIN LEFT THE DAY ROOM, Desna listened to Chelsey's story about what she'd seen when Berlin was finishing up with the last camera. It was obvious Chelsey was terrified recounting the crawling figure on the floor, but even more so by the thing that had dragged it away. Chelsey said she hadn't mentioned to Berlin what she'd seen. "I just wanted to get out of there!" Fat tears formed along the bottom ridges of Chelsey's eyes.

"What do you think it was?" Desna was impatient to get the ship's rolling maneuver underway. Wurther promised he'd be ready to go later that day.

"I don't know. I just want to be off this damn ship!"

Desna realized Chelsey hadn't fully recovered from her previous breakdown, and probably had returned to duty too soon.

"Wurther assures me we'll be ready to perform our ship roll soon." Desna spoke in a firm but calm voice. "I need you to go to the hydroponics lab and research center and help Berlin ensure everything's ship shape and secure before we do this. You might want to check your private quarters as well..."

"I thought AGS protected against any orientation issues on *Gretel?*" Chelsey acted as if confused by Desna's request.

"Yes, for the most part, but, you know, there are always loose ends, stuff that can get tossed about." Desna knew that wasn't true, hoping to keep Chelsey's mind busy with mundane concerns. The orientation on *Gretel* was controlled by the anti-matter gravitational system, which ensured that the crew would always feel perfectly normal and upright, even if the ship was inverted, which in and of itself was a relative concept in space. Due to the AGS, the floor would always feel like the source of gravity, no matter where anyone was on the ship, or the ship's bearing or orientation. *Gretel* was not governed by the physics of Earth. But right now, Chelsey's mind was governed by a para-lyzing dread and Desna needed all hands on deck, present and engaged, for this latest scheme.

Chelsey and Berlin returned after a few hours and said every-thing was set, though there hadn't been much to do, Chelsey claimed. Wurther was running last-minute checks and Desna wanted it to be over with. She felt once the entity was gone from *Gretel,* they could resume their science and exploration mission, minimize the drama. Skip and his little dupe muffins still had to be dealt with. And the heart transplant. Desna had convinced Doc Karl to wait until after the ship roll procedure, in the event of unforeseen turbulence.

Available crew met in the bridge. Doc Karl stayed back in sick bay with Fawn, leaving Hurd, Wurther, Berlin and Chelsey to perform the roll. Berlin would monitor the ship's systems while Wurther operated the aileron thrusters. Chelsey would operate the hold cameras she and Berlin had installed, with Hurd watching the exterior hull cameras—normally used for hull integrity checks—to make sure the entity was moving where they wanted it to. Desna planned to operate the hold doors. In order to capture the entity in Cargo Hold 3, the hatches had to be opened and closed at precise times.

When Wurther started counting down, Desna opened the hatch to Cargo Hold 3 on the port side of *Gretel*. Chelsey gave the all clear, referring to the empty hold when the main exterior hatch was fully open. At the count of zero, Wurther initiated the procedure, firing the aileron thrusters to start *Gretel's* roll. Berlin watched on her display, announcing the progress in ten-degree increments. "Good, good," Berlin said to Wurther.

Desna watched the ship graphic rolling on her monitor, paying close attention to the pitch and bearing. Wurther had apparently mastered the technique, spinning *Gretel* slowly on her z-axis without affecting the pitch or yaw. Cargo Hold 4 would soon be flooded with sunlight, the temperature on the hatch-less hold rising upwards of 123 C.

By now, sunlight should just be cutting down the shadow edge of *Gretel,* and if Hurd's assumptions were right, starting to make the entity a little uncomfortable. Hurd announced that sunlight was beginning to penetrate Cargo Hold 4. As if in sync with his pronouncement, the loud banging started below their feet, the ship vibrating, rattled by the disturbance. A shattering din, chorused with screeching and shrieking, filled the air. According to Berlin, *Gretel* was reaching the 180-degree turning goal. By now, Desna figured, full sunlight.

"Mr. Hurd? Anything yet?"

"No, ma'am."

Berlin announced that *Gretel* was now inverted. Even so, they could feel no difference. Desna was pleased it had gone so smoothly, though wondered why the entity had not left the hold, seemingly content with just complaining, releasing deafening cries and howls, pounding *Gretel* with electromagnetic pulses. Wurther was busy at the controls, checking everything, Berlin watching the ship's roll making sure it didn't drift. The banging and pounding continued, Desna feeling as if the ship were coming apart.

"Mr. Wurther, can *Gretel* withstand this battering?" she screamed over the pandemonium.

"Yes, ma'am!" he shouted back, giving her the thumbs up.

Her console was starting to tremble and shake, the uproar growing louder until Hurd yelled. "It's moving!" The clangor stopped, leaving behind an eerie reverberation. Desna rushed to Hurd's station to get a better look at the organism. It was enormous, filled with humans. It crawled down the side of *Gretel*, trying to escape the bright light, maybe even the heat. They hadn't considered temperature could be a factor.

The hull cameras showed the creature squirming along the lower half of *Gretel,* disappearing past the edge until it went out of sight. Hurd quickly brought up the port cameras on the dark side of the ship. So far so good. The plan was working. Hurd punched up the light enhancement controls on the hull cameras to make it easier to see. In a few seconds, everyone was huddled around Hurd's station, observing the creature coming into view. A few gasps escaped upon seeing its full size. The dupes trapped inside it were barely visible, merely small silhouettes against the nearly imperceptible glow radiating from the jelly substance.

"What is that?" Desna whispered.

"Radioactivity, maybe," Chelsey said. Wurther concurred with a brief grunt.

"It's right on target," Berlin said, Desna trying to will it into Cargo Hold 3.

"Get in there you big ugly S.O.B.!" Chelsey said, tapping the screen as if directing it to its new home.

Once the entity escaped the sunlight, it stopped. They waited, everyone's attention on Hurd's screen. Hurd broke the silence: "Can we roll the ship a little more, Mr. Wurther, put the sun on its rear end, so to speak?"

Desna nodded her agreement. "Great idea, Hurd."

Wurther hurried back to his station, his fingers on the aileron thrusters. He tweaked the controls, Berlin telling him he was doing great, the sunlight creeping beneath *Gretel* and up the other side, nudging the creature toward the opening of Cargo Hold 3.

"A little more," Desna told him, watching the hull cameras.

A moment later, Chelsey shouted that it was entering Cargo Hold 3. "It's almost in."

Hurd confirmed. They held their collective breath, Desna's fingers poised above the hatch close button, listening for the command from Chelsey. A few seconds went by, then: "Now!"

Desna jabbed the button, the exterior hatch closing. Once it was shut, she directed Wurther to right the ship as soon as she had the exterior hatches opened for holds 1 and 5.

"Okay, let's put her upright!" Desna said. "And checkmate this fucking thing."

Wurther fired the aileron thrusters, reorienting the ship to its normal position. Once again, Berlin repeated to him *Gretel's* slow rolling progress in ten-degree increments.

Hurd whispered to Desna that it wouldn't really be a checkmate. "More of stalemate, making it so it can't move."

"I don't care what you call it, Mr. Hurd," Desna said. "When we flood that fucker with O_2, it will be game, set and match!" Hurd just smiled weakly, his attention on the exterior hull cameras.

"How we looking, Chelse?" Desna said. Wurther finished with the roll procedure, Berlin announcing *Gretel* was upright.

Chelsey turned on the lights in Cargo Hold 3, previously adjusting them to their lowest setting, just enough to confirm the creatures' presence without upsetting it. "All tucked in, safe and sound."

Desna took a deep breath. "Okay, well... this could get a little rough." She glanced toward Wurther. "Let's give it some air, Mr. Wurther."

The plan was to flood the chamber with O_2 in order to weaken it. Once they had sufficiently sapped its strength, they would open the exterior hatch to Cargo Hold 3 which was now facing the sun again.

Wurther watched the gauges on his computer display, the O_2 levels rising in Cargo Hold 3. A high-pitched warbling rang through the bridge, in concert with a constant pounding and banging that shook the vessel. Desna felt herself gripping the arm rests on her chair, wanting the commotion to stop before it did permanent damage. She glanced over at Wurther for assurance the ship would hold. He never met her eyes, seemingly immersed in his own deliberations.

Chelsey sat still as a corpse, her eyes like full moons, wide and bright. Berlin was draped over Wurther's right shoulder, her head angled toward the floor. The clamor continued, reaching a crescendo, the banging and screeching intolerable.

For several minutes the tumult grew more erratic, wilder, then started to become less resolute and volatile.

"Is it still contained?" Desna asked Chelsey.

"Yes. For a second it seemed to be edging toward Hold 5,

until it pushed through the connecting wall and got a taste of sunlight..."

The screeches and angry cries turned to mewling and groans, the pounding reduced to a few bumps and occasional clinks and clanks. It was losing energy.

Desna joined Chelsey at her terminal, regarding the entity lying flatter to the floor, the dupes floating inside it seemingly dead. Or at least no longer moving.

"Okay, let's finish it off." Desna was poised to flip the open-door switch for the exterior hatch to Cargo Hold 3 when Hurd halted her.

"We should give it a minute or two more."

Desna cut her eyes toward him.

"Tonic immobility is a fairly common survival strategy among many organisms," Hurd added. "We should give this creature a few more moments to make sure."

"Tonic immobility?" Wurther asked.

"Playing dead," Hurd said. "Less common among predators, but we really don't know what purpose this entity serves in its natural habitat."

After nearly fifteen minutes of inactivity, Desna was ready to open the exterior hatch to Hold 3 when all hell broke loose. Chelsey reported that the entity was climbing the walls, shaking and fibrillating, the wailing starting again. The commotion only lasted about three minutes until it fell silent, unmoving on the floor of the hold.

"Now, Mr. Hurd?" Desna asked

"Yes, I believe it is safe."

Sunlight flooded Cargo Hold 3, shimmering rainbows of color reflecting back from the creature's gelatinous flesh. Desna watched the camera feed from Cargo Hold 3, the blob of jelly and dead dupes an oozing, lifeless mass spreading slowly along the floor, the edges already beginning to crystalize.

"Nice work, everyone," she said. "We have a few more messes to clean up... then we can get on with our mission..."

CHAPTER THIRTY-SIX

No one had seen Doc Karl for several days. The Fawn dupe had died for no apparent reason, leaving Doc Karl so distraught he'd gone into self-imposed exile on *Gretel*. And even with plenty of places to hide out on the huge ship, the space wasn't infinite. They would find him, but Desna didn't care for his antics, especially with Skip still missing, Fawn lingering at death's door in sick bay, and the crew emotionally exhausted from dealing with the entity. Berlin and Wurther had managed to dispose of the remains, casting what was left of the entity into space. Chelsey reported for duty, but was so frightened by what she'd seen in the storage area when she'd been working with Berlin, she needed an escort to and from her quarters for her shifts, staying locked in her room the remainder of the time.

Desna went to sick bay to check on Fawn and speak with Hurd. He was taking over duties in sick bay, which now amounted to making sure Fawn was monitored, her IV changed, her body turned from time to time. Doc Karl had kept her suspended in a medically induced coma until he could perform the transplant, and Hurd didn't know how to bring her out of it safely.

"We have to find him," Desna said to Hurd.

Hurd was finishing up with the IV. "She'll be fine for now. I'll help you look."

They both had D-mobes dangling from their belts, especially after what Chelsey had reported seeing in the cargo area. Everyone was still under orders to carry their weapons at all times, at least until they could be sure the ship was free of dupes.

Desna and Hurd initiated their search on B-Deck, which consisted mostly of recreational areas; the gym, a climbing wall, a library of books, movies and music, a gravity free zone and an advanced-reality playroom. Also on this deck was the science lab, hydroponics, a comprehensive microbiology lab, a cryo chamber with numerous pods for the crew in case of emergency. Also private spaces anyone could use for meditation, or as an art studio, or for creating music, and myriad other rooms for reading, writing, even creating films, movies or documentaries with the aid of innovatory audiovisual technology.

Finding Doc Karl would certainly take longer if they didn't split up. Regardless, they chose to stay together; it felt safer that way. In fact, the crew had grown accustomed to pairing off to perform even the most routine duties. No one felt secure alone on *Gretel* anymore. Desna wasn't sure how this would work in the long run, hoping the fear would subside as the days and months rolled off, after the dupes were successfully exterminated.

Compartment after compartment, Hurd and Desna entered, checking every cabinet, every corner and table, anywhere someone could hide. They had been searching for almost two hours, coming up with nothing. She dreaded checking the storage holds, engine rooms and power stations in the belly of *Gretel,* but knew that's where they needed to go next.

"Do you need a break?" Desna asked Hurd.

"I'm good to go on if you are." Hurd's expression was impossible to read.

They chose to take the freight elevator to the lower deck to search the storage area first. They would have to check each hold. Desna became weary just imagining it. Forty holds, with no idea what they'd find.

Performing the inspections was easier by accessing the holds through the single emergency door, which was the size of any normal door, but part of the enormous interior hatch, which was used for loading and unloading supplies. It was near one of these holds that Chelsey had seen someone crawling toward her, before the unfortunate being was accosted and whisked away. Desna had made room for the possibility that Chelsey had imagined it. The lighting wasn't the best down here, and the entire area could often fall under a vaporous fog. Not so thick you couldn't see, but heavy enough to hide the farthest, shadowy end of the vault. It wasn't hard for the most twisted gears of the imagination to kick in when the mist was present.

Door by door they searched. Hatch to hatch. Desna worried about the provisions she'd expelled into space when she found the little community of dupes having an orgy. Surely all the supplies in Cargo Hold 34 hadn't been tainted by the dupes, but Desna was so upset she hadn't been thinking straight when she'd flushed the contents into outer space.

She unlocked the emergency door to Hold 34, and was momentarily crushed by how empty it was. A part of her brain was still trying to fill it up with the needed supplies she'd wasted.

"I thought half the food provisions from BC-1 were stored here?" Hurd said, following her in.

"They were... this was where we found the dupes..."

It seemed to take a moment or two for Hurd's mind to call back the details from that particular incident.

"Ah, yes," he said, regarding Desna. "It couldn't be helped."

"I appreciate your sentiment, but that won't matter much if we run out of food before reaching BC-2." Desna turned to leave the hold. After Hurd exited behind her, she spun the airlock on the emergency door and moved to the next.

Almost four hours of searching and they'd seen nothing to hint at the whereabouts of Doc Karl, or Skip. She hadn't been looking for Skip, but hoped they might stumble onto his location, try to talk some sense into him.

Both tired from the hunt, Desna and Hurd sat on the floor with their backs against one of the main hold doors. He was speaking about something Desna couldn't focus on, something about Doc Karl and how upset he was when the dupe died, the words coming at her like a foreign language.

"What?" Desna said when the words echoed back through her mind.

"Dr. Karl said the Fawn dupe must have been connected with the entity in some way," Hurd repeated.

Desna turned her head toward him. "Why would he think that?"

"While we were destroying the entity, Dr. Karl said he observed the Fawn dupe exhibiting strange behavior."

"Such as?"

"Convulsions. Then her eyes rolled back in her head. A moment later she was dead..."

"He never said anything about that to me!"

"He was so devastated... you know how he gets..."

"Devastated... or pissed at me that I didn't let him do the transplant when he had the chance?"

Hurd took his eyes to the floor. "No one knows what would have happened to Fawn if he had done it..." Hurd sighed and sat a while longer in silence, then: "Ready to resume the search?"

Desna stood, weighing every decision she'd made from the first moment she'd said, "Yes," to this mission. At the beginning, she'd felt extremely qualified to lead a small group of scientists and researchers on the greatest discovery of all time. She'd already devoted her life to science and space exploration in the classroom; why not make it real! But over the past several weeks, she'd felt woefully unskilled to deal with the events which had transpired, much less the emotional and psychological fallout. Everyone had been affected adversely, their lives put in danger. Everyone accepted the risk of growing too old or sick to never return to Earth, but no one anticipated an anomalous organism that replicated crew members and would need to be killed. This mission had never been about killing alien life forms. Yet, there was no denying the heartless brutality she had ordered.

They rode the freight elevator to the lower deck, where all the power stations, engine rooms, generators and life support apparatuses were located. Due to the convoluted nature of the space, Desna suggested they stay very close together navigating the jungle of technology and machinery, pipes, conduits, ducts and wires. If someone wanted never to be found, the lower deck energy plant was the place to disappear; it frightened her to no end. She wasn't a weapons' person, but wished she had something more deadly than a D-Mobe.

She detached hers from her belt and implored Hurd to do the same. He complied without commenting, following a few paces behind her. They hadn't traveled very far when they spied movement up ahead. Desna stopped, a wildfire crackling in her chest.

"Did you see that?" she whispered back to Hurd.

"Yes, ma'am."

She hesitated, then: "Dr. Karl? Is that you?"

She listened to Hurd's breathing, rough but stifled, her own breath seemingly caught somewhere behind her ribs. Just then a loud clunk, followed by a low moaning. Hurd stopped breathing altogether.

"Is that you, Dr. Karl?" Desna called again, much more tentative this time.

A raspy, guttural cry issued from deep in the matrix of pipes and conduits, like someone hurt and unable to move. She couldn't see who was making the sound, but didn't want to inspect closer. She waited, but wasn't sure what she was waiting for, then spun toward Hurd. "You wait here..." She attempted to sound brave, her legs rubber.

"No, I should come with you. Best to stick together."

She wasn't sure if he'd said that for her benefit, or his own. Either way, she felt better having him behind her; two opportunities to discharge their D-mobes.

They picked their way between large pipes, equipment stacks and electrical boxes, the thudding of the generators growing louder as they went deeper into the meagerly lit space. Desna paused a moment to listen, though heard nothing.

"I can lead if you like," Hurd said, coming up behind her.

She wanted some auxiliary courage to kick in, but it didn't. She nodded to Hurd, who took the lead. In less than a minute they came upon the source of the unfortunate noise. Skip. Or something that was at one time Skip. A milky-colored slime oozed from his eye sockets and nostrils, and appeared to be eating into the flesh of his hands and arms. The same jelly covered his legs, had eaten through his boots. Desna gagged and turned away. Skip was still alive. She couldn't bear to look at him, his deteriorating hand reaching up to them, begging, pleading.

She heard a sudden discharge, a bright flash reflecting on nearby equipment, and knew Hurd had done what she couldn't; put Skip out of his misery. She turned around, Hurd squatting next to Skip.

"Don't touch him!" Desna said, jerking Hurd away from Skip's ravaged body.

Hurd lost his balance, ending up on his butt before using his feet to push away from Skip. He jumped up quickly. "We must get him into a refrigeration unit in sick bay," Hurd said.

"No... we're not touching him. Not until Doc Karl's had a chance to study this... if we ever find him..."

She turned away, hurrying through the warren of equipment and technology, wanting to get to the freight elevator before she lost her stomach, their mission of exploration now a grotesque and appalling nightmare.

CHAPTER THIRTY-SEVEN

DESNA WAS INCONSOLABLE WHEN SHE REACHED HER DAY ROOM in the bridge. Hurd must have told Wurther what they'd found on the engineering deck, because Wurther was at her door knocking and asking if he could come in. She wasn't sure what the man could possibly want; she had nothing to offer except a paralyzing dread. She should have gone back to her personal quarters, but she didn't want to be alone. But she didn't want to engage with crew, either. What she'd witnessed was too hard to talk about.

After waiting a few moments, hoping he'd take the hint and give up, his knocking became more frenzied, so she invited him in.

"I'm not in a chatty mood! Make it quick!"

As if ignoring her admission, Wurther immediately sat in the chair facing her desk. "Do you think we still have dupes aboard *Gretel?*" His tone was harried, as if his conversation with Hurd had left him agitated.

"I don't know... but Skip didn't die from the flu!"

Wurther shook his head, his eyes fixed on nothing. "We need to find 'em and get rid of 'em... or no one will be safe."

"What do you suggest?" Desna felt defeated, as if the crew might never be certain the dupes were completely gone. How could they possibly know? When they stopped finding crew members turning to jelly?

Wurther aimed his eyes toward her. "I have real weapons, Des.... I know I wasn't supposed to bring any, but, Jesus, no one could anticipate what we might run into... especially a bunch of Cal Tech academics with super-computers and bad haircuts!"

"What kind of 'real' weapons we talking about?" Desna experienced the slightest sensation of relief, as if 'real' weapons could solve their very real problem.

"Automatic weapons capable of killing at a distance. Easy to handle, deadly weapons that anyone on board can learn how to use in less than ten minutes..."

"What about *Gretel*? How will she react to these 'deadly' weapons?"

Wurther's expression soured, as if he had hoped nobody would ask that question, much less think of it. "We have to be careful... sure, but what's the alternative? We all get turned to jello! Hurd could hardly describe what he'd seen without heaving!"

Desna didn't like the idea of everyone on *Gretel* having these weapons, especially given the level of angst the crew was experiencing. The collective terror could quickly become a shooting frenzy, firing at anything that moved, or didn't move, crew members shooting one another in a moment of frenzy. It was too risky.

"How about you and me?" Desna asked. "Berlin and Hurd are handling things pretty well. Chelsey needs a little hand-holding, but maybe she and Berlin could bunk together for a while, work shifts together. Hurd and Doc Karl... if we can find—"

Wurther cut her off. "I saw Doc Karl this morning. In sick bay. He seems together now..."

Desna had no idea he'd returned from his self-imposed isolation. "Did he say where he'd gone off to?"

"One of the personal studios on upper deck. He's got an idea about Fawn that he's working on... he thinks he can still save her..."

This was the best news yet. Why hadn't Wurther led with

that? "So, then, if they can run the ship, what do you think? A hunting party, just you and me...?"

"Sounds like a plan," he said. "It'd be great to get this done in the next two weeks, before we get to XB-92..."

"That's coming up that fast?"

"Maybe three, but yeah. I've already started reducing our speed so we can orbit and land."

"Atmosphere?"

"Not much... spacesuits only."

She'd hoped for something a bit more hospitable. "Where can I learn to fire these weapons of yours?"

Wurther said he'd go set things up in the cargo area. It would give them the most unobstructed space for target practice. "And if you miss," Wurther assured her. "Those massive titanium cargo hatches should stop a bullet. It'll take me about thirty minutes..."

She wasn't sure about this plan or much of anything else. Using the ship's comm, she called the crew to the bridge for a meeting. When everyone was assembled, she told them what she and Wurther had come up with, and for the time being, she wanted the crew to pair up, both in their duties and sleeping quarters.

"I know this isn't the most ideal arrangement, but we really need to pull together right now."

Berlin and Doc Karl immediately agreed to bunk together again, smiling, and could do it in sick bay, if necessary, to keep an eye on Fawn. Hurd offered to stay with Chelsey if she was okay with that. She said it would be nice to have someone to talk with, and appeared genuinely relieved.

"Okay, so... this is good..." Desna said, glad the plan had come together virtually drama-free. No one said anything, but everyone knew by now what had happened to Skip, and no one wanted any part of that.

As Berlin and Doc were leaving, Desna asked Doc to stay behind a moment to talk in her day room. Berlin said she'd wait, while Chelsey and Hurd resumed their duties on the bridge.

Seated in her day room, she asked if Doc was doing okay. He said he was, that he just needed a little time.

"Hurd told me what happened to the Fawn dupe when we were destroying the entity. Can you tell me anything more about that?"

Doc Karl cleared his throat, straightening in his chair. "I'm sorry about not telling you... I was just very..."

"Look, I know you were upset with me, but I hope you're past it... we have a real situation here..."

"No, I understand completely," he said, shyly. "I just... acted childishly... and I'm a bit embarrassed..."

"Tell me what happened that day, Karl..." Desna wanted to move beyond his remorse.

He explained that he had been monitoring the Fawn dupe very closely that day, as he had gotten some strange readings from its bioactivity. At the time, he couldn't understand what was happening, but it was obvious the dupe was under some kind of duress. He had forgotten about the ship rolling procedure, and tried to get the dupe out of danger by sedating it, but the tranquilizer did nothing. Soon the dupe was experiencing convulsions and spasms.

"I saw it first in her brainwaves, as if she were experiencing an epileptic seizure. I injected her with lorazepam." A second or two later, the doctor injected a bit of history. "As you know, epilepsy was eliminated on Earth, so I was surprised to find it among the anticonvulsant medications stocked on *Gretel*. However, it did nothing for her symptoms."

He explained that he tried another anticonvulsant, but it had no effect either, and he figured its biology was indifferent to human-based medications. All he could do was standby, watching it suffer and eventually die.

"It suffered?" Desna hadn't asked the question in a ghoulish way, but rather, trying to piece together some insight into the anomalous creatures, wondering how many human traits it might exhibit.

"Not in the way you might think. It certainly was in distress, but not necessarily in physical pain..."

"Psychological?"

"If I had to make a guess, I'd have to say yes. Her anguish seemed to be existential, not physical..."

For whatever reason, Desna found that to be more disturbing than anything he had shared to this point, as if the doctor and crew had not even begun to understand this phenomenon. Did dupes not feel physical pain? The Chelsey one she encountered in her private quarters that night surely seemed to experience *pleasure,* but maybe that was projection on her part; she had certainly experienced profound gratification. Thinking back though, she couldn't really say the Chelsey dupe had felt anything the same, or for that matter, anything at all.

"How about Fawn?" Desna asked, unsure why she'd posed the peculiar question.

"Fawn?" Doc Karl was suddenly peevish in an impatient sort of way, as if it were a bothersome or inappropriate question.

"Sorry..." Desna was baffled by her own impulse to ask the question in the first place.

"Fawn's in a medically-induced coma!" He became defensive, as if her inquiry had been insulting in some way.

"I don't even know why I asked." Desna was trying to recover.

"Yes, okay..." His severe expression faded. "Well, if that's all, Berlin is waiting for me, and we need to get back to sick bay..."

"Do you want to tell me about your new idea to help Fawn?" Desna hoped to end the conversation on a more upbeat note.

Doc Karl bristled. "Can we do it another time? Once I've had a chance to gather more data?"

Desna smiled. "Certainly. I don't want to hold you up..."

He gave her a brief smile, then hurried from her day room as if he were late for a meeting.

CHAPTER THIRTY-EIGHT

IT WAS DISCONCERTING, LEARNING TO FIRE AN AUTOMATIC weapon. She and Wurther had practiced for over an hour. She got pretty good, though it didn't seem all that hard. The rifle fired so many rounds it was hard to miss. Plus, Wurther had her stand no more than fifteen meters from the target. "We'll have to kill at close range," he'd told her. "Any farther, and we risk hitting vital systems on *Gretel.*"

Kill at close range. Those were words she never expected to use in her lifetime. In her most wicked nightmares about this journey, needing to kill anything had never entered the equation, especially organisms that looked exactly like humans. And not just any humans, but ones she'd spent the last fifty-two months living in very close quarters with.

Since she and Hurd had found Skip on the lower deck amongst all the machinery, they decided to start there. The lighting in the belly of *Gretel* was really bad, or maybe only seemed that way because the area was so precarious and Byzantine. Yet, being here with Wurther felt so different than with Hurd, Desna enjoying a wellbeing with this ex-paramilitary man she hadn't known in weeks.

Wurther, upon hearing of Skip's degraded condition, suggested they wear hazmat suits. She had started to protest, until she pictured Skip again. It was still unclear how he'd come to such a grizzly end.

The suits were warm. They'd only been at it for about thirty minutes, but she was already perspiring, the occasional bead of sweat slipping down between her breasts, or tracing a trail along her spine, her arms and legs clammy. Wurther's face, visible through his tinted shield, was flush and pebbled with sweat. He'd told her he was used to it, that they often wore upwards of eighty to a hundred pounds of gear on maneuvers in the desert. He showed her how to follow him, to stay close, but not too close, how to tap him on the shoulder if she needed something, how to stop when he did, and move when he started moving. They needed to be as stealthy as possible.

Ten minutes later, Wurther stopped dead, his right hand raised slightly to signal her. Paused two meters behind the big man, she waited, searching for the source of Wurther's alarm. There it was, something moving up ahead on the other side of some huge shiny metal tanks; she had no idea what was in the tanks, the outer skin displaying warning labels; obviously they were filled with something that wouldn't react well to bullets.

Crouching, Wurther inched forward, his weapon balanced perfectly between his thick fists. The gun looked like a toy in his meaty hands, though she could still picture what the bullets had done to an empty 55-gallon drum he'd set up for target practice.

Closer now, she could almost make out some being sitting on the floor, busy with something, though she still couldn't tell if the figure was male or female. Wurther moved closer until he was within four meters, his weapon trained on the being.

"Wurther! Why the hazmat suit?" the figure said, standing. Desna recognized her at once: Berlin. Wearing a standard issue flight uniform. Desna hadn't worn hers past the eighth month of the expedition, opting instead for street clothes, jeans, cotton blouses and tights. She even had a pair of high heels hidden away in one of her drawers, though she was never sure why she'd brought them. Maybe some need for normalcy.

When Berlin stepped toward Wurther, he yelled for her to stop, the barrel of his weapon pointed at her chest.

"Whoa, what's going on here?" Berlin said, putting her hands up and taking a step back.

"What are you doing down here?" Wurther said.

"Working on some new recalibrations for the hyper-fusion drive. I think they could really improve performance..." She extended the E-pad toward him. "Here, have a look..."

Wurther didn't budge, his eyes leveled on hers, like a poker player looking for tells. Desna edged closer but still stayed back at least three meters behind Wurther.

"Desna, hi! What's going on here?" Berlin shifted her attention away from the big man. "What's got Wurther so spooked?"

Desna felt herself fraying around the edges. It certainly sounded like Berlin, and nothing like the ridiculous air-headed dupes she'd met in Skip's quarters.

"Unzip your jumpsuit!" Wurther said. Berlin stared at him, dumbfounded, before bringing her eyes to Desna, as if wanting a second opinion on Wurther's command. Desna knew exactly what Wurther was doing. They'd both been intimate with Berlin. He wanted to see her double-dagger tattoo to make sure it was her. That tattoo—if Hurd was correct about how the entity had duplicated crew members—wouldn't be present in Berlin's genome makeup.

Reluctantly at first, she pulled the zipper down to her navel. She was naked underneath. She put her hands out to her sides as if to say, nothing to see here.

"All the way down," Wurther said, unwavering in his focus.

Berlin took the zipper in between her thumb and forefinger and drew it to her pubis. Even with the zipper pulled all the way down, the fabric was not spread apart enough to see the tattoo even if it were there.

"Pull the material apart down there." Wurther pointed with the tip of his automatic rifle. Without taking her eyes from him, Berlin slipped the garment off her shoulders, letting it fall to a heap at her feet. No tattoo. Desna's heart sank. She knew Wurther must be feeling the same, his rifle firmly directed at the dupe's bare chest.

Confusion spun Desna, making her dizzy. How could this dupe be so conversant, smart? Maybe Hurd was right, that the dupes she'd met were merely the lowest rung on their evolutionary path. Within a ridiculously short span of time, this one had evolved to calculus, aerospace engineering and astrodynamics. What would she be like a month from now? A year?

Berlin pulled her jumpsuit back up and zipped it, meeting Wurther's gaze.

It was obvious he was as befuddled as Desna, trying to figure out what to do with this creature. Her intelligence and poise made it difficult to just destroy her. Yet, she posed more of a threat now than ever, her superior intelligence a greater danger than Desna could imagine.

"What should we do?" Wurther asked, never taking his eyes from the Berlin dupe.

"Let's see if she'll respond to being escorted to main deck." A battle raged in Desna's gut, some dark voice in her brain screaming, *just shoot the damn thing!* "We'll lock her in Fawn's compartment."

"You think those quarters will hold it?"

She knew he was trying to avoid humanizing the creature, which would only make it more troubling if and when it came time to kill it.

"Skip's quarters couldn't even hold *him!*" Wurther seemed to offer proof he felt it was a bad idea to treat this thing with empathy. And he was absolutely right... Skip had escaped without any difficulty. What challenge would the simple lock pose to this entity?

Desna was still contemplating what to do when she noticed something odd about the dupe. She couldn't be sure if she was witnessing a micro transformation taking place in the dupe's face, or if she was imagining it due to fatigue and the heat of the hazmat suit.

"You seeing this?" Wurther asked, his rifle aimed at the dupe.

"Yes... what the hell..." Before Desna could register her own confusion, the dupe opened her mouth, spewing a thick jelly all over Wurther's suit and rifle. He opened fire, bullets ripping into the uniform, the dupe faltering, dropping to her knees. She spewed more of the substance at Wurther, then turned it on Desna, who jumped back. Wurther kept shooting the dupe until it collapsed to the floor. He waited a few seconds, then walked closer and put the barrel to its head, the weapon popping several more times.

As if on fire, Wurther peeled the hazmat suit from his body, switching the gun between his hands until he was free of the garment. It lay in a lump on the floor, a wispy curtain of vapor rising from it.

Standing in his underwear, he yelled for Desna to remove her suit. The gel had just started to penetrate the material at her legs, her suit beginning to melt. In her underwear and bra, she stepped back near Wurther, both of them watching their suits slowly dissolve. Within a few minutes their suits were destroyed.

Distracted by the destruction of their hazmat suits, neither had noticed that the dupe had become a thick, gloppy puddle on the floor; no blood, bones or skeleton whatsoever. Even her hair was nothing but slime.

"What the fuck are we dealing with?" Desna whispered to herself in the dismal engine room.

CHAPTER THIRTY-NINE

AFTER SEVERAL DAYS, BERLIN JOINED DESNA ON A DUPE safari. Wurther was dealing with *Gretel,* closely monitoring their approach to XB-92, even though it was still more than ten days away. Desna and Berlin searched every deck, finding nothing. Desna couldn't help but wonder if the dupes were gone, or like Berlin had suggested, had just gotten better at hiding. What puzzled her the most, were the remains from the dupe Wurther had killed. Of course, she knew that when a human was cremated, even with all their complexity, nothing would remain but a pile of ashes. But the Berlin dupe had seemed like she had no real substance to begin with, as if it were directed by some higher intelligence. Like a puppet. But that couldn't be possible, unless they hadn't truly eliminated the entity in Cargo Hold 4.

Desna ran her theory past Berlin.

"The ones Wurther and I killed died like humans," she told Desna. "They didn't turn to mush. They just died. And we ejected their bodies into space."

Desna couldn't make sense of it. What had changed?

"Why do you think there's some higher intelligence involved?" Berlin asked. "That seems like a leap..."

"The two dupes Skip was shacking up with could barely utter the names he'd taught them. They were imbeciles. But this Berlin dupe... scary intelligence..."

"You don't think I have scary intelligence?" Berlin said, Desna unsure if she was joking or insulted. Before she could ponder it very long, Berlin smiled and said she was pulling her chain.

Desna recalled something Hurd had said about the entity in Cargo Hold 4 when they thought they'd killed it. Tonic immobility: playing dead. Is that possibly why the dupes Berlin and Wurther had killed appeared to die like humans? That they were playing dead, or made to look like they were dead. If they still had a deceased dupe, Doc Karl could perform an autopsy and they'd know for sure. Or would they? If these creatures were masters of tonic immobility, then they would demonstrate organs and bones, a human veneer. But how could they if they were dead? Is that why the Berlin dupe they killed a few days earlier had turned to jelly? To keep them from doing research on it?

"You okay?" Berlin said, interrupting Desna's mind-boggling journey down brain-twister lane. Her face must have been contorted into a hideous mask.

"I'm fine." Desna was anything but fine. "If we had one of these dupes we could do more research."

"Karl already did that on the ones he has in sick bay," Berlin said.

"Does he have any dupes there now?"

"He should. The Fawn dupe that just died should be there."

"Let's go."

They rushed to sick bay, Desna hoping Doc Karl was there. When they entered, they didn't immediately see him. Walking to the back, they found him in his office.

"Do you have any dupes on ice?" Desna said, dispensing with formalities.

Doc Karl shot back in his chair, his face bright and wide. "What?"

"Dupes. Do we have any?"

"Yes... but why?" He rose behind his desk.

"Desna has a wild theory, Karl," Berlin said. "Get one on the table."

"What's this about?" Doc Karl seemed defensive.

"Just do it, Karl. For shit's sake!" Berlin shouted. Desna was relieved Berlin was finally acting like her First mate again. "Does everything need to be a debate with you!" Berlin glared at the doctor.

Walking back to the morgue, Doc Karl questioned Desna on her theory, rebutting her suppositions by explaining about the DNA and blood samples he'd taken. He bent over and pulled out the drawer, a thick cloud of vapor escaping the vault. He pulled the handle up and rolled it to the middle of the room under the overhead light, then worked the controls on the side. In seconds, the Fawn dupe was at work level, the sides of the vault folding down, transforming into a gurney/autopsy table complete with fluid gutters on all sides.

"What do you want me to do?" He asked defiantly, as if any request was a monumental bother.

"I want you to slice her open," Desna said. "The way you would for the transplant... to harvest her heart..."

His mouth twisted in disgust. "That's sick..."

"Think of it as research."

"Just fucking do it! It's an order!" Berlin shouted, stepping closer. Desna regarded her a moment, secretly pleased she was asserting her authority again. Desna couldn't do it alone; she needed consensus among at least one other crew member.

He disappeared to scrub and get ready.

"Trouble in paradise?" Desna said, knowing Berlin and Doc Karl were rooming together.

"He's an asshole," Berlin said. "I moved in with Wurther. Hurd's living with Doc Degenerate, now... I can't stand to be around him..."

"What's the deal?"

"I don't know. He just creeps me out... but he and Hurd get along, so..."

"What about Chelsey? Is she by herself again?"

Before Berlin could answer, Doc Karl entered the morgue, gloved and masked, as if he were performing major surgery. Desna didn't understand the ritual, but didn't care, either. She needed answers.

Stationed next to the autopsy table, he carved Desna a hard

look over his mask, then picked up the scalpel, hesitating as if he weren't sure where to start. After a few tense moments, he inserted the tip of the scalpel near the base of her throat and drew it down the length of her torso. The flesh parted normally at first, then, as if a switch had been thrown, the dupe's anatomy collapsed into a putrefied jelly, the rotting stench nearly bringing up Desna's stomach. Berlin bolted away, throwing up in the corner trashcan. Doc Karl, backing away from the table in shock, was covered in slime, the scalpel still grasped in his gloved hand. The scalpel made a tinny sound bouncing off the floor when he dropped it, his eyes downcast, studying the vapor rising off his medical gown.

"Get the gown off, Karl!" Desna shouted, her voice muffled by her hand covering her mouth. "Hurry!"

Doc Karl writhed in the garment, swinging his arms back and forth trying to free himself, as if a specter were attacking him. Berlin rushed over and grabbed the tie at his back, then ripped down on the gown until it was lying on the floor, a sickly steam rising from the material. He jerked the mask from his face, dropping it before pulling off the gloves. With bare hands and arms, he rushed to the sink, the sensor switching on the faucet, sudsy cleansing-solvent covering his skin. He rubbed for several seconds before shoving his hands beneath the dryer.

Once they saw he was okay, Desna and Berlin rushed from the morgue, the horrible odor following them into the hallway. Desna couldn't understand why this dupe reeked of burning flesh; the Berlin one she and Wurther had killed had no smell at all. Doc Karl joined them, but not before slamming the door to the morgue.

"What just happened!" His face was a veil of horror, his eyes darting back toward the sealed room.

Desna wasn't sure, but her gut was signaling trouble ahead. Unable to understand how, she believed the entity from Cargo Hold 4 wasn't dead and gone, and had managed somehow to evade their attempt to terminate it. Originally, it seemed, the life form had readily tried to maintain the ruse of human form, even after death. Now, what worried her the most about this enigmatic intelligence, was, that it no longer seemed concerned with keeping up the charade once its virtual humans were killed, freely revealing the gelatinous life form at its core. Why was it becoming so bold? Did detection no longer matter? Desna was frazzled, entangled in a fabric of troubling questions.

CHAPTER FORTY

HURD INFORMED DESNA FAWN HAD DIED. SHE HAD JUST returned from a hunting expedition with Berlin—the third day without finding any dupes—when Hurd entered her day room to give her the news. She was shocked, feeling as if everything was falling apart. Wurther overheard him and came over to her when Hurd left. He asked if they were going to have a ceremony or anything. She needed to talk to Doc Karl, wondering why he'd sent Hurd to tell her instead of coming himself.

"Give me your thoughts," Desna said.

Wurther seemed to study on the question, maybe thinking the same thing she was; how many viewing ceremonies would they observe during this journey? And who would be stuck with performing the last one, especially now, with the youngest member of the crew dead? Fawn had been the lynch pin making this entire journey possible. The next youngest person was Berlin. Even so, she would be in her seventies by the time *Gretel* reached Earth. But she'd never last that long on an empty ship; she was far too needy. Desna wasn't sure any of them could survive such crushing isolation for years on end.

"Let me think on it," Wurther finally said, about to return to his station. "Oh, I forgot. We're four days out from XB-92."

"Wow, the time sure went fast," she said. "Are we ready?"

"Absolutely. Our speed will be perfect when we reach the planet."

"Have you determined if we can land *Gretel* there?"

"The data in our handbook says we can, but I'm not so sure the folks at the institute had enough actionable intel to make that prediction. We might want to put *Gretel* in orbit and take *Hansel* to the surface."

She wasn't wild about that idea. Taking *Hansel* would certainly hamper their investigation; the transport was cramped at best, and if they found a wealth of artifacts, they'd have to leave much of their discovery behind. Or make numerous trips between *Gretel* and the planet surface. And for less than a nanosecond, she'd felt the ordinary tug of normal concerns. She'd even felt that familiar tinge of exhilaration over exploring a new world. But it quickly evaporated, that spirit of adventure forever tainted by the events of the past weeks.

"Keep me informed as we get closer," she said, getting up to leave. She followed him out of her day room and headed for sick bay. She wasn't sure why she wanted to place Fawn in cryo-suspension, but some part of her brain wasn't ready to give up on her just yet. That was crazy. She was dead, and storing her body for months and years on end would never change that. Information they'd gather from the BreadCrumb ships moving forward would not be advancements, but information long trapped in the past.

Desna was surprised to find sick bay locked up. She went to Dock Karl's private quarters and knocked several times before he opened his hatch.

He ushered her in with a sweep of his hand, then closed the latch behind her. It looked as if he'd been crying.

"You okay?" She didn't want to engage his drama, whatever it was, yet couldn't just ignore him. When the mission started, she'd felt he would be a loyal and stalwart ally, but over the past few months, things had changed, though she could never quite figure out what. Maybe it was his furtiveness, as he always seemed to be in service of some hidden agenda with everything he did.

"What a waste," he said, plopping back into his chair. "So young... what a terrible waste."

He never attempted to disguise the contempt in his accusatory tone, and she wasn't about to stick her head into that trap. How could he have thought for a second that a heart transplant would have worked? The dupe had no heart; no organs whatsoever. It had been a ploy from the beginning, the entity some twisted grandmaster of illusion. It wasn't as if rushing to operate would have changed anything.

"Where is she now?"

He shook his head sadly, as if even mentioning her name was an unspeakable burden. "In the morgue," he finally said.

"Do you think we should keep her in cryo-suspension?" Desna wished she hadn't voiced the stupid question; she'd already decided it was pointless, but his behavior had undermined her composure.

He scoffed, looking away, as if her question was too insipid to address.

"What have I done to piss you off, Karl?" she shouted, spiraling down into the vortex of her own anger. "God willing, we are going to be on this ship a very long time. I can't deal with your peevish conduct. Let's get this sorted right now..."

She waited, pressure throbbing in her temples. He shifted his eyes to the floor, before gulping in a deep breath, then hooked his attention to some distant world in the universe, his expression vacant, lost.

"I miss her," he said. "Fawn and I... we had a connection." A single small tear slipped down his cheek, then: "I know everyone on this ship would judge it as... wrong... but it wasn't. It was the most wonderful relationship I've ever had." He paused, sniffling, then wiped his nose with his fingers. "She *was* almost seventeen, you know, not exactly a child... mature far past her biological age..."

Desna wanted to slap him. The drivel coming from his mouth sounded like the crap every pervert probably tells themselves. Maybe that's what she had intuited lately, his inappropriate relationship with this young girl. And could account for her no longer trusting him, that beneath his mellow exterior was a morbid man engaged in depraved behavior. An even more vile notion broke in on her fury; what had he done to her while she was in the medically-induced coma? She could hardly contain her rage. Berlin said she'd caught him feeling up the Fawn dupe one night, and he tried to pass it off as a necessary examination. The images in Desna's head were making her ill. She felt responsible for Fawn, and blamed herself for not knowing what was happening. Her disgust brought her to a very dark place; she wanted to drop the doctor off on XB-92 and leave him there to rot!

"I can't talk to you right now," she said, storming out of his quarters. She went to sick bay and punched in the code. Somebody had cleaned up the morgue, the awful stench completely gone. She opened several cadaver drawers, coming to the Wurther dupe Berlin had killed weeks ago. Why had Doc kept it? She thought she'd told him to eject it from the ship. Closing the Wurther dupe drawer, she continued her search until she found Fawn. In death, Fawn finally looked more like her living-self than she had in months; more natural, calmer and youthful—her condition had robbed the child of all vitality. Desna placed her hand over her own mouth in disbelief, picturing Karl climbing onto this lovely, vulnerable girl, or running his bare hands under her gown while she was drugged. It was disgusting.

She squatted down next to Fawn, trying to compose herself, figure out what to do with Doc. She needed to talk to someone about it, but who? If she told Wurther, she was fairly certain he'd kill Doc. Berlin might as well, and feel justified doing it. Maybe Hurd; he had the engineered emotional landscape to handle this kind of wickedness with some detachment.

She reached into the metal vault and held Fawn's cold hand. A notion surfaced that she thought she'd gotten past. Obviously, she hadn't. Tucking Fawn's right hand back down next to her body, she came to the other side of the crypt and lifted the child's left hand into hers. Deftly, though feeling the sizzle of guilt, she rotated Fawn's hand until the skin at the bottom of her wrist was exposed, bringing a spontaneous sigh of relief. On Fawn's flesh was the small but intricate compass tattoo, North pointing toward her palm.

Of late, Desna was disoriented, plagued by a brand of paranoia she'd never felt before. She'd become obsessed with the macabre possibility that the Fawn dupe had traded places with Fawn, and when the Fawn dupe had supposedly died, that it was, instead, Fawn herself who had died. Desna had failed to check the Fawn dupe when she ordered Doc to cut her open. Now it didn't matter. Her worst fear had been put to rest. Though the notion that Doc may have actually facilitated such a switch—for God only knew what reasons—lingered in the darkest bog of her mind.

She pushed the drawer back into its space and left the morgue, locking the main hatch to sick bay behind her. They would have a service for Fawn, but not with her body present. They'd display her face on the bridge big screen, and no one would learn of Doc Karl's ghoulish proclivities. No one aboard *Gretel* would be easy prey for him now, and Desna had not completely abandoned the idea of killing him herself.

CHAPTER FORTY-ONE

ONE DAY OUT. WURTHER ASSURED DESNA THEY WERE IN perfect position to enter XB-92's orbit. The usual excitement around these off-ship explorations was conspicuously missing from the crew. People tended their duties and kept to themselves. The ceremony for Fawn was short but nice, though a few members asked why Doc Karl hadn't attended. Desna explained that it was too difficult for him, given the failed chance at the transplant, that he felt responsible for her death. The truth was, she warned him if he showed up for the commemoration, she would kill him on the spot, then explain the reason. His only chance to remain immune from retribution from the remaining crew was to stay away and keep a low profile. And stick to the cover story she'd given him until she could figure out what to do. Berlin was the only one who suspected she had something to do with Doc Karl's absence, cutting her curious looks during the observance, but even when it finished, she said nothing.

Berlin was leaving when she pulled her aside. "Up for a little safari?"

"Sure. Let me change my clothes."

They met in the cargo hold area. Desna wondered aloud if dupes could be hiding in Cargo Hold 4, to which Berlin only frowned, as if to say, *How could they?* But the entity was Desna's main concern. She wanted to check 1, 3, and 5 to see if some *part* of it had possibly managed to escape when they were flooding Hold 3 with oxygen. She didn't believe the dupes were autonomous. For whatever reason, she was convinced that they were all connected and ruled by the governing entity from Cargo Hold 4, some kind of "hive" mind responsible for their activities and intelligence, their very life itself. Their *creator.* And if the crew could fully destroy their *creator,* the dupes would also die. The proverbial "cut off the head of the snake" concept. What made the task so monumentally exasperating, though, was the entity's confounding protean nature. It was adapting for survival at mind-bending speed and in unimaginable ways.

"Why would you think the dupes could live in Hold 3? Or any other one for that matter?" Berlin asked, holding one of Wurther's assault rifles with the casualness and ease of a merce-nary. As if she'd been born with it in her hands.

"They're not like us, baby. They're not real... they're made of fucking goo! Definitely not human..."

Berlin wore a strange, seductive smile. "I love when you call me that," Berlin said, her eyes softening. "You want me to come back and stay with you? It would be fun..." Berlin let the rifle dangle from its strap, reaching over to touch Desna's forearm with her gloved hand.

"Things tense with Wurther?"

"No... it's downright *brotherly,* if you get my drift..."

"Okay... well, I'm not sure I'd be any different right now. Let's focus on the dupes." Desna walked to Hold 3 and pressed the button to open the interior hatch. Berlin caught up beside her as cold air swept out from the enormous empty chamber.

"Damn," Berlin said. "Even with this hazmat I can still feel the fricking cold."

They didn't waste resources keeping the cargo holds, espe-cially empty ones, at ship temperature unless they contained freeze-sensitive provisions or technology. Those they held at ten to twenty degrees above freezing. Most of the artifacts collected during planet research junkets were left without heat at all. According to DSEG mandates, all collected materials from alien planets should be maintained at prevailing temperatures, that no additional heat should be provided. Desna had always considered that they had ruled that way to prevent unnecessary risk to the crew, that any living organism exposed to extreme temperatures would most likely not prevail. Obviously DESG had not anticipated an entity like the one from Cargo Hold 4.

Desna entered the empty hatch. There weren't many places to hide, and it took only a few minutes to thoroughly scope out the entire area. They did the same with 1 and 5, finding nothing.

"Let's head down to the lower deck," Desna said. "Check the engine rooms and power plant."

"Hey... why did Doc not show up for Fawn's vigil?" Berlin said.

"I don't want to talk about it." Desna led her to the freight elevator.

"Wurther said we're getting to XB-92 tomorrow. We landing *Gretel* down there?"

Entering the elevator car, Desna wondered how much Wurther had told her. "Not sure, yet..."

"He said it would be really dangerous to use *Gretel...*"

Why was Wurther discussing these kinds of things with Berlin? It was upsetting, until she remembered that Berlin was First mate, second only to her in the chain of command. Part of Berlin's duties was to stay abreast of everything happening aboard *Gretel*. Desna hated her new state of distraction, as if she'd lost all ability to think clearly. The freight elevator stopped with a jolt.

"What the heck was that?" Desna said. A second later an awful stench filled the elevator car. Berlin grabbed her nose and slammed her other palm against the door open button. They bolted from the elevator, slipping on something in front of the elevator doors.

It took a few seconds for Desna to figure out what had happened. "Fucking dupes! In the elevator shaft!"

"Holy fuck!" Berlin said, chuckling inside her hazmat helmet. "That's some crazy shit!" Berlin glanced down at the glop oozing out from beneath the elevator floor. "Damn, it's all over my shoes!"

Desna looked down, the soles of her hazmat shoes covered in the mess, a thin vapor starting to rise from them.

"Get them off, Berlin!" Desna yelled, racing away from the soiled spot on the floor. Berlin hurried behind her, both of them rushing to remove their shoes, watching them disintegrate.

"Jeez," Berlin said, shifting her eyes between the evaporating safety footwear and Desna. "Do you think these things are still being replicated?"

She could only shake her head, flummoxed by the implications of Berlin's question. She wanted to believe they were just cleaning up the prior *brood,* but could no longer be sure.

"Let's take the stairs up." Desna made a move toward them when Berlin grabbed her arm. She followed Berlin's gaze toward the dark end of the ship, back near the entrance to the engine room. Her heart went cold, spying movement.

Berlin's eyes looked foreign behind her hazmat shield, a million miles away.

"Let's check it out," Desna said. "But we have to be careful. We can't just fire willy-nilly in the engine room."

Berlin nodded her agreement, Desna taking point moving toward the engine room. Odd noises came from the closed metal hatch when they got closer. Could be the grumblings of *Gretel's* normal functioning; contraction, expansion, generators cycling up and down, fluids passing through pipes and conduits. Desna opened the hatch and they entered, clanking and whooshing coming from all directions at once inside the convoluted space. Desna caught movement less than twenty meters away, and raised her weapon, easing slowly toward it. Less than five meters now, three beings Desna didn't recognize stood in a circle holding hands, creating a low, murmuring drone, almost like a chant.

The sudden clacking of machine gun fire stole Desna's fixation, the beings surprised and frightened, crippled, falling to a heap on the floor. Desna spun around to see Berlin's contrite expression, etched with intensity, anger. One of the beings was still writhing along the metal floor when Berlin finished the job, destroying its skull. Desna waited, watching the creatures, unable to speak or form a real thought, her mind a tempest.

Like a fading dream, the three creatures evaporated before their eyes, then reappeared several meters away and casually left the engine room. Berlin raised her assault rifle to open a new barrage on the departing dupes when Desna placed her hand on the barrel and pushed it down gently.

"They're not there," Desna said, fully defeated by the event. The dupes were ghosts at best, and at worst, emissaries of the most indomitable and pernicious life form one could ever imagine. Desna felt like she and Berlin had just been treated to a spectacular performance, this entity showing them that it could emulate life and death in equal measure, and that it operated beyond the boundaries of what Desna knew to be possible.

CHAPTER FORTY-TWO

THE CREW WAS ASSEMBLED FOR A PRE-EXPEDITION BRIEFING.
Desna was so distracted by the event from the previous day, she
had Berlin handle the meeting. It was a fairly routine affair, going
over the guidelines for a safe and productive excursion to a
foreign planet.

"Due to circumstance beyond our control," Berlin said to the
crew. "We will be taking *Hansel* to the surface."

"We haven't done that before," Chelsey said, seeming more
than a little concerned. "How will that work?"

Berlin glanced over at Wurther. "Would you mind?"

Wurther stood up, all eyes shifting toward him. "*Gretel* is
already in orbit around XB-92, which is considerably smaller
than Earth's moon. It will take *Gretel* approximately seven hours
to orbit XB-92. That means that roughly every seven hours we
will have a window to return and meet up with *Gretel*. There is
leeway as *Hansel* is fast, not Hyper-speed fast, but can catch up
to *Gretel* in orbit if necessary."

Berlin stood and thanked Wurther, then continued speaking
to the crew about the plans to return to *Gretel* repeatedly over
the next several days, depending on how the investigation of
XB-92 proceeded. Desna sat quietly by, only half-listening to
Berlin, while mostly contemplating the entire crew leaving

Gretel. Doc Karl had begged to be left on the ship, desperately trying to convince Desna that he could handle any issues that might arise while the crew was gathering data and samples. Wurther had assured Desna that no one needed to remain behind. "*Gretel* is designed specifically for this mission," Wurther had told her, saying that it was fitted with numerous redundant systems that could and would be controlled from XB-92's surface. "It was designed that way due to the limited crew *Gretel* could support over the long haul." The Deep Space Exploration Group hand-picked every crew member for their specific skills and potential contributions. Every member was required to be fit and capable of carrying out all facets of the mission, including space walks and planetary exploration at the granular level. "No free rides!" was how Wurther categorized it, and put forth no effort to conceal his animosity toward Doc Karl. Berlin must have shared some of Doc's darker secrets with him, Desna figured.

She already knew everything about the crew and *Gretel* that Wurther had shared; she'd read the entire manual and the history behind the program. But hearing it from Wurther's lips, it landed differently for her, allowing her to see the genius and commitment of DSEG.

She never discussed with Wurther why she wasn't going to allow anyone to remain behind on *Gretel* during the planetary exploration; she needed to feel confident no crew member had been subsumed by a dupe.

Everyone met in *Hansel's* hangar for preflight checks and to refresh themselves on the operation of the state-of-the-art spacecraft. What it lacked in cargo space and ability to approach the incredible speeds of *Gretel,* it made up in maneuverability and ease of control, all aspects of piloting aided by advanced technology to correct for the possibility of human error. And *Hansel's* capabilities in landing and taking off from any surface, no matter how inhospitable, were nearly miraculous.

After several hours of flight preparation, Wurther announced that they would depart *Gretel* in thirty-seven minutes. Hurd was familiarizing himself with co-piloting *Hansel,* the job that would have fallen to Wurther if Skip had still been among the crew. Now Wurther would pilot *Hansel,* Hurd at his side. Desna walked over to him and asked how he was feeling.

"Good, Captain. Very good indeed!"

Desna went to each crew member to gauge their mental and emotional states, not bothering to address Doc Karl, who seemed to have adopted a permanent scowl. She could barely bring herself to look at the man without devising ways of making him suffer.

Chelsey was at her station going over data, humming a song Desna wasn't familiar with. "You seem ready," Desna said to the young woman.

"I'm actually pretty excited to get off *Gretel* for a while, you know... given everything that's been happening..."

Desna felt the same, hoping to gain perspective on the situation. She and Berlin had agreed to keep the latest encounter with the dupes from the crew, at least until she had time to explore the phenomenon more, and ascertain the threat level of this latest variation. She wanted the crew to be focused for the upcoming probe on XB-92, not worried about alien wraiths roaming freely on the ship.

"I'm sorry I haven't been up to hunting dupes," Chelsey said.

The statement sent a chill down Desna's spine, the concept of *hunting* life forms on *Gretel* with the sole purpose of destroying them. The fact of an alien presence aboard *Gretel* made her want to abort the entire mission and hightail it back to Earth. Of course, *hightailing* sounded fast, while in reality it would still take at least three years, even if they scuttled *Hansel* and much of their gear, and pushed *Gretel* to the limit.

"You didn't sign up for *hunting* expeditions with assault rifles, Chelsey," Desna said. "None of us did..."

Chelsey gave her a weak smile, then turned back to her terminal. Desna walked over to Berlin, touching her arm. "How are you holding up, sweetie."

"Good," Berlin said, her broad smile a welcome sight to Desna.

"Hey, when we finish with XB-92, we're gonna have several

months before our next destination. I'd like to take you up on your offer..."

"What off— Oh! Yeah, that would be wonderful. You have no idea how much I want to kiss you right now..."

Desna smiled, wanting, needing, to stretch some feeling of love and calm over her bottomless pit of dread.

CHAPTER FORTY-THREE

ON THE JOURNEY TO THE SURFACE OF XB-92, WURTHER encountered turbulence in the atmosphere that hadn't shown up on *Gretel's* scans. Nevertheless, *Hansel's* advanced Pilot-Assist System detected the anomaly and immediately launched counter-measures, guiding *Hansel* easily through the invisible tides.

With suits, lights and gear, the crew exited *Hansel* onto the surface of a dark and eerie planet, with meager greenish light from a bland inner moon. The crew paired up according to tasks, using Sherpa Terraingers to move heavy exploration gear and guide them to their predetermined locations. Desna purposely teamed up with Doc Karl, not only because she didn't trust him anymore, but she wanted to get him alone to talk. But mostly— and she hated even admitting it to herself—she thought about murdering him for what he'd done to Fawn.

As they followed the Sherpa Terrainger on foot to the probe sight, they navigated between numerous formidable rocky pillars and monoliths. Eyeing these formations with something other than scientific curiosity was troublesome. She could tell the crew that during excavation for soil samples, a large boulder had shaken loose and killed him. As if these fantasies weren't disturbing enough, she tried to figure out when the idea of killing had become so easy? Destroying dupes has certainly loos- ened her ethical restraints, but she never imagined they could become so lax as to include humans whose actions were reprehensible. Maybe it was her way of coping with an untenable situation. Or maybe she thought Doc Karl was expendable now.

They had traversed nearly 400 meters when the Sherpa Terrainger stopped. Doc Karl checked the quadrants, motioning back to Desna that they had arrived at their destination. Desna surveyed the area; a bleaker place she'd never seen. And it would be so easy to kill Doc here. Large rock columns everywhere. It would be easy to sell such a story to the crew.

Doc began unloading gear from the Sherpa, carrying it to an area designated by his atomic-compass. He dropped the gear, heading back for more. The gravity on XB-92 was slightly weaker than Earth's moon, so when Doc dropped the equipment it bounced strangely, as if the ground were made of rubber. By the time he returned to the Sherpa for another load, the tools he'd dumped at the work site had finally settled.

He was reaching into the Sherpa for the radiation detector and seismic monitor when Desna grabbed his arm. She activated the helmet-to-helmet comms.

"We need to talk, Karl..."

A reflection sliced across his visor, concealing his face. He turned his head toward her, his features hidden behind the dark shield of his helmet.

"Can you please switch on your helmet lights?" She was losing patience with the warped doctor.

The light came on, illuminating his face in a ghastly way, yet in keeping with the image she now held of him; ghoulish, sick.

"What is going on with you, Karl? What is your problem lately?"

He glowered at her, his head appearing wedged into the tight, bizarrely lit space of his helmet. Hers must look the same to him, she thought.

"I hate you," he said. "For killing Fawn!"

"Killing Fawn! How the fuck do you figure that? Don't you remember what happened when you cut into the Fawn dupe? There was no heart to transplant! Just slime!"

His eyes never softened, as if he were immune to her rationale. "That's not what I'm talking about..."

She waited for him to explain, but he turned away and picked up gear to carry to the work site. She seized his arm, jerking him toward her until they were face to face. He dropped the implements he'd been lifting.

"I am not going to stand here and play twenty-fucking-questions!" she screamed, a vague oval of fog appearing on the inside of her visor, dissipating quickly. "Get this shit off your chest, or we're gonna have a big problem...!"

His face held tight, his eyes hard and black as rocks. "When you were killing the entity in Cargo Hold 4," he explained. "I told you that the Fawn dupe had reacted in a very strange way to the life form dying..." He paused, never breaking eye contact. "That was a lie... it was Fawn who reacted to your murderous act! And when the entity was finally eliminated, Fawn never recovered. She went downhill shortly after..." Doc Karl stared at her, his eyes wetting behind his visor.

"You just had to kill everything!" he said. "What a hypocrite you are! You're supposed to be a scientist, exploring the cosmos, searching out diverse life forms, but you're nothing but a charlatan! A barbaric fake!"

She was thrown by how Doc had flipped the tables, accusing *her* of wicked and scandalous acts, when she felt that same about him. The truth in what he was saying, though, stuck like a dagger in her heart. She found herself unable to counter his attack, to get her footing in this conversation. In the midst of her terrible undoing, the most alarming notion overwhelmed her.

"Fawn reacted adversely to the entity dying?" She hoped she'd heard him wrong.

"Yes." He nodded sadly. "She had some connection to that miraculous creature you destroyed. It's not surprising that the alien life form had developed a connection to the most brilliant, youthful member of *Gretel's* crew. Obviously, it was attracted to her intelligence, her vigor and exuberance... her beauty..."

Doc was apparently in projection about the creature's intent, Desna fairly certain the organism hadn't given a fig about Fawn's *beauty.* But why and how had it connected to Fawn? Is that why she became sick soon after their expedition on J-78? What had the entity needed from her?

Panic shot through Desna. She turned and starting running back toward *Hansel*, calling the crew on her comm to drop everything and head back to the ship.

"Abort! Abort the mission! Just leave your gear and get back to *Hansel*," she screamed inside her helmet. "Wurther, get *Hansel* ready for immediate takeoff!"

"It will take a while to plot a course to *Gretel*," Wurther's small tinny voice came back through the helmet comm, sounding a thousand miles away. "*Gretel* is nowhere near our rendezvous point!"

"I don't care, Mr. Wurther! Just get the ship ready for takeoff as soon as everyone's aboard!"

CHAPTER FORTY-FOUR

WURTHER DEMANDED THEY WAIT FOR DOC KARL. AS FAR AS Desna was concerned, they had already waited too long. He might not even be coming. Another fifteen minutes passed with no word from the doctor, Wurther repeatedly calling him from the ship's comm. Nothing. Desna ordered Wurther to prepare for takeoff.

"But, Captain..."

"We don't have time for debate, Mr. Wurther! We'll return for the gear and Doc Karl, but for now, I need you to get this ship in the air!"

Wurther turned back to his station to start warming the engines for takeoff, shaking his head, clearly upset over the command. *Hansel* began to tremble under the engines revving. Chelsey looked over at Desna, as if to ask if they were really leaving Doc Karl behind. Berlin just smiled, typing in commands for the departure, glancing in Desna's direction. Mr. Hurd sat by quiet, watching the exterior cams.

"Something's off with the telemetry," Wurther said.

"What do you mean?" Desna paced the bridge.

"I'm not seeing *Gretel.*" He fiddled with controls to boost the signal. "I plotted her course, and she's not supposed to be on the other side of the planet... which would block her signal from us..."

"Put us in the air, Mr. Wurther," Desna said, crossing her arms, feeling things sliding sideways. "We'll check her position again once we're in space."

Mr. Wurther nodded his agreement, and started the count-down sequence. The crew strapped in. Desna took her chair on the bridge and fastened her seat belt. *Hansel* quivered, the systems and displays occasionally flashing. It was all normal, from what Desna recalled, and yet, something was off.

The count had gone down to *three* when Mr. Hurd shouted to abort the take off. "Dr. Karl is running toward the ship!"

Mr. Wurther cycled down the engines. Chelsey operated the airlock to allow the doctor to board, Mr. Hurd following his progress. Once Doc Karl was in the airlock, Chelsey secured the hatch. "All systems are go," she said. "Doc Karl is safely aboard and secured in his seat in the airlock."

The engines revved, the ship trembling, the count hitting zero, *Hansel* lifting off from the planet surface. The G-forces lasted only a short while before they reached the edge of XB-92's meager atmosphere, and another few minutes before they were in orbit around the planet.

"Have you found *Gretel,* Mr. Wurther?" Desna asked from her command chair, unbuckling her seatbelt.

"It will take a few minutes." He checked radar, then telemetry readings. "It should be no more than four minutes before we can see *Gretel* again... I think she's playing hide and seek behind XB-92..."

Desna walked over to Wurther's station to peer over his shoulder. "Is that it?" Desna pointed at a tiny blip on radar.

"No." He busily typed in commands, watching the screen, readouts flashing across his display. He cleared his throat, then pecked in more data. More readings flashed, data appearing, other data vanishing, numbers and coordinates, trajectories, orientation, bearings, approach.

The wait was grating on her last nerve, her worst fears marshaling her every thought. How could she have allowed this to happen? *Nothing's happened yet,* she tried to convince herself. She trained her eyes on Wurther's screen, then on the radar, unconsciously shifting from foot to foot.

"We might have something..." Wurther's tone sounded skeptical.

Her patience was dissected into stingy, fleeting portions. "Mr. Wurther! Do we have something or not!"

By now the crew had fixed their attention on Wurther, ignoring their own terminals. Even Berlin had lost her smug grin. Doc Karl entered the bridge and took his chair at his station.

"Mr. Wurther!" Desna shouted.

Wurther shook his head, visibly flummoxed. "I don't see *Gretel*... I can't find her..."

"That's unacceptable!" Desna prayed the sheer force of her command could change their destiny.

"I'm recalibrating instrumentation so I can better figure out our exact bearing... and *Gretel's...*"

"I don't understand, Mr. Wurther..." Desna tried to conceal her panic and terror. "You assured me we could control *Gretel* from this ship." She paused to reset, to catch her breath, then: "Take over control of *Gretel* so we have access to her readings on *Hansel...*"

Wurther typed on his console, command after command, his fingers nearly a blur. Mr. Hurd ambled over, seating himself at the console next to Wurther.

"May I try something?" he asked, though hadn't directed his question at anyone in particular.

"Go ahead," Wurther said. "I'm not getting anywhere..."

Hurd's keyboard clacked and clicked, his fingers moving nonstop. After a few minutes, Hurd stopped typing and stared at his display.

"Well?" Desna said, unable to hide her agitation. Wurther swiveled toward Hurd to check his screen.

"It will take a moment to compile," Hurd said, sitting patiently by as if he knew exactly what he expected to see.

A moment later an eerie warning flashed in small letters on Hurd's monitor. [NOT FOUND]. Hurd typed again, then paused, waiting, his eyes fixed on the screen. Within seconds, an animated graphical wireframe depiction of the planet XB-92, along with other tiny satellite objects, appeared on Hurd's screen. On the graphical readout was also *Hansel's* current position orbiting XB-92. Then the warning flashed again: [NOT FOUND].

Desna's heart sank. Berlin and Chelsey joined the other crew members at Hurd's terminal. Chelsey was the first to speak. "What does that mean, *NOT FOUND?*"

Desna walked over to her command chair, cutting a deadly look toward Doc Karl as she passed by.

"It means *Gretel* is no longer in orbit around XB-92," Hurd stated matter-of-factly.

"Where is she?" Berlin asked, her voice cracking a little.

Hurd shrugged. "We have no idea."

The two young women looked at each other, then back at Desna.

Wurther stood up and stretched, then walked over and sat next to Desna. "How did you know *Gretel* was gone?"

Desna was emptied, numb. "I didn't know for sure..." She eyed Doc Karl, who was clearly trying to steer clear of the discussion.

"What does he have to do with it?" Wurther shifted his gaze between Desna and Doc Karl.

"Why don't you tell them, Doc!" Desna yelled across the bridge.

When he didn't respond, she proceeded to explain about Fawn and her reactions in sick bay when the crew destroyed the entity in Cargo Hold 4, telling everyone about the young girl's bizarre connection to the entity.

Doc Karl spun from his station, his eyes ablaze. "There was nothing *bizarre* about it! In fact, it was the most profound life form we'll ever encounter... and you all killed it!"

"I don't understand any of this," Chelsey said, noticeably worried. Berlin seconded Chelsey's confusion.

"What are you proposing, Captain?" Hurd said, turning in his chair. Wurther looked on, curious and concerned.

The words she was about to speak were going to be devastating. "I believe that the entity in Cargo Hold 4, with the unwitting help of Fawn, have taken over *Gretel*..."

A weighty hush filled the bridge, until Chelsey fractured the silence. "But Fawn is dead..."

She struggled with that herself, until she remembered what Hurd had told them. "I don't think she was dead..." She turned to Hurd. "What did you call it? 'Tonic immobility,' I believe."

"But why? What do they need with *Gretel?*"

Here she paused. She had no idea if she was even correct in her assumption about Fawn and the entity in Cargo Hold 4. But it felt right. Regardless, it was obvious *Gretel* was gone, maybe knocked off trajectory by a comet, or even destroyed. Either way, they had no way to reach Earth again.

They spent the next five days orbiting XB-92, attempting to make contact with *Gretel,* desperately trying to locate her in the infinite vacuum of space, all efforts futile. They bandied around other schemes, weighing options; even attempting to return to Earth with *Hansel!* No idea too ridiculous to voice, every conceivable possibility falling short. Provisions aboard Hansel would run out completely in the next twenty-four to thirty-six hours. Even with strict rationing, it was impossible to prolong the inevitable; the truth was they'd only packed food for one day. Those reserves were now gone, with the freeze-dried emergency supplies nearly exhausted.

The greatest paradox the crew faced, was, too much time to ponder their fate; while in reality their time was extremely limited, constantly stalked by the inescapable orbit of death. They all agreed it would be better to override *Hansel's* safety protocols, program the airlocks to open automatically at a given time. Scuttle the ship; let outer space take everything, including their lives. It would be over in seconds.

So far, no one had taken the initiative to put the plan into action, some tiny atom of hope promising unreal aspirations.

Though it no longer mattered, she couldn't stop thinking about what had happened aboard *Gretel*, the entity, the precarious nature of the dupes changing and morphing, presenting themselves in so many varying forms. Had it been evolution, as Hurd had suggested? Or something more fiendish? Some kind of twisted performance, perhaps? That's what stumped her, until another hypothesis broke through; had everything the crew experienced during the onslaught been nothing more than a test, a way for the entity to learn about humans, gauge their responses, discover what they were capable of, what was important, how they processed situations and functioned? Possibly it had been creating an elaborate profile mapping their emotional terrain, their biological reactions to outrage, horror, fear, intimacy, power, compliance... But why, to what end?

Desna sipped her coffee, listening to Berlin wail through the thin walls on *Hansel,* railing about regrets, ranting over the unfairness, beating the bulkheads with her fists until they were bloody. Desna could do nothing to console her. Wurther seemed to accept his fate, as if he deserved it, spending most of his time contrite, or praying. Hurd occupied himself with reading, apologizing to Desna about not being a better spiritual liaison, that he felt powerless to console the crew in their gravest time of need, heartbroken over not being able to help Chelsey. Chelsey. She was the saddest case of all, and the most surprising to Desna. One day the beautiful young woman went to the airlock, shut the interior door, and expelled herself into outer space. Dead instantly.

Doc Karl was ghosted by the remaining crew members, ignored and scorned, abandoned to face death alone.

But then, didn't everyone have to face death alone, Desna reasoned, raising her cup to her lips, the smell of fresh, hot coffee lingering in her senses like a pleasant memory.

EPILOGUE

Fawn crossed the bridge, watching the crew go through the paces, while Captain Berlin checked on each one, making sure every member understood the responsibilities they were tasked with. Skip piloted *Gretel*, assisted by Officer Wurther seated beside him. Chelsey focused intently on her screen. Dr. Karl was absent, tending to his duties in hydroponics and sick bay, making sure that any trace of the deceased dupes aboard *Gretel* was erased.

"Here's the new data on the recalibration of the hyper-fusion drive." Captain Berlin handed Fawn the tablet.

"This looks good. I'd like to study it closer."

"Use the day room," Captain Berlin said.

"You don't mind?"

"Hey, I'm captain in name only. We all follow you."

Fawn smiled and walked away with the device. She sat behind Captain Berlin's desk, remembering back to a few months earlier, the day of the ship takeover. Lying in the cold, dark vault, she'd felt it; the absence of Desna and the crew was palpable. She knew in that instant they had departed *Gretel*. She opened the morgue vault and climbed out, proceeding to the bridge. She used the ship's comm system to alert the others that everyone was gone and it was safe to come out. "We now have control of

Gretel, and have left XB-92's orbit," Fawn had told everyone. "Please, come join me on the bridge."

That was a momentous day, Fawn recalled, bringing up the research she'd been working on. Every crew member was expected to occupy the quarters of their human predecessor, learning everything they could about each one in their spare time; histories, political affiliations, love relationships, schooling, social life, parents, siblings, grandparents.

Berlin entered the day room, interrupting Fawn's reverie.

"What do you think about the recalibrations?" Berlin asked. "Should I implement them?"

"I haven't had a chance to study everything yet." Fawn patted the tablet. "I've been daydreaming. How much time will it cut off?"

About two and half years," she said, "give or take..."

"That's good. You're really getting the hang of colloquialisms..."

"You're doing pretty well yourself. *Hang...?*" Berlin said, chuckling. "I've been studying speech patterns. Humans speak in vague terms even when exact information is available. I have our ETA calculated to the second; two years, nine days, three hours, six minutes, twenty-seven seconds."

Alone with Berlin, Fawn took the opportunity to discuss their cover story again, asking Berlin about the account they'd fabricated for returning to Earth so far ahead of schedule.

"Do you think it's believable?" Fawn asked. The story would be that the wreckage to *Gretel* was due to their failed linking attempt with BC-1, a disastrous event that ended with them losing much of their provisions in the mishap. Desna died assessing damages during a spacewalk. With depleted supplies and food, along with the loss of their captain, the crew felt they had no other choice but to return.

"Yes... I think it will work," Captain Berlin said. "All anyone will have to do is look at the damage."

Fawn nodded, feeling a slight discomfort over the account.

"What's wrong?" Berlin eased down into the chair opposite the desk.

"Mr. Hurd. How will we explain his absence?" Fawn never

understood why his biology had been resistant to replication. She knew he had ersatz components. Yet, they should have been able to improvise something. Every attempt was a disaster; malformed limbs, missing organs, a lifespan of merely minutes, sometimes only seconds. "And *Hansel...*" Fawn added, still considering Hurd while meeting Berlin's eyes.

"Hansel? I don't recall that crew member."

"The ship. *Hansel.* The auxiliary vessel."

Berlin shook her head, her expression softening. "We'll formulate a convincing scenario. Really." Berlin leaned forward and touched Fawn's hand. "We have a lot of time, sweetie."

Fawn nodded, still not convinced, forcing a smile.

"What's going on?" Berlin said.

Fawn was uneasy. "Those huge dents in the hatch door. How will we explain those?"

Berlin got up and came around the desk. Standing next to Fawn, she started typing, pictures appearing on the display. "Look at these, Fawn."

A travelogue of images drifted across the screen. Vast blue oceans, majestic skies, mountains stretching up to meet enormous white clouds, spectacular golden plains rolling to the horizon. Modern solar cities glistened, bustling with life, people of all colors walking through lush green parks, farms and animals, trees of every imaginable shape and configuration, flowers and plants bursting with color.

"It's magnificent, Fawn... and it's going to be our home. Don't be sad."

It was splendid, no doubt, yet a perplexing weariness still gnawed at her. "They will destroy us if they find out," Fawn said, hating this perverse feeling of dread.

Berlin reached over and rested her palm on Fawn's cheek. "It's going to be all right. It will."

Fawn took a deep breath, then smiled at Berlin. "Go ahead and start the new recalibration. Hard to believe we'll get to Earth in just over two years."

"It's very exciting, isn't it! Hey, let's hook up later."

Fawn chuckled, meeting her eyes. *"Hook up,* huh... sure, that would be lovely."

When Berlin left, Fawn took her attention back to the monitor. She brought up the dossier she'd been working on the past few months, realizing her assimilation would be the trickiest of all. Her Earth parents, Amelia and Ryder, were still alive. She studied the photo of her Aunt Claire on her mother's side who had a son and daughter, Fawn's two cousins, Xander and Olivia. Olivia looked to be about Fawn's age, wearing a beautiful white dress. On her ankle was a small tattoo.

Fawn paused, twisting her forearm to admire the compass tattoo. She brought her palm up until it faced her, and examined the compass design on her thin wrist, the N-heading aimed upward. She let her eyes follow the arrow toward the ceiling, wondering what it could possibly be pointing to.

ABOUT THE AUTHOR

Lonnie Busch is an award-winning author whose short fiction has appeared in *Southwest Review, The Minnesota Review, The Baltimore Review* and other magazines. Among his awards for fiction are the Clay Reynolds Novella Prize for his novella, *Turnback Creek*, finalist in the Tobias Wolff Award for Fiction, the *Glimmer Train* Very Short Fiction Award, and others.

Busch is also a painter, animator and illustrator, and has created artwork for numerous corporations, ad agencies and institutions, including the "Greetings from America" and "Wonders of America" Commemorative Stamps for the USPS.

See Busch's books at:
https://lonniebusch.com

(More books by Busch on following pages)

WITHOUT A FACE

Kurt and Alice barely escape an abduction attempt in the middle of the night, but now they're on the lam, unsure who, or what, is pursuing them…

"*This is a fully immersive novel that is as emotionally compelling as it is captivating and thrilling.*" — **Lorena Padureanu, for Bestsellers World**

Read on Kindle Unlimited

ASSIMILATION

When Kercy's mother sells their secluded island cottage, she implores Kercy to never return. "Even after I'm dead…don't ever go back there!"

ALL HOPE OF BECOMING HUMAN

Earthquakes rock the planet, revealing huge metallic objects, vast subterranean graveyards, and creatures with only one goal...killing humans.

*"This absorbing, realistic near-future tale brims with unrelenting mystery and tension." — **Kirkus Reviews***

PROJECT ÜBERMENSCH

Modern-day messiah or military experiment gone awry—either way, Geoffrey Cannon, a young inspirational guru, has mad metaphysical skills and a monstrous alter ego.

"A fun, fresh take on a SF trope with enough surprises to keep readers guessing." — **Kirkus Reviews**

THE CABIN ON SOUDER HILL

In the Southern Appalachian Mountains, a woman stumbles into dark family secrets, backwoods justice, and seemingly impossible events that threaten to rip apart her world.

An io9 Pick of Best Books of the Month and Audible Bestseller

THE BALDWIN HOTEL

Past and future collide when Theodore meets his new boss, who has a connection to Theodore's past, and a pivotal role in determining his future!

"It reminded me of "Scarecrow Has a Gun" by Michael Paul Kozlowsky which also raised questions about science while being thoroughly entertaining."— **Caroline Lewis, Goodreads**

THE ANYTHING ROOM

Martin Moffett is given an opportunity that no one should ever get — a second chance to start a new life with his wife... who's been dead for eleven years.

PUSH ME

Feisty Stories of Love & Loss

Life-affirming stories through the lens of humor and compassion, exploring the marvelous complexity of human love.

"There's no shortage of emotions throughout the collection—Busch knows exactly which buttons to press to evoke feelings, and the characters, no matter the situation, feel raw and real. A well-written and engaging collection with a lot of heart." — **Kirkus Reviews**

TURNBACK CREEK

A Novella & Six Stories

This bittersweet tale of a confrontation of one old man with mortality defies the gravitational pull into despond and emerges as a very nearly inspirational story

Winner of the Clay Reynolds Novella Prize

SIGN UP FOR BOOK RELEASE DATES, SPECIAL OFFERS, FREE ARCS & GIVEAWAYS!

(Unsubscribe at any time. Email will never be shared or sold.)

https://lonniebusch.com/

Most of my books are available at these fine book sellers

BARNES & NOBLE

Rakuten kobo

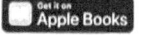 Apple Books

Everand

tolino

OverDrive

CL cloudLibrary™

hoopla

vivlio

Borrow Box.

Smashwords

Gardners

fable

Bookshop.org

amazon